HOT AND BOTHERED

HOT AND BOTHERED

DIANNE CASTELL

BRAVA

KENSINGTON PUBLISHING CORP.
http://www.kensingtonbooks.com

BRAVA BOOKS are published by

Kensington Publishing Corp.
850 Third Avenue
New York, NY 10022

All Kensington titles, imprints and distributed lines are available at special quantity discounts for bulk purchases for sales promotion, premiums, fund-raising, educational or institutional use.

Special book excerpts or customized printings can also be created to fit specific needs. For details, write or phone the office of the Kensington Special Sales Manager: Kensington Publishing Corp., 850 Third Avenue, New York, NY 10022. Attn. Special Sales Department. Phone: 1-800-221-2647.

Brava and the B logo Reg. U.S. Pat. & TM Off.

ISBN-13: 978-0-7582-2359-3
ISBN-10: 0-7582-2359-5

First Kensington Trade Paperback Printing: April 2008
10 9 8 7 6 5 4 3 2 1

Printed in the United States of America

HOT AND BOTHERED

Chapter 1

Springtime in Savannah with pink, purple and white azaleas, magnolia blossoms the size of punch bowls and a warm breeze declaring winter never really happened at all. With things this perfect outside RL Investigations, how could it be so pitiful inside?

An empty in-box, an empty out-box, no phones ringing and—was that a spiderweb across the monitor? The online course said, "Imagine yourself a PI and you'll develop the instincts of one." Propping her feet on the oak desk like some gumshoe from a dime novel, Charlotte deShawn grabbed her coffee, and doughnut, and pictured a gray fedora and crumpled trench coat, as Griffin Parish III hustled into the office.

Dripping red jelly onto her white blouse, she stared at Savannah's primo bachelor. Next time she'd imagine a Porsche and being a size four. Jerking her legs from the desk, the chair reeled over, spewing coffee across the room.

"Sweet Jesus!" Griff hunkered down beside her sprawled body. "Are you okay?"

She faked a grin. Appearances mattered in Savannah no matter how painful or embarrassing the situation. "Caught me a little off guard is all." She scrambled to her feet and kicked doughnut shrapnel under the desk. This never happened in those dime novels. There it was a pack of Camels, a dark alley and a secretary named Trixie.

Griff loosened his tie and handed her a handkerchief. April in the Low Country was hot but not that hot. "I need some investigating done, and I need it to be kept private."

"In this town? Good luck." She paper-toweled the mess as he paced the office of metal file cabinets, two pleather club chairs and a percolator with a broken switch that did up the best coffee east of Bull Street. West of Bull, bragging rights went to Scrumptious Savannah, but the point was, *Griff fit in as well as she did at his hotel.* So why *was* he here?

"As much as I appreciate the business, you need to know that Daddy's the real investigator and he's laid up with a broken leg and I'm filling in and, truth be told, not doing all that great a job, as everyone realizes since I mistook Mr. Austin's visiting mother for his current mistress, though in my own defense, she was wearing pink spandex. So if it's something small, I can help, but if it's big, then—"

"I want you." His eyes met hers, and he didn't blink. She blinked a lot because she never expected to hear those three little words from Griff Parish's sexy mouth. For a split second, fifteen years of glances across crowded rooms and accidental-on purpose passing touches all came crashing together. She figured the two of them would go on secretly flirting forever. Urban sport, hunting and fishing city-style, except no one got caught or stuffed and mounted, though the mounted part crossed her mind a time or two.

"I suppose you've heard the conditions of Otis's will," Griff said, snapping her back to the moment with legal stuff about his stepfather while she contemplated sex and the single guy. Little wonder they never got together.

"Latest word from the kudzu vine is Otis bequeathed Magnolia House to you and Jaden Carswell, daughter of his old partner, who was murdered along with his wife twenty-five years ago, and your mama emptied a Thirty-eight Special into Otis's gravestone when she found out you weren't sole heir. Blew it to smithereens, marble chunks everywhere."

"Thirty years ago," Griff paced the other way, "the baby daughter was sent up east, but no one knows where she is now, and Camilla's in Tuscany. Her nerves are . . ." His brow furrowed.

"Shot?"

"I'm truly getting to hate that word." He ran his fingers through his thick black hair, making it not quite so perfect and a lot closer to tool-belt-and-T-shirt Griff Parish, restorer of historic treasures. Indiana Jones meets Casanova meets grits and pecan pie. "The bank along with my suppliers are getting antsy, with me not owning Magnolia House outright."

"But you managed to break the will—least, that's the latest buzz."

"I'm the one who started that buzz, and now I have to find this daughter without stirring up any more talk." He gave Charlotte an intent look. "The bottom line is, I need to buy her out so I can get on with business."

Okay, how was she supposed to say something with those big blue eyes focused straight on her? "Uh . . . meaning no one will suspect you'd hire the likes of me when you have lawyers on retainer."

"I'll pay you well." He took a check from the breast pocket of his suit coat and handed it over. "This should cover your expenses."

Pay? Well? Her heart raced, blood pressure surged, and it had nothing to do with gorgeous Griff but more with his gorgeous bank account. "There is an abundance of zeros on this paper."

"It's settled then. You can start today, and I mean really today and not Savannah today, which can be anytime in the next month or two." He held out his hand to shake. "There is absolutely no breaking the will. God knows I've tried everything, and I do mean everything." He muttered, "I can't believe it's come to this."

She studied the check, thought of rent on the office, taxes, Daddy's no-insurance medical bills and her little white lie to him about how great the agency was doing. What was there to consider except she wasn't exactly Sam Spade? Heck, she could imagine Spade! "You got yourself a deal."

She took Griff's hand, their fingers and gazes meeting, her heart flipping even worse than it did in the chair.

"You sure you're okay? You look . . . confused."

So much cash and maleness in one place was enough to confuse the stuffing out of any girl. She pulled her hand back and slapped the handkerchief in its place. "PI cover. I'm practicing."

"Terrific." Except his *terrific* sounded more like a *good God, what have I gone and done!* He headed for the door, calling over his shoulder, "I'll be waiting."

"But . . . but . . ." Griff was gone, his footsteps retreating down the hall, her pulse thumping to the cadence, a million questions humming in her brain about the case but the biggest question of all being, Why was she so fascinated by this guy? Always had been. She fanned herself with the check. "Holy Moses."

"Honey," said BrieAnna Montgomery as she backed into the room pointing through the open door. "I don't know who you're looking at, but the only thing Moses and the Biscuit have in common is one went and got the commandments and the other breaks them on a regular basis, and everyone around here knows who's who."

BrieAnna parked her perfect size six next to Charlotte's size twelve on the edge of the desk as they considered the doorway. "The man surely does deserve his name. Whenever I lay eyes on him walking off like that, I'm reassured Griff

Parish has the finest butt in all Savannah. One yummy Southern Biscuit, just what every woman around here wants to sink her teeth into, especially you, since you're the one who went and gave him that name."

Together they exhaled an appreciative sigh over broad shoulders, tapered waist and superb ass. "I came up the front stairs to drop off these garden-tour flyers and saw him going down the back. So, what's his excuse for sneaking around and making you dribble jelly? Something a little . . . clandestine, I hope? Finally? At last!"

Charlotte handed over the check. "Forget the hanky-panky eye roll. This is business, all business. Besides, we both know Camilla would rather her only beloved offspring be cloistered in a monastery than the Parishes have anything to do with the deShawns, and on this particular issue Griff seems content to honor his mama's wishes. Just last week, the woman tried to run me over with her Caddy right there on Abercorn. Tire tracks still on the sidewalk. I wonder what got me caught in the crosshairs of Camilla's Escalade?"

"A three–vodka gimlet lunch, no doubt." BrieAnna peered at the check and frowned. "What would make the Biscuit give you all this money?"

"My superior investigative skills, which he's in dire need of."

Prissy St. James floated into the office like springtime does Kate Spade, or at least a Kate knockoff. "Oh, now that is a hoot. You can't find your way around Target without getting lost. And did you know there are bare-chested, well-tanned and probably very well hung males in hard hats digging up Broad Street, and the good lunch tables at the Pirate House suitable for afternoon viewing will be taken if we don't get a move on? And why are you wearing coffee and jelly, Charlotte deShawn?"

"Less fattening than eating it, and they moved the shoe department at Target, so it wasn't my fault for getting lost."

BrieAnna flashed the check at Prissy. "Looky here. Charlotte's springing for lunch."

Prissy snagged the paper and gasped, dropping the check on the desk. She jumped back, losing her left shoe, and held out her arm to Charlotte. "Look, goose bumps. My goose bumps have goose bumps. Burn it! Burn that check, Char, right now, before it's too late. It's bad news!"

Charlotte snagged the paper. "It's signed, and the commas and periods are in the right places. This is alleluia and bless-the-man's-hide all rolled into one."

"And such a nice hide, too," Brie added as Priss pulled in a deep breath, her black eyes clearing. "You're right. It's me, all me. Sometimes I just get this . . . feeling."

"Me, too, honey," BrieAnna sighed, hooking her arm through Charlotte's and handing Prissy her shoe. "Not having a date in three months can do that to a woman. Long time to be without some. We are so in need of lunch and those hard hats on Broad Street."

What the hell had he started, Griff wondered as he cut across Oglethorpe Square fighting the damn top button of his damn shirt to get it damn-well closed and colliding head-long with Daemon Rutledge. "Holy hell, if you're here, who's minding the hotel?"

"With some luck, not a new owner. So, did she take the case? Did you persuade her?"

"I think my checkbook did the persuading." Griff focused on the ever-present fresh red rose in his manager's lapel and remembered the red jelly on Charlotte's T-shirt about where her nipple would be. Nipple . . . Charlotte . . . Oh, damn! He tried to concentrate on the coffee smears instead of the jelly, like that was going to happen. "Let's hope her investigative skills are considerably better than her doughnut skills or this plan to keep things quiet and find Jaden is going to fly like an albatross."

"Your daddy's will sure did throw a monkey into the mix, all right. I've been at Magnolia House since Otis opened the doors and never expected he'd leave things brewing the way he did."

They crossed State, then rounded the corner to the hotel, yellow pansies spilling from flower boxes, wrought-iron porch and the brass and glass double doors twinkling in the sunlight. "I'm thinking Otis was cramming for finals. Afraid if he didn't give William's daughter her rightful share, he'd get a one-way ticket straight to swindler's hell."

"Seems to me that what happened in the past should stay where it belongs."

"Hell, all of Savannah is running around in the past. The place is one big time warp. Just look at this hotel. If the mortar on the back wall isn't crumbling, there's a new crack in the foundation. And who knows what's happening on the second floor with things moving around. Lee had his last picture taken here, and I think he decided to stay. Least he didn't bring his damn horse."

They helped the doorman unload luggage from a BMW idling in front, then Griff cut across the lobby to the back courtyard, making note of the smudge on the marble floor, a light out in the brass chandelier and the need to give the doorman a raise. Guests lunched under blue umbrellas, and he clued the waiters to water Mrs. O'Hara's martinis or she'd wind up face-first in her okra soup or maybe dancing on the table. Hard to tell which way she'd go.

Heading for the back alley by the ivied carriage house, Griff wondered how much longer he'd be in charge of the hotel. He'd worked at Magnolia House his whole life, lugging suitcases at twelve when they couldn't afford a real bellhop, or much other help for that matter. Griff Parish could scrub a tub, do up a bed and put mints on pillows with the best of them.

It hadn't been all that many years ago that Savannah

teemed with gangs instead of tourists, the big old decaying homes with their wide verandas, winding stairways and high ceilings setting empty and selling for tax money. He thought of his seventh birthday, sitting on the steps of Lillibridge House playing Go Fish with Otis so the bulldozers couldn't tear the place down before they scared up a buyer. He and Otis saved more than one place that way—though Go Fish morphed into poker—but Magnolia House was always the prize, their lady. Griff intended to keep her, even if it took every blasted penny he had to buy Jaden Carswell's share and—

His neck snapped as someone grabbed his tie and yanked him inside the carriage house, the dark interior making it impossible to see who did the yanking.

"What the—," he gasped as the wood door clicked closed. He stumbled, his body flattening a woman's against the wall, giving him a soft landing that made the choking worth it. He caught the faint aroma of coffee and doughnuts as breasts swelled against his chest, his body reacting as if he hadn't had sex in months. Hell, maybe he hadn't. "Charlotte?" he croaked through a shrinking trachea.

"We need to talk."

"Wish I could." He loosened his tie and gave a quick glance around the narrow hall, his eyes adjusting to the dim light. "Consider using a telephone?"

"Someone might overhear and I know you don't want that, and I was heading for my house to change and I saw you coming and . . ." She took a deep breath, her face scrunched in question as she peered up at him. "So why did you really come to the office?"

"The will? The missing daughter? Keeping things quiet? Stop me if you've heard this before. You sure you didn't whack your head when you fell off that chair?"

Her breath came fast and was getting faster. Her eyes lit with fire—even in the dim light he could tell. "Why me?"

she whispered, the implication having nothing to do with the case but with the two of them together now in this hallway after all these years of dancing around.

His brain refused to function, probably because the part of his anatomy below his belt was overfunctioning. "You run an ad in the yellow pages." Maybe. He had no idea about anything right now except Charlotte and wanting to kiss her and knowing he shouldn't. Things between them were complicated—always had been and getting worse by the minute. He studied her delicious mouth, wanting and waiting for his. Make that getting more complicated by the second, and if his plan worked, *complicated* would be a huge understatement and their lives would be totally fucked.

He touched Charlotte's cheek, her skin soft and smooth, as her body leaned into his, setting him on fire.

"We don't have an ad." She bit her bottom lip. "You're right, I should have phoned," she said with a shiver. "But we're here now." She yanked his tie again, bringing his face to hers, and she kissed him right on the mouth, her lips full and moist and delicious and opening. Did they have to open? Closed lips were a lot easier to dismiss, but this was not a dismiss, kind of kiss, especially since he'd wanted it for so many damn years he'd lost count.

She released his tie, her arms sliding around his neck as his tongue touched hers and he lost his mind. Dumbass!

Their tongues mated, and his hands dropped to her sweet round bottom, pressing her softness to his hardening dick. There'd always been an attraction between them, but this was pure jump-her-bones-and-do-her-right-now lust . . . and he liked it more than he ever imagined.

She sucked his bottom lip into her mouth, the motion suggestive as hell as her legs parted, nesting his erection tight against her heat. God, she had great heat! He slid his hands into the waistband of her skirt, her firm rump fitting

so well into his palms. His mind warped, there was a ringing sound . . . no kiss or ass-grabbing had ever made his
head ring before, especially to the tune of "Moon River" . . .
a Johnny Mercer song . . . his favorite. Ah fuck! His cell!

It was like a bucket of freezing snow dumped on his
head. The instant sanity kicked his gut-tightening lust
through the goal post of are you out of your freaking
mind. He stepped back, his vision clearing, his body in big
pain from what it wanted but couldn't have.

"I . . . I didn't come here for this," Charlotte panted as
she raked her tangle of red curls away from her flushed
face. "Least, I don't think I did, not that I'm complaining.
I am so not complaining."

"It has nothing to do with thinking. In fact, not thinking is what got us both to this point." Did that make sense?
Nothing right now made sense.

She stared at him, her eyes green pools, her lips parted,
"Moon River" jarring his brain. He wanted nothing more
than to stomp the phone flat and take her fast and hard and
deep right here against the wall, satisfying what they've both
ached for, for half their lives. Instead, she yanked opened
the door and ran off into the bright sunlight, leaving him
with the biggest hard-on of his whole damn life.

He had known when he stepped into that office that
only Charlotte would be there—alone, without RL—and
that he didn't have a choice in what he had to do, and that
things could get sticky. He hadn't planned on it getting this
sticky this fast. Damn Otis! Damn Griff's damn cock. He
snapped open the phone and growled, "What?"

Charlotte took the shortcut through the alley, then stopped
under the oak on the corner. She gave three tourists directions to Paula Deen's Lady and Sons over on Congress
Street, warned of the two-hour wait, ballyhooed the bread
pudding, then pulled in a few calming breaths, though it

would take a lot more than breathing to get her calm right now.

What in almighty blazes had she been thinking to kiss Griff? All she'd wanted were some answers about the case.

Oh what a bunch of blewy! She'd wanted that kiss and followed him to get it like some two-bit hussy. She blushed and nibbled her bottom lip, tasting Griff all over again, making her head foggy. This couldn't happen every time she met up with him about the case. Didn't that online PI course say something like "Thou shall not kiss thy client"?

Things between her and Griff had to be strictly business from here on out. She'd find Jaden Carswell, cash the fat check and get on with her life without having to file for bankruptcy. Good plan. And it shouldn't be all that difficult after the kiss ... that steamy, sexy, yummy, completely satisfying kiss that fulfilled all her desires for Griff now and forever, right? Right! She could move on, put that part of her life right out of her brain.

She crossed Habersham to the gray clapboard with white shutters she'd called home for all thirty years ... well, at least for twenty-nine of the thirty. And technically, it wasn't exactly her home, since when she turned twenty, RL decided he'd had enough of sharing a bathroom with Clinique, Revlon and Tampax and Charlotte redid the garage out back into a white-and-yellow cottage.

Charlotte took the mossy brick sidewalk and pushed open the front door to Daddy in a wheelchair, leg extended, and LulaJean Wilson, practical nurse by day, divine jazz singer by night. LulaJean called from the kitchen, "Nuh-uh, no one's better at being Bond than Pierce Brosnan. Some PI you are if you don't know that much."

"Pierce?" Daddy countered. "How can James Bond be a Pierce? Sissy-boy name, if you ask me. That new Bond guy is a real bad-ass, the way Bond should be."

"Except he looks like he got hit with the original ugly

stick," LulaJean said, and Charlotte added, "When they get Johnny Depp as Bond, he'll get my vote."

She smoothed Daddy's wiry gray hair and then planted a kiss as he faked a strangling sound over her choice of Bonds. LulaJean answered, "Depp? Mr. Fancy Pants? Look what he did to being a pirate. They should have gotten our own Ray Cleveland or that good-looking boy of his out there on Thunderbolt Island for their pirate. The real deals, that's what they are. Yummy as all get-out, a little shady and a lot involved in who-knows-what. Yessir, real Savannah pirates."

Charlotte sat down on the blue corduroy ottoman next to Daddy and clicked off *Wheel of Fortune*.

"Hey, I was watching that, little girl." He gave her a once-over. "Did that old coffee pot finally explode?"

"Guess what, I got a gig."

"We've always got gigs—least, that's the story you're telling me." He gave her a questioning look, and she quickly swiped the liar-liar-pants-on-fire expression from her face. He shifted in his chair to get comfortable, which couldn't be easy with his leg sticking straight out like one of those railroad-crossing gates. "So I'm guessing *gig* means you're finishing up your teaching degree. Something more to your taste for when I get out of this here chair and you can get on with you life?"

"The junior high inner city middle school kids ate me alive, remember? I learned how to hot-wire a motorcycle and pick locks, and they learned nothing."

He rubbed his chin. "Then you're heading on back to school to finish up your culinary degree?"

It was the usual litany of what is Charlotte doing with her life," probably brought on by sitting here with nothing on his mind and watching Dr. Phil. "I gained ten pounds the first month, kept eating all my mistakes. But before you bring up the vet assistant thing and interior decorator stint, there's good news. What I have to show you is better paying than any of them, actually the best paying job we've had so far." Least that part wasn't a lie.

"Know how we heard that Griff Parish broke the will leaving his hotel to his daddy's partner's daughter? Well, it's not true at all. He made it up to keep the finances of the hotel on an even keel. Griff wants little old me—" She pointed to her chest, remembering being pressed tight to Griff's and kissing him, and suddenly she couldn't breathe, her mind fuzzing out, the sensation of Griff's lips on hers taking over.

"And?" Daddy coaxed. "Yoo-hoo, Charlotte, honey? You okay? What in thunder does Griff want you to do?"

Probably the same thing she wanted, if their kissing was any indication. She should never have done that kiss. She wasn't satisfied one lick! Blast! "He wants me to find that Jaden girl for him." Charlotte turned toward the kitchen. "Are you catching all this, LulaJean?"

"Uh-huh, and I know enough when to keep my mouth shut tight, just like your daddy does. Everybody in this town knows he's the only man who can do that."

"Griff." RL went as white as his cast, then bellowed in his two-by-four voice, "Like heck!"

"I know you don't much care for the Parishes," Charlotte said, "but their money spends just fine and—"

"Why is that boy dragging you into this? He knows better. Why can't he just break the dang will? Thought he was supposed to be so smart. Doesn't sound so smart to me. Sounds like his name should be Pierce."

"I heard that, too."

RL slapped the side of his wheelchair. "Damnation!"

Charlotte pulled out the big guns—the check with all the zeroes. "This is not damnation. Look at this little bitty piece of paper."

"Big Al was just saying last week that he has an opening

in his carpet business. He'll teach you about carpet, make you a partner in no time, as soon as I get back on my feet and can take up the business. Uncle and niece—a perfect family-business combination."

"I'm not a flooring kind of girl. I hate carpet and vacuum only when the dust bunnies plan mutiny." She shook the check in front of Daddy's nose, making it do a little dance. "You're not looking here. Finding Jaden can't be that hard. And the only reason Griff chose me is to keep things on the QT around here because no one would expect him to hire me, being a small agency."

LulaJean came in from the kitchen and handed Daddy a sandwich plate. "I recollect there were a lot of unanswered questions when Otis's partner and his wife got murdered. Happened in the old morgue. They were meeting someone to sell a right expensive necklace. Otis and William needed money to finance Magnolia House. Course, all that happened when I was just knee-high to a grasshopper." She grinned and winked.

"That's it," Daddy yelled. "You are not getting involved with this. I'm putting my foot down, Charlotte."

They all stared at his protruding leg.

"What is the world coming to?" Daddy groused. "Nothing but disrespect in my own home."

"I'm just taking a job," Charlotte soothed. "Except this is a mighty good-paying one."

"You cannot carry off finding this woman on your own. It's a big case, and if you mess it up," Daddy continued in a rush, "it'll . . . it'll give me a bad name, ruin the reputation of the agency, scare off all of our clients."

Clients?

The pulse in his neck beat hard, and he was getting more perturbed by the minute. "You've got enough business to keep us afloat and pay bills. That'll have to do. I . . . I don't want you having anything to do with the Parishes.

Stay away from them, Charlotte. You hear me, girl? I don't trust them, dammit! What the hell do you think you're doing?"

Dammit? Hell? Charlotte froze. LulaJean did likewise, her eyes huge. RL never cussed. Even when he got hit by that moving van when doing surveillance two weeks ago and wound up in the ER at St. Jo's he still didn't cuss. But now? Why now?

Chapter 2

And Daddy wasn't eating the fried oyster sandwich that LulaJean made. It was his absolute favorite. What if his cholesterol dropped? He got skinny and healthy? What kind of a Savannah body was that? But he was right about it being his agency and finding a missing person being out of her league. She couldn't even find missing shoes at Target. RL was getting more agitated by the minute. He didn't need agitating; he needed to get well. Putting his mind at ease was the very reason she made up the string of lies about business being good in the first place.

"All right, all right. You can rest easy. I'll return the check after I have lunch with BrieAnna and Prissy. No need to throw a hissy."

"I am a grown man and I do not throw hissies!" he hissed.

LulaJean tiptoed back to the kitchen saying, "I'm getting myself out of your hair right now, so there's no need to be crabbing at me."

Charlotte gave her daddy a quick kiss on the cheek, then zipped out the rear door before he went ballistic over something else. He was not in a good mood. Being laid up was really getting to him, even more than when she decorated his bedroom in puce and mauve. Decorating wasn't her thing. Neither were cooking and teaching. The question was, did she have a thing?

She headed for the cottage, took a minute shower, then tossed her blouse into the washing machine, watching the water run over the jelly smear. Griff made her brain sizzle, made her want to put on lacy panties instead of cotton and made it impossible to drink coffee and eat a doughnut. No other man had ever interfered with her doughnut eating. And now she was kicking him out of her life. Rats!

For sure she'd missed lunch at the Pirate House by now, so she might as well return the check. Slipping it in the front pocket of her peasant skirt, she took the sidewalk to the street and spied BrieAnna walking her way. Actually it was more of a stomp, her strappy sandals smacking the pavement as if they'd done something bad.

"Well, where in the world have you been?" she said, hands to hips. "We waited and waited." Her frown morphed into a little smile. "And I must say, you missed one very fine parade of male loveliness."

"I have an excuse." They continued down Habersham. "RL wants me to give the check back to Griff and take up installing carpet."

"Carpet? Does he know about the dust bunnies? I'm desperately sorry, Charlotte, I truly am. Prissy and I were talking at lunch and there's more to this Jaden person than you think. Her parents were killed, of all things. Think of that." BrieAnna shivered. "I'm sure RL doesn't want you getting mixed up in anything involving murder and mayhem."

"He'd rather have me in the land of premium installation, services guaranteed. Go with me to drop off the check?" Least with BrieAnna along, there'd be no yanking ties and canoodling in hallways.

They took the shortcut through the alley, BrieAnna continuing, "I guess this means the Biscuit is off your radar again. You know, I don't think I even have a radar any-more, or maybe it's just on the fritz. I haven't had so much as a blip in a long time, and I think Mama's determined to marry me off before this summer ends, and that means someone rich and connected and probably old and—"

Charlotte grabbed BrieAnna's arm and yanked her behind a Dumpster.

"What in the world are—"

"Shh." Charlotte did the finger-to-lip sign while nodding at a clump of bushes behind the carriage house. Griff and Daddy, wheelchair and all, deep in conversation. Neither looked one bit pleased about talking with the other, and intent on arguing and not being noticed.

BrieAnna gasped, "Well, I'll be. Since when are they so chummy?"

"Shh," Charlotte insisted as her father shook his head about something, then turned his chair, making Charlotte duck behind the Dumpster, dragging BrieAnna with her. The wheelchair crunched over the loose gravel as it rolled down the alley, Daddy grumbling under his breath. She waited till the crunching faded, then peeked to make sure Griff was gone as well. BrieAnna said, "What was that all about? I've never seen Griff and RL in a conversation before."

"Not unless there's growling and snorting involved. Twenty minutes ago, Daddy was lecturing me not to have anything to do with Griff, and now he's the one who's out here shooting the breeze with him."

"From the looks, I think they'd prefer to be shooting each other."

Charlotte took the check from her skirt and stared at it. "I get a really good job and suddenly there's two Savannah warlords doing battle in the alley. Seems a tad strange, don't you think?"

BrieAnna swiped at a dirt smear on her pink-flowered dress where she'd brushed against the Dumpster. "Ask Griff about it when you give him the check." She stopped swiping and cut her gaze to Charlotte. "Honey, you are giving him the check, aren't you? What are you going to say when RL asks, 'Oh, Charlotte, my precious little girl, did you go and give that big old check back to Griffin Parish like I asked you to?'"

"I'll do what I've been doing all along. I'll lie. I've got the lying part of being a PI down pat."

"Except you're not a PI, not really and truly."

"Brie, I didn't go looking for this case. It just got dumped in my lap. And RL sure isn't leveling with me about whatever, and Griff's no better. They're having clandestine meetings in alleys. And for Pete's sake, I've got to pay some bills somehow around here. Money's not falling like manna from heaven, and no second job I can take is going to pay me enough to afford RL's therapy."

BrieAnna put her arm around Charlotte. "I can lend you money. I have Gram's trust fund. I can help."

"You know RL would blow a gasket if he ever suspected, and it's not what I want to do either. Nope, this is my turn to help out, to make things right. RL took me in when Mama ran off to who knows where, and now I'm going to pay him back. It's my chance to take care of us for a change."

"Well, I know all about old houses and raising money to save them, but I don't know the first thing about finding missing babies. That's Bebe's department. She never made it to lunch either, so I'm guessing she's at the station. Having a police person for a best friend may not get us out of speeding tickets or those pesky parking tickets no matter how much we beg and whine and bribe with Godiva, but she might help on this."

BrieAnna bit her lip. "Murders and missing people . . . I bet you'd be a fine carpet salesman . . . saleswoman."

Charlotte conjured up an evil expression, and BrieAnna held up her hands in surrender. "Right, no carpet. I'll pretend the stuff doesn't even exist."

Brie headed for Magnolia House, and Charlotte turned toward Bull. With luck, she'd find Bebe. Hunting her down on the job was always dicey. You never knew what you were walking into—burglary, assault, double homicide, a Big Mac and large fries. What in the world was a blue-eyed blonde of model proportions doing as a police detective, anyway? And those horrid suits she wore. You'd think that after twenty years of the four of them being together, some of Prissy's prissiness would rub off.

Charlotte eyed the red brick building that was once a hospital during the northern unpleasantness but now the police station. She spied the answer to J.C. Penny's catalogue centerfold hurrying down the front steps, blonde hair streaming out like some Hollywood nymph. If Joan Rivers appeared, microphone in hand for an interview, Charlotte wouldn't have been surprised one bit. 'Course "The Rivers" would have totally ragged on Bebe's suit and gravel-gripper shoes.

"If you're here to drag me off to lunch, forget it, no matter how delicious Prissy's latest man report. I have to work, for heaven's sake. I—"

"What do you know about the Carswell murder thirty years ago and their baby?" Charlotte asked in a lowered voice as she tugged Bebe off to the side behind a lilac bush, letting others pass.

Bebe's sparkling blue eyes laughed. "Well, that's a greeting I didn't expect. Did you happen to bring me a cheeseburger? I remember a lot better with a cheeseburger in my hand. Or a malt. I could do with a chocolate malt. I'm starved."

A well-deserved pout formed on Charlotte's lips. "Okay, that does it. How can you be a size two and devour burgers and chili fries like no tomorrow? What happened to metabolisms slowing down when we got to thirty? Mine sure did. But nooooo, you still eat like when we were fourteen. I just look at fast food now and might as well slather glue and paste fat and carbs directly to my hips."

Bebe twitched hers. "I got some fantastic genes. Whoever they might be from, I'm truly thankful. I'd die without cheeseburgers and chili fries, my two favorite food groups. As for the Carswell murder, it happened the same year I was adopted, which makes it the same year all four of us were. Otis's death has gotten people talking, particularly the older officers who were around then and . . ." Bebe's face took on a blank cop stare. "What's all this to you, Char?"

"Tell me about the Carswell's baby."

"That's Social Services. What are you up to?"

"Would there be anything on the Internet about the case or the baby?"

"Everything's on the Internet, especially something that caused such a stir and didn't get solved and is back on the front burner now."

Bebe took Charlotte's hand, a touch of worry in her eyes. "Someone has a lot at stake with a murder and very pricey jewelry gone missing, and just because it's an old case it's no less dangerous. Whatever this is you're working on, and I'm guessing you're working on something, leave it for RL and the police."

Charlotte reclaimed her hand and plopped it on her hip. "Excuse me? What kind of confidence is that? I need a little support here. We're friends to the end, remember? Or did you forget that night in Bonaventure Cemetery when we did pinky swear to stick together, be family for each other and never find our no-good parents who gave us up.

We cut our little fingers." She held up her scarred digit. "Shared blood and—"

"And Prissy fainted dead away and BrieAnna threw up and you got lost, and the cops found us and dragged us home. Yeah, I remember. Look, Charlotte, with your daddy in a wheelchair, that means you're on your own. This is not the case to start your career on."

"I need money. RL's going to need physical therapy. Ever see what one of those bills looks like?"

"Ever think about going back for your teaching degree? You're older now. I bet you could whip those bratty kids into shape in no time."

"Tell me, oh skinny one, ever think about being a model?"

"Me? Oh good God, no."

"Well, that goes double for me and teaching. I can handle this case. And if you say one word about me getting lost in that store with the red bull's-eye, I'll scream."

"RL doesn't know how bad things are financially for you all, does he?"

"And he's not going to."

"Keep my number on speed dial."

"You know, that is the ugliest brown suit I ever did see. Worse than your others."

"It's my favorite. And the first rule of being a PI is never insult someone with a nine-millimeter strapped to their waist."

"Great brown suit."

"Much better."

Streetlights blinked on and a gust of wind carrying a warm spring shower rippled through the trees as Griff pulled his pickup into the carriage house. After Charlotte commandeering him in the hallway, he'd never think of this place the same way again. Damn, she was something.

More accurately, Charlotte was major trouble, and he better remember that part of her being around and not her lovely face or terrific ass. Think of something else. Anything else besides necking with Charlotte.

He cut through the alley to the back of Magnolia House. No one needed to see the owner dirty to the bone. He smiled into the night thinking of the Thomas Square row houses he'd just bought. Much safer than dreaming about Charlotte.

The houses had bracketed eaves, original two-over-two windows. He had no business laying out money with things so dicey in his financial future, but if he didn't the houses could be bought up by some high-end developer and the humble folk barely managing to afford to live there now would lose their homes for good. He couldn't let that happen. Hell, Otis would haunt him something terrible if he let that happen, though getting haunted by Otis wouldn't be all bad. Griff missed him, missed him a hell of a lot.

Griff kicked off his work boots to minimize the trail of dirt, then carried them up the service stairs to the third floor. He unlocked his apartment and went inside, someone stepping in right behind him. "Otis? Hey, I bought the row houses. That should make you happy."

"Why?"

Griff spun around. "Charlotte?"

"Why would buying the row houses make me happy? Though BrieAnna thinks you're a candidate for sainthood for doing such a thing, even though she doesn't know you're the one who did the buying."

"If you're here to return the check—"

"And just why in the world would I go and do a thing like that, hmm?"

Damn good question, and the answer was that RL had said he told her to. 'Course Griff couldn't say that, since Charlotte didn't know he'd talked with RL in the alley.

Griff was tired clear through, the risk of him saying things he shouldn't high. "I thought maybe you were getting cold feet about working for me, is all."

"You're the one without shoes." She closed the door and suddenly nothing on him was cold. The dim glow from the streetlights slid through the blinds, making horizontal lines of gray and gold across Charlotte's eyes, her lips, her breasts. Why couldn't it highlight her forehead, her nose and her chin? They were a lot easier to ignore . . . maybe.

All he'd wanted was for Charlotte to take a few days to find Jaden and then he would get on with owning the hotel outright. But now her daddy was involved, and Charlotte was here, and Griff wanted nothing more than to continue where they left off in the carriage house.

Rain pattered the windows, blurring the shadows, giving the room a quiet sensual quality. Now he was tired and horny as hell.

"We need to talk, and this time I mean it." Except there was a spark in her eyes that said she wanted more than talk.

His vision hazed as he fixated on the rapid rise and fall of her nicely rounded breasts, which he could still feel pressed to him. "What do you want to know? Otis didn't tell me all that much except that Jaden was taken to Boston, where her grandparents were."

"She didn't get there by herself. Who took her?"

Couldn't she just shut up and jump into his bed? This night was made for loving. Hell, Charlotte was made for loving. "I'm guessing Otis paid someone or the family hired someone to come get her."

"Doesn't this seem a little strange to you? I'm guessing the family probably came to Savannah for the funeral. Why didn't they take the child with them?"

Ah hell. All these damn questions. That's not how it was supposed to go. Well, actually it was. He simply underestimated how being near Charlotte so often would affect him. He thought he'd get used to her, get over her, not have any trouble concentrating when she was around. She had to stop asking him for information before he said something he shouldn't and blow everything from here to kingdom come.

"Do you know the name of the grandparents? Where in Boston they lived? Did Otis ever visit the girl? Do you have a picture of the missing necklace? Why were you talking to RL in the alley?"

His gaze fused with hers. RL? The meeting? She knew! Fuck. He couldn't think of a lie and he sure couldn't tell her the truth, so he went with plan B and took her in his arms and shut her up with a mind-numbing, heart-racing, it-was-really-a-great-plan-B kind of kiss. Hell, he should have done this the minute she walked into the room.

She tasted incredible. Even better than in the carriage house, and that was going some. Her body formed to his as his tongue seduced hers, then got seduced in return, making every inch of him stone-hard and hungry . . . very hungry. He braced his hands against the door, caging Charlotte between his heated body and the cool oak. Her breaths came fast, her fingers twisting into his hair. Her lips tasted sweet and wet as he took them again and again.

"We shouldn't," she panted, her gasps on his mouth, "do this."

"Too late." He bunched her skirt up in his fists; she undid his jeans. "I'm hot and sweaty."

"Oh thank God, I thought it was just me."

"I mean . . ." He couldn't think of what he meant because his jeans and briefs were now down around his hips and his dick right out there, in the open air. "Oh my God," she said on a sigh.

"That's my line. Oh Lord, is that my line." She was staring at him, his erection thick and rigid and ready. His fingers connected with her . . . panties? Damn panties. There should be a law against them.

She touched his erection and he nearly dropped dead from the sheer pleasure. "I want you now," she whispered in a shaky breath. "I want this."

"Bedroom?" He could barely talk. If he got any harder he'd rupture something.

"Too far."

He backed her to the hall table and slid her up onto the smooth dark mahogany.

"Nice bowl." She pushed it aside.

"Nanking Cargo, in the sea for two hundred years. When you dine on it, it seeps salt. It's a perfect bowl." He gazed down at her bare, parted thighs and the dark patch under the white lace. He wanted that patch. "You are a perfect woman." He cupped the triangle hiding her secrets, and desire shot through him hard.

He ripped her panties and she gasped, "Thank heaven for cheap underwear."

"Thank heaven for you." Her scent of blatant female sex filled the foyer, and he wrapped her legs around him, her heat scorching his erection, so close now, his need to be in her overpowering.

"Protection?"

"We have a doorman."

Her eyes cleared for a moment. "Condom?"

"His name's Rick."

She framed his face with her palms, her green eyes wide and blazing and wanting him. "You're teasing me at a time like this?"

He kissed her, the rain making him feel totally alone with Charlotte, just the two of them, no one else in the city, no one else in the world. "I want to make this last just a little longer, Charlotte, and I need a little diversion. Damn, girl, I've wanted you since forever, since high school, college, last week when you were at that bar on Whitaker and now. God, I want you now."

There was a terrible pounding on the door, making Charlotte jump, and his insides freeze when he heard . . .

Chapter 3

"Griffin? Griffin," Camilla called, then she hammered the door again. "Are you there? One of the waiters said he saw you come up here. My plane just got in from Rome, and I need to see you immediately. What's going on with our precious Charlotte? What have you done?"

Griff felt every muscle in Charlotte's body tense at the mention of her name connected with *precious*, one of those words that could be nice or not nice at all. His mother never used it in the good way, and it was obvious this time more than ever.

Charlotte pushed him back and slid from the table. "Never mind."

He swallowed a string of curses. "Never mind? What do you mean, never mind. Hell, I mind!"

"Well, goodie for you."

He ached, and Camilla bellowed, "Griffin, I hear you in there. Why aren't you answering the door?"

Charlotte took her panties and stuffed them in the pocket of his T-shirt, then jerked open the door. Camilla stumbled inside with the next knock as Griff turned his back and did the fastest and most painful zip job in history. Camilla looked from one to the other and yelped, "Bless my soul, what's going on here in this room?"

"Have a nice flight, Mother?" Griff kissed her on the cheek, listening to Charlotte's footsteps fading, knowing that if Otis's death hadn't been so recent and Camilla wasn't threatening a nervous breakdown every few days, he'd make the carriage house over into an apartment in record time and move out there. "You're home early."

"And you're up to no good with, with . . . with *that* woman. Are you—"

Griff cut her off by taking her elbow and ushering her into the hallway. He nodded to her apartment at the other end. "I'm sure you have unpacking."

"But—"

"And you want to rest after your long journey."

"Why was Charlotte deShawn . . . And you have white . . . Are those—"

"I'll see you tomorrow, Mother. Welcome home. I hope you're well rested."

"But . . . But . . ."

Griff went back inside his apartment, closed the door and yanked the slip of white lace from his pocket. Fuck! Double fuck! Exactly what he wanted to do and didn't, and now he had lacy panties to remind him of that very fact.

Charlotte sipped sweet tea as she sat at the polished mahogany bar at Magnolia House. Mahogany . . . the same wood as the little table in Griff's apartment.

She tried to forget that yesterday she shared it with some exotic salty bowl, her bare legs around Griff's hips and her womanly attributes almost around his fantastic manly one. She swallowed a whine. Not that this was her first guy, but probably her first big guy. Her insides throbbed and moistened and swelled in anticipation just thinking about Griff and his . . . penis. Something that satisfying needed a better name, and if she kept thinking about him, about *it*, she'd have an orgasm right here in the bar.

Blast Camilla for interrupting! Charlotte bit the side of the glass. If that woman wasn't trying to mow her down with her big blue Caddy, she was killing her with frustration. The Caddy was definitely an easier way to go. All she and Griff needed was five more minutes. Her mouth went dry at the thought. Right now she'd need about three minutes to make it happen. Maybe less.

She had to think about something besides Griff and last night and that table. Like the piano music in the background that came from the real deal and not some second-rate recording, the complimentary cheese and fruit, perfect and expensive, or the reason she was here now, to talk to Daemon Rutledge. She had to steer clear of Griff no matter how much willpower it took.

Across the entrance hall that separated the bar area from the registration desk, the faultless hotel manager with graying temples and a perfect red rose in his lapel signed in another guest. There'd been a steady stream checking in during the late afternoon, but there seemed to be a lull in the action. As he headed for the glass double doors at the end of a hallway that led to the courtyard, now twinkling with candles under crackled glass globes and sparkling cream china, Charlotte followed. "Mr. Rutledge."

He turned and smiled his manager smile, which always seemed to be in place and made everyone feel welcome. "Why, if it isn't Miss Charlotte. What a pleasant surprise. How's your daddy getting along these days?"

"He's managing, thank you for asking. Can I talk with you for a minute? It's about the Carswell baby."

"My, that was some time ago, now wasn't it." Daemon ushered her down the short hallway, lined with framed photos of Magnolia House before and after its restoration. He opened the door to a small office under the staircase marked "Manager" that was across from a door marked "Griffin Parish." Daemon said, "I'll be glad to answer any questions you have, but I honestly don't recollect much."

"I'm trying to help Griff find the missing daughter, but that's just between us."

"Of course. I understand completely." He nodded and smiled. Everyone knew Daemon Rutledge to be a man of his word, completely discreet and manners fine enough to write the book on the subject. He stood by the window that overlooked the gardens, his attention on the waiters setting up for dinner. "Let me see now. As I recall, the babe was in Otis's care for about four months, then he hired someone to take her up east to Boston. He wanted to raise the little girl himself, as he and William were dear friends and William left him guardianship. But being a single man, and with the huge job of restoring Magnolia House and no money, he had his hands quite full and realized he was not cut out to be a daddy after all, least not at this stage of his life. He didn't feel he could do right by her."

"Who was supposed to take the baby to Boston?"

Daemon turned, his right brow arching a fraction. "Supposed to?"

"I know. Surprised the daylights out of me, too. I got Adie's maiden name from the death notice in the *Herald* and called her parents. Seemed like a logical thing to do, and the simplest. The grandmother and grandfather, Edwina and Shipley, have no idea where Jaden is. And you're going to love this: Jaden never lived with them, and from what I could tell, that was just fine and dandy. Children were not their thing. Guess that's why Adie moved to Savannah. The only reason the old bat grandma talked to me at all was to see if I knew anything about the missing necklace."

"Well, I . . . I had no idea. If that doesn't beat all."

Daemon stroked his chin. "Grandma was definitely not a milk-and-cookies kind of lady."

"More a diamond-and-ruby kind of lady, and she wants the necklace back. Seems it's museum-quality. Louis the something had it made for a mistress. Edwina didn't say how it came to be in her family."

"But where is Jaden?"

"Did Otis ever say anything to you? You were with him since back in the day when he and William bought this hotel and started fixing it up."

Daemon smiled. It was a reminiscent one, the kind that accompanies good memories. "We hauled bricks and lumber and plaster right along with the workers. Whatever it took to get the job done." He affectionately patted a wall as if it were a living, breathing thing. "Otis never mentioned the baby after sending her off."

"But why would Otis let everyone believe Jaden was in Boston?"

"You know," Daemon said as he straightened his rose. "Now that I'm considering all the details, I imagine it was for protection. Her parents were murdered, and if the baby just disappeared, Otis probably believed that was the safest path to follow. It was always suspected that William and Adie were murdered for the necklace, but actually there's no way of knowing for certain that was the only reason. In those days, William and Otis did almost anything to get cash. The renovations took more money than they estimated and they were flat-out broke. Maybe William got mixed up with a loan shark and couldn't pay up? That's all I can figure."

Daemon eyed his watch. "Oh my goodness, the dinner guests are arriving presently. If more comes to mind, I'll be in touch. You take care of yourself now, you hear. Give your best to your daddy for me, and let me know if you discover anything about Jaden." He clucked his tongue. "Poor little thing. Where could she be all these years?"

Daemon took the door to the courtyard, welcomed guests, then escorted them to their tables. Dinner at Magnolia House promised more of an experience than simply eating great food, especially if the weather allowed the garden open. Daemon Rutledge made it all that was expected and much more. Griff was lucky to have him.

Charlotte looked at the photos of the hotel in the hallway as she left. Thirty years ago, the place was a shambles, with boarded windows, iron railing falling off the second story, decaying brick. Word had it that when they went to fix the back wall, the whole thing collapsed into a big heap right there in the courtyard where dinner was now being served.

There was a picture of Otis and William shaking hands and a woman looking on. Adie probably. The hotel in the background looked like a war casualty. Next, a picture of Otis and Camilla and Griff. Otis tall and handsome and serious; Griff a cutie clutching Camilla's hand. What was he then, three or four when Camilla and Otis married? Camilla had that same huffy look about her, and the hotel in the background didn't look any different.

Charlotte checked the date. The picture of Camilla and Otis was six months from the picture of Otis and William together, meaning Otis and Camilla were married soon after the murder. Like a few months after.

The next picture was three months later and showed considerable progress on Magnolia House, least on the outside. So, what happened after Otis married Camilla that let this happen? And did Camilla know Jaden? The timelines could overlap.

"Hi," came Griff's deep voice behind her, making her heart dance and her insides get mushy. Wanting to get laid by Griff Parish hadn't diminished one bit in twenty-four hours, except right at this moment she had questions that needed answering, and they weren't of a sexual nature. "How'd Otis fix up Magnolia House?"

"With a lot of sweat and taking big chances." He backed her into his office, dropped the blinds and kissed her socks off. . . . He'd already kissed her pants off last night.

"What are you doing?"

"Picking up where we left off in my apartment. Damn sorry about that, I really am. I hope you're not wearing underwear. I'm getting to hate that stuff."

"Whether or not I wear panties has nothing to do with you," she lied, thinking of the pink lacy ones she chose. She picked them with him in mind, for reasons she didn't want to think about . . . like would Griff like the pink ones or the yellow? Gads, she was pathetic. "Where'd the money come from to restore Magnolia House?" she blurted to get her mind off Griff and panties.

His expression looked the same as when Camilla pounded on the door. "Pardon me?"

"The money to fix this place up? Where'd it come from? Otis was broke."

"How the hell should I know?" His face went unreadable. He and Bebe took expressionless lessons from the same teacher.

"You're lying. I can see it in your eyes, and since your lips are touching mine, your eyes aren't far away."

"Why would I lie?"

"Do you remember Jaden?"

"I was three years old when Mother married Otis. I remember wedding cake and candy."

"What kind of game are you playing, Griff?" She should step away, but wanting him rode her hard, and instead of running off like a sensible woman, she ran her hands under his suit coat. She wanted to believe him because of the kiss, but his eyes . . . those tell-all blue eyes . . . said something else was going on. Blast something else. Blast this case. But bless his great build and hard muscles.

She stepped away. "You kiss me one minute, and then go and lie to me the next. And what were you talking about with RL in the alley? What's going on around here?"

"He wants me to get you off the case, but I want you to find Jaden. That's the truth."

"But not the whole truth, is it? And you're not going to tell me for reasons I intend to find out." She grabbed the door handle, considered her options, turned back and kissed Griff with lots of tongue and lips and a little nibbling and incredible cooperation. Then she tore open the door and raced down the hall before she turned back once more and threw herself across the desk saying, "Take me, you no-good lying bastard."

Depriving herself of great sex called for a big piece of peanut butter pie. Lots of it. It wasn't as good as sex by any stretch, but it would give her a nice sugar high and help her figure out what was going on. She and Griff had chemistry that went back years and had worsened to the point of terminal frustration. So what should she do? Un-frustrate or un-Griff? And how could she un-Griff when she worked for him?

She considered that question as the city faded in the dusk and she made her way up Bull. She took an outside seat at Six Pence, under the scrawny locust tree by the sidewalk. Everyone came here for shepherd's pie, but who wants a shepherd when there's peanut butter to be had. The waiter brought the order, lit the votive candle in the middle of the little white metal mesh table and gave her the evil eye for taking up space and not ordering dinner.

"Oh thank God I found you," Prissy said to Charlotte as she trotted up the sidewalk in four-inch heels, purse flapping at her side, gauzy shirt slipping off her shoulder. She pulled out the chair on the other side of the table as the waiter served Charlotte's pie, almost dumping it in her lap while drooling over Prissy.

Priss took the fork from the plate, dug into the pie and said around a mouthful, "I'm a complete wreck. What seemed like a great idea yesterday in broad daylight is a little scary now no matter how hot the Biscotti guys are."

"Biscotti like the cookie?"

"Biscotti like the new owners of the old morgue. I'm on my way there right now to try and land the decorating job. Good gravy, Charlotte, what was I thinking? It's a morgue, for pity sake, and I'm getting those bad vibes again just thinking about that place."

"Priss, does anyone have good feelings about a morgue?" Charlotte tried to reclaim her fork, but Prissy chowed down another piece. "Besides, you're making your mark on Savannah with this job. The morgue is really old and I'm guessing on the registry of Savannah historic homes. This is your ticket out of the paint department of Home Depot. Your big chance to prove yourself. And if you eat the last bite of my pie, I'll hurt you bad."

Priss forked another chunk. "You gotta come with me. The place is creepy beyond words."

Charlotte watched the last bite disappear, then Priss licking the fork back and front. "Me a decorator? Remember the mauve-and-puce bedroom?"

Prissy shoved her notebook across the table. "Carry my stuff. You can fake it as my assistant. I'll highlight your hair."

"I don't want my hair highlighted."

"Well, you should, and the feeling I have is more creepy than downright life-threatening." Sometimes it just comes to me out of the blue, like with that check of yours."

"This time it's indigestion from pilfered peanut butter. And what would I do with highlighted hair?"

"Seduce the Biscuit. Priss wiggled her brows up and down.

"How does that sound? Pretty yummy, huh? You, Griff, great hair. Bet you're wearing hot pink panties from just thinking about the man."

Charlotte held Prissy's hand. "The hottie owners have been in the morgue for three weeks and are still alive and doing well, so there's no reason for me to tag along or for you to be afraid. In fact, everyone in Savannah loves the brothers to death."

"Can you leave out the death part?"

"They stroll the city every night, attend jazz clubs, chat with the locals, leave big tips, drink red wine, then go home before midnight and work till dawn on their place. All very respectable."

"Think about what you just said, girl. Stroll at night, work till dawn, no mention of daylight. Not your typical townsfolk. And think about this: The morgue was where William and Adie were murdered, remember?"

"I'm not investigating the murder, just the whereabouts of Jaden, and I guarantee nothing about her is in that morgue. Heck, she's not even in Boston. She never got there to begin with."

Prissy's lips formed a perfect O and she sat back. "Well, my goodness, what happened to that little baby? See, you need inspiration, a connection to the case, and this is the way to get it up close. Besides, there's no reason for you to hang around here. You already finished up your pie. Come along with me. It'll do you a world of good."

"It'll do *you* a world of good, you mean." But Priss was right as rain about the pie being gone. And there was no need to go home and check on RL, since Big Al was visiting, probably to discuss her future in floor coverings. "All right, all right, I'll go."

Prissy beamed and stood. "You really need your hair done, and for heaven's sake, leave a big tip. The waiter's a real cutie."

They headed for the morgue, cutting through Forsyth Park, the white tiered fountain in the middle of grass and trees sending sprays skyward, droplets reflecting moonlight. A stillness settled over the city. Daily hustle and bustle . . . at least as much as Savannah ever hustled . . . set aside till tomorrow. Prissy slowed, then came to a stop, Charlotte beside her, both staring through the moss and muted streetlight to the neglected building. Prissy whispered, "The morgue part's in the basement, with an old casket room in back, offices in the front." She pointed to the second floor. "Anthony and Vince live up there, over their . . ."

"Funeral parlor."

"Yeah, funeral parlor." Prissy swallowed. "Think Chicken in a Bucket has openings?"

"And just what kind of impression does cooking chicken parts make on the rich and snobby unless you want to be their cook?"

"What I need is their business. The nuns are desperate for a nun-mobile and a new kitchen. They've been making pralines and boysenberry jam and doing their Sweet Sisters gift baskets to make ends meet. They've been taking in runaway teens—three this past month alone—and . . . look, there's a light on the porch. They're expecting us."

Charlotte felt a bone-deep chill. "These better be some memorable highlights." She hitched her pocketbook under her arm, then trotted across the street, Prissy in tow. They took the crumbling brick steps to the covered porch, white paint peeling from the header and jamb, suspended wrought-iron light swaying gently overhead, dancing the shadows to and fro. Overgrown bushes and trees crowded in around them.

Prissy whispered, "If one of those Addams Family people comes to the door, I am so out of here."

"You have to knock first."

"I need a margarita. I have a lot more courage with a margarita in my hand."

Charlotte picked up the heavy iron knocker and let it drop with a solid thud that made them both jump as Charlotte's cell chirped "Sweet Georgia Brown."

Prissy glared. "Don't you dare even think about answering that thing, Charlotte deShawn. I absolutely forbid it. Whatever it is, you'll use it as an excuse to go and leave me here all by myself."

Charlotte flipped open the phone. "It's BrieAnna. She's checking on something important for me."

"We've known each other for a million years. She'll be around tomorrow."

Charlotte read the text message. "There's someone on the garden tour from South Carolina and she wants me to meet them, and they're in town only for this one night. It's about Camilla."

"But I've got first dibs on you and I want you here now, and how'd Camilla get mixed up in all this, anyway?"

"I'll fill you in later." Charlotte pointed to the door. "I hear footsteps."

"Oh Lordy. You can't do this to me," Prissy whined in a stage whisper. "Friends don't let friends do spooky places alone."

"It's not spooky. It's your imagination and a house that needs a coat of paint and a city that has a whole bunch of tourist hype about haunted stuff because it's so darn good for business. Do you know how many ghost tours this city has? Haunted Savannah, Savannah Happenings, Savannah Midnight, Savannah—"

"I don't care!"

"I'll come with you next time. Bring peanut butter pie, your own fork, a garlic necklace."

"That is so not funny, not one teeny little bit. And you

can just forget all about those highlights and keep living with your old auburn hair."

Charlotte turned, hand on hip. "It is not old, it's . . . understated."

"Bet that's not what the Biscuit thinks. He's thinking highlights and how sexy Charlotte would be if she stayed and helped Prissy."

Chapter 4

Prissy sucked in a deep breath through clenched teeth to keep them from chattering like that plastic windup toy her dentist kept on his desk. Her mouth went dry, knees knocking, and not just because the place was eerie but because this could be her big break . . . if she lived to tell about it.

The knob turned, her stomach did the same and the door opened to—well, glory be to Mary!—to the most handsome man God had seen fit to put in the grand state of Georgia. A Goth version of George Clooney, widow's peak and all. The man at the door flashed a dazzling smile, the inside hall light shining in his black hair, his superfine build relaxed and friendly. Friendly counted for a heck of a lot right now.

"*Buona sera*, Ms. Pricilla St. James," he said in an expensive Chianti kind of voice. He took her hand and kissed the back as hammering sounded from the upstairs. "Welcome to our mess," he laughed. "I am Anthony Biscotti. My brother, Vincent, is attempting to fix the stove. We are hoping to offer you sweet tea. We are addicted."

"Everyone calls me Prissy." She forced a smile in return as he stepped aside. Oh dear, did she really have to go in? "You've been without a stove all this time?"

"We survive."

On what? Canned goods? Bread? Veggies? Body parts? But he didn't look the body-part type. Then again, what was that type?

"And we are pleased you could come. You are very persistent."

More like desperate. Anthony took her hand and she had no choice but to enter. He nodded at the center hall and the room to each side. "So, now that you are here, tell me what you think of our fine home. There are many more rooms, of course, but mostly they are like these. So perhaps the job is too big for you? Too impossible?"

Holes in the plaster, stained hardwood floors—she didn't want to think about what stained it—peeling wallpaper, crumbling ceiling and the most fabulous crystal chandelier in a crate in the corner. Well, that was good news. Someone who had this wonderful antique must have good taste and couldn't be into plastic flowers or flocked wallpaper. She hunkered down by the box. "It's a real beauty. Venetian amber glass. Where'd you get it?"

"A gift from Napoleon to Vincent and myself for helping with his unification of the arts project when he was in Florence and—"

"Actually, Anthony meant to say the fixture is from the Napoleon Foundation," added a shorter, slightly balding but still good-looking guy strolling down the stairs. "But there are several nice chandeliers in the house already, some in need of much cleaning and repair from a fire in the back rooms long ago, but we will get to them someday."

He wore perfectly pressed pants, a black silk shirt and incredible Italian leather shoes that had to cost the earth. No knockoffs here. He kissed the back of Prissy's hand, but his fingers were cold and clammy and had a smear of blood. "I am Vincent."

I am toast!

He took a handkerchief and swiped the blood away. Least he didn't lick it! "I nicked myself fixing the stove. So, do you think there is any hope of salvaging our new home? A very big job for one girl to handle. Perhaps you should rethink. We have made the upstairs somewhat livable, but everything else is in need of much help."

And she needed to get out of here. Then she thought of Sister Ann, who taught her how to draw; Sister Clementine, who taught her about color; and Sister Florence, who took her by bus to Atlanta to the art museum when she was eight. Prissy needed this blasted job!

She pointed to the cherry staircase to draw their attention there. "Well, I can tell you, this is a jewel. No one knows how the craftsmen made them with the perfect arc. The art was lost with time."

"You see," Anthony said, now holding the door open for her to go. "It's all in the materials."

The brothers obviously didn't want her there. She didn't want to be there, but there, was the issue of a double oven, a Sub-Zero fridge and a Viking stove.

"But the true problem," Vince added, "is that the banks won't lend us money. The new president of Low Country Federal Bank and Trust himself would not loan us more money. So I suppose Anthony and I will have to do the repairs ourselves. It will take time, a lot of time, but we will manage."

"But I can help. And . . . and I work cheap. And the sooner we get you open for business, the sooner you can make money." She gave them a reassuring grin. "Let me see the next room." She closed the one door, then tugged Anthony into the room down the hall. Dark, their footsteps echoing, her ever-dry deodorant pooping out as every hair on her head stood straight up. She flipped the light switch and the whole house went totally dark. Was that scream her own?

"It is all right, Miss Prissy," Anthony soothed. "Do not be alarmed. This happens all the time. The wiring is not up-to-date, is all." His hot breath fell over her cheek, his body close. He lit a match, the orange glow illuminating his face against the night. Oh crap! Oh crap! Oh crap!

She ran, tripped, fell flat on her face, swore never to wear platform shoes again for the rest of her life no matter what the style was, then flipped over to see Anthony, his face gleaming in the flickering light. "Are you all right?"

"No!" She scooted back, her heels peddling fast against the hardwood floor, ruining her new poly skirt that really did look a lot like silk.

He approached and held out his hand. "I want to help you."

"You want to suck my blood! You're . . . you're vampires!"

Anthony stopped, a slow grin sliding across his face, his teeth white, his eyes laughing. "Vampires? You truly believe there are such things?"

"This is Savannah. We're all about parties, food and anything haunted, and you bought this old morgue and you're up all night and black is your favorite color. That's quite a damning list. And your hands are cold."

"We drink the sweet tea," Anthony offered as the lights blinked on. Vince sat down in an old Victorian love seat with original horsehair upholstery, and Anthony leaned against the white marble hearth. "We are just regular guys, as you say. We are awake at night because Anthony lost his beloved Celeste two years ago and the nights are lonely for him. So we work the nights."

"I am sorry for your loss," she said to Anthony, but she wasn't buying it and wanted to run and forget all about this place. Except Sister Anita, praline diva of Savannah, would love marble countertops. Priss could imagine her with gray veil pulled back, white sleeves rolled up, sugar and butter creaming in the industrial-size Kitchen Aid Professional 600.

"I'll get you financing," she blurted without a clue to how she'd do it. "I have a friend who has connections. We'll throw a party, show off the attributes of this place and how having a funeral here is a grand last tribute to a loved one. The bank will lend you money when they see there is interest and more money to be made. And you can't renovate the whole place by yourselves. It'll take years. That doesn't make good business sense especially with me here to help out."

The brothers exchanged looks, and Anthony said with a resigned sigh, "If we want to be businessmen in the community, we have to act the part or people will not believe we are who we say we are."

She wasn't sure what that meant, but it sounded like a good omen for a job.

Vince said, "A garden party, outside perhaps?"

"Sure, outside." Or on the roof or in the middle of the street, or on the sidewalk or in Timbuktu. "So does that mean I'm hired, or what?"

Sam Pate sat at the crowded Magnolia House bar and ordered another Rolling Rock beer as he studied the papers in front of him. He should be in the office dealing with more pressing matters, but he'd had it with those four walls, even if two were floor-to-ceiling windows overlooking the Savannah River. He needed a break.

Closer to the truth, he needed a woman.

Busting his butt to get ahead landed him in a sweet position in Savannah but didn't allow time to land a sweet babe in his bed. He wasn't just a working machine, dammit. He was thirty-five and a horny male and in need of female companionship of a carnal nature . . . and he spotted just what he wanted walking into the bar right now.

"Hi," he said as she strolled by, suddenly wanting to make a connection. She paused, turned, gave him a quick once-over, not seeming to mind his jeans and T-shirt. She flashed a smile, his heart flipped, her eyes darkened. Well, hot damn! Southern hospitality was alive and well in Savannah. "I'm new in town."

"I know." Her cheeks pinked just a touch under her lovely amber skin, a shade or two lighter than his own. "I mean, I would have remembered seeing you around."

There was something about her. An instant link he'd never experienced, an unusual bond. No doubt brought on by his abject horniness and her sophisticated scent and incredible hair. He was a curly-hair kind of guy, always had been since middle school when he caught a whiff of Lilly Moore's ginger locks and nearly had his first orgasm. Someone pushed against the babe, knocking her into him, allowing him to capture her in his arms. Her eyes danced, and his heart stopped. Dang, he wasn't all that far from the orgasmic state now. *What was with him and this woman?*

Sex!

"What would you like to drink?" he managed without sputtering too much.

"You," she whispered in a breathy tone, her words flowing across his face. She blushed to her hairline this time. "I mean . . ." She nibbled her bottom lip, looking confused and sexy as hell. "Actually I don't know what I mean. I never say things like that to strange men . . . even unstrange men. I don't even kiss on the first date."

He smiled at that, and she swallowed, her innocent air a real turn-on, though he wasn't needing any help in that department. "Maybe we have met before," she said. "I don't know. There's something about you. . . ." Her hand tightened a fraction on his arm, her eyes dark as the river at night, his brain in meltdown, lust gnawing his gut.

He kissed her, not caring squat that this was unbecoming behavior for a business guy striving to make a good impression in a new town. And then she kissed him back . . . with gusto. Well hell, he really liked the gusto part. Except every muscle in his body went rigid and he didn't give a rat's butt if they ever met before or who saw them, and from the way the babe responded, he doubted she cared about those things either.

"I have a room," he mouthed against her lips. Holy shit, did he really say that?

"Close by?" she panted, her eyes not focusing.

He stood, snagged the papers, stuffed them in his back pocket, then cupped her elbow and headed them for the elevator. "Do elevators always take this long?" he muttered as they stared at the closed double doors, the electricity between them enough to light Savannah for a year. How'd this happen? Why her?

"We could take the stairs," she whispered.

"In my condition I . . ."

"Me, too." The elevator doors finally slid open and they stepped inside. As the doors closed, so did his brain, and when the car rose, he backed the babe to the wall and hit the stop button. An alarm went off somewhere . . . in the hotel or in his head. Either way, he wasn't paying attention to it, or to anything else, just the babe. He bunched up her skirt and brought her sweet body hard to his as their lips mated. The warmth of her skin seared his, her scent drove him wild. His hands cupped her firm little rear, the thong panties giving him sweet access.

"What are we doing?"

"Anything you want, sweetheart, anything at all. Name it, it's yours." He could barely get the words out. She kissed him again, her tongue halfway down his throat this time. A hell of a way to show agreement, and he liked it! But not nearly as much as he liked the fact she was undoing his belt. His dick swelled, and he was surprised he had enough skin left for it to get any bigger.

He lifted her onto the hand railing and she grabbed it. "Wrap your legs around me, darlin'." She did, and in an instant he pulled aside the slip of panties. "Oh crap."

Her eyes widened. "This is not an *oh crap* kind of moment!"

He wiggled his wallet from his back pocket, located a condom. She bit back a grin. "Right. Just hurry, okay?"

He dropped the wallet to the floor, ripped the package and covered himself. Then in one long, even stroke, he slid into her, the sensation mind-blowing. A perfect fit, they were made for each other . . . least, right now they were.

She gasped, the pulse in her throat throbbing. She bit his shoulder to stifle her cries as she came, her whimpers filling the small room, her hips thrusting hard against him. His brain fried and his body exploded in an orgasm that shook the whole damn hotel.

"Oh God, the elevator's moving."

Moving! So much for a shaking orgasm. "Must be an override."

"I hate overrides," she panted as she slid down. He wrapped the condom in the papers in his pocket . . . the most exciting thing to happen to mortgage rates in years. He zipped up and she smoothed down her skirt as the doors to the lobby opened and the manager with a red rose in his lapel asked without raising a brow, "Are you folks okay?"

Define *okay*.

Red Rose continued in an even voice, "We do seem to have difficulties with this elevator from time to time."

An elevator club like the Mile High Club? "No harm done," Sam managed. He took the babe's hand and stepped out into the hall trying to act normal, and that was a damn tough thing to do with his heart in hammer mode, the babe at his side and wanting to take her again right here in the hotel hallway. Did he remember to zip?

"Sir," the manager said as he drew up beside him. Oh God, he did forget to zip! And now the manager was going to tell him that his dick was hanging out there for all the world to see and—

"I believe this is yours." The manager discreetly slipped the wallet into Sam's hand, a corner of blue foil barely visible at the side. Sam felt light-headed with relief, and he tried to pick a fifty from his wallet to pay the manager for his most excellent discretion, but the manager just smiled. "Everyone at Magnolia House considers our guests family, and we take care of family. Enjoy your stay."

Which was concierge-speak for "Your secret is safe with us." Thank God. Now Sam could concentrate on getting to know the babe, and that would be the most enjoyable thing he'd done in a long, long time. They had this connection that went beyond sex, beyond anything he'd ever experienced before. He turned back, anticipating her great smile, flashing eyes, incredible scent . . . except she was gone. Totally vanished. Not at the bar, or in the courtyard or the lobby, or even in the upstairs hallways, where he thought she might be waiting for him. How could he be doing her one minute, thinking she was the hottest thing around, and she up and disappears on him?

Finally giving up, he returned to his room. Did he just dream the babe? Effect of an overactive, horny imagination? Hell, no one dreamed sex like that. But where was she? He could ask the bartender or the manager, but that would draw attention to the elevator incident, and he did not need that dredged up. But why did she leave?

And by the next morning, not only did he still have no clue where she'd gone or why, he had damn little sleep to compensate for it. Sam gazed out his office window to the

Savannah River flowing below and an ocean freighter growling its way into port. Was he that bad of a bed partner—or in this case, elevator partner? From her sizzling responses and intense orgasm, that didn't seem to be the problem. He got hard just thinking about what went on between them. Probably be hard as a damn brick all the damn day.

Savannah wasn't that big of a town. He'd run into her again, he was sure of it. What would he say? Nice panties? Hope I can see them again sometime? Unless she was passing through town. Then he'd never see her again. He didn't want to consider that possibility. He had to see her! More than that, he had to have her again!

A knock at the door drew his attention to banking business and the South's answer to Rosie O'Donnell with big hair, who happened to be his secretary. She drawled, "Ms. St. James is here to see you about a loan, sir. She's insisting on speaking only to you, that you were already familiar with the present situation."

Then the babe walked in, and he nearly slid out of his chair. He stared, unable to breathe, his brain whirling, and finally reality hit him upside the head like a two-by-four and everything became crystal clear. He managed a smile. "Yes, I'm familiar all right."

Rosie shrugged, then left. The babe seemed almost as surprised as he was. "Well, who would have thought," she finally managed.

"Nice try."

"Excuse me?"

"So that's what last night was all about." He stood, came over to her and said in a low voice, "You do me in some elevator and show up here wanting a loan? Couldn't you be a little more original than that?"

"What? Are you out of your mind?" She held up her hand. "I had no idea who you were last night."

"And that's why you left?"

"After what we . . ." She blushed. "I was a little embarrassed that . . . I'm not the kind of girl who . . . And I was so tired and . . . Hey, you picked *me* up, buster, remember?"

"And you're the one who strutted her stuff in my face to get my attention." And she did have terrific stuff, in and out of the elevator. He dreamed about her damn hair all night and—

What the hell was he doing? Fantasizing about her all over again? Hadn't he done enough of that last night? "That crap about not knowing me was a nice touch. The innocent game? Been a long time since I had that one pulled on me." Actually he never had it pulled on him because he was too busy being a damn banker.

"Oh, for Pete's sake, I didn't know you, and that's the truth."

"Honey, I was reading mortgage specs. You just told my secretary that I was familiar with the situation."

"You know the property I'm here to discuss. You already turned it down for a loan. I wouldn't know a mortgage spec if I tripped over it."

"If you're wanting a loan, you know what's involved."

Her lips thinned, her eyes flashed "I decorate stuff like me, rooms, anything that stands still." She waved her hand over her clothes. "See? Gucci, Prada. Well, actually they're knockoffs and the scarf's from Target. And who in the world decorated this office?"

"I did. And you probably had someone point me out to you. Well, let me tell you, sister, I am no fool—"

She jabbed her finger to her chest "Oh, I am so not your sister. I do not have genes that include olive-drab drapes and a brown couch." Her fist tightened around her handbag. "And you are the biggest fool I ever met if you think I'd screwed you for money."

"Then why the hell did you?"

"Obviously a case of temporary insanity."

"Or blackmail. If I don't approve your loan, you go running to the bank home office telling them I'm bedding the clientele. And you've got the hotel staff to back you up."

Her hand went to her heart. "Oh my stars, you think I'm a . . . a . . ."

"The easiest way for a woman to get what she—"

She slapped him hard. "You . . . you . . . no-good, low-rent Yankee pip-squeak."

Ouch! "Hey, I'm from Atlanta."

"Well, it's not Savannah and that's all that counts around here." She jutted her chin, turned on her very high heels and strode to the door, snatched it open, stopped and slowly turned back. "So." She put her hand to her hip. "Are you going to give me the loan for my restoration project?"

Okay, she had balls, he'd give her that. Actually he was the one with the balls, and they ached from thinking about her and not getting any. More than anything, he wanted to say "Hell no, I'm not giving you a loan," but that was too much drama considering the number of bank employees and customers now at the doorway to check out the commotion. "I don't even know which property you're talking about."

"The morgue on Drayton Street, which will make a simply lovely funeral parlor. Saturday night the Savannah Historical Society is having a gala to show support for the project. Come to the event, then you'll see it's a sound investment."

The morgue wasn't a sound investment, it was a money pit. But the new guy in town peeing all over a local gala and renovation project was not good business, especially with his audience growing by the minute in his doorway.

What happened here would be all over the city before noon, and a run on the bank was not how to grow his career.

Sweet stuff gave him a little gotcha smile. Damn the woman! She knew precisely what she was doing.

"See you on Saturday, Mr. Sam Pate." She offered a little finger-wave, and he nearly popped an important blood vessel somewhere.

Fuck! Damn! Hell! She used him. She played him. Somehow he had to steer clear of getting the bank involved with the morgue-rehab project, and he had to steer himself clear of the conniving babe because every time he saw her, he got into big trouble. There'd be no more of that.

Prissy trotted down the steps of the bank, then stood in front of the old red brick Cotton Exchange enjoying the griffin fountain spewing a steady stream of water, the iron fence with medallions of poets and presidents, the incredible Savannah spring flowers and an altogether superb spring day. Well, she did it, she got the loan—or at least, she avoided a flat-out loan rejection. That was the good part, but that she now had no future with Sam Pate was the rotten part. No male would have anything to do with a woman who shamelessly used him like he thought she used Sam. But by the stars in heaven, he was one yummy piece of mankind.

"Prissy St. James," came a voice behind her. "You just wait up a minute now, you hear me."

Prissy turned as Camilla Parish bustled up the sidewalk, every gray hair bouncing in time to her stomp. "I want you to go and tell that friend of yours to stay away from my Griffin," she panted without so much as a "Hello, and how are the good sisters these days?" Camilla straightened her purple linen suit, then stiffened her back. Catfight mode? "He does not need her causing trouble and interfering in his life."

"I imagine we're talking about—"

"That Charlotte deShawn girl, of course. You just tell her I don't want her at Magnolia House and I especially don't want her in Griff's room ever again. Of all the nerve. Simply scandalous, if you ask me."

His room? Prissy squelched an eyebrow raise. "And the reason you're not telling Charlotte this yourself is . . . ?"

"Because I'm talking to you, of course. Because you're here now and this issue needs tending to immediately. Griff wants nothing to do with her, and she should . . . should leave town and go find herself another place to live." Camilla jutted her pointy chin.

"You want Charlotte to leave Savannah?"

"Be the best for everyone, especially if she knows what's good for her. She shouldn't be here anyway. So there. I said it, and I'm mighty glad I did. Now you just give her my message to steer clear of my boy."

Camilla stepped around Prissy and pranced off down Bay. A chill snaked its way up Prissy's spine. Condescending Camilla, the reigning Savannah queen, she knew—everyone did—but an out-and-out threat? Going to Griff Parish's room had frightful consequences, made the elevator event with the bank president seem like small potatoes.

Prissy dodged an orange open-air tourist trolley bellowing information about the cannon being named George and Martha, and she threaded her way through clusters of cameras and maps and water bottles till she flung open the door to RL Investigations. "Well," she said to Charlotte, sitting behind the desk staring at a picture of JLo. "This day is off to a rousing start. It's not even noon, and I've just been called the town lady of ill repute and you've been tossed out of Savannah, and why are you staring at that picture?"

"I'm imaging myself a size four."

"Imagine a banana for breakfast instead of a doughnut."

"Good grief, why?" Charlotte jerked her head up. "Someone called you . . . the nun's kid . . . a . . . What exactly did you do at that morgue last night?"

"Not the morgue. The bank or the hotel, depends on what you're referring to. And it's all about that new bank president, to be precise. And it's your fault because I was looking for you at Magnolia House to whine about not going with me to meet Vince and Anthony and then this guy . . ."

"The bank president?"

Prissy sat on the edge of Charlotte's desk and sighed. "He was at the bar, and we sort of did the deed in the Magnolia House elevator."

Charlotte's eyes overtook her forehead.

"I still don't know what happened. There's something about him. A real connection."

"No kidding."

Prissy conked Charlotte on the head with a pencil. "Not that kind of connection. Something metaphysical, almost spiritual, ethereal."

"Yeah, that's what we all say. Just another name for wanting hot sex."

"It was more. Like we were drawn together. And not that it matters, because we hate each other now and he thinks I used the elevator event to soften him up for a loan."

"I don't think *soften him up* is the right description, honey."

Prissy rushed on. "And I sort of ambushed him into attending a society party at the morgue on Saturday."

BrieAnna entered with, "Party? What party? And who in the world is the *him* you're talking about?"

Charlotte nodded to Prissy. "The guy she boinked in the Magnolia House elevator."

BrieAnna's jaw dropped, and Prissy said, "Will you forget about the elevator event for just one minute?" She looked pleadingly at Brie. "I need you to throw an event Saturday to get the rich and snobby's support for the new funeral parlor so the bank will know there's money to be had and give us the loan."

"Sweet mother," BrieAnna said as she sat down on the other corner of the desk. "I take it this means you got the job and you have been busy this morning."

Prissy tossed back her hair. "A Starbucks Espresso Macchiato with double whipped cream for breakfast can do that to a girl. And I think I've got the job if I can get the money for it. Can you pull off the party, Brie? The Montgomery name has clout."

"Well now, Savannah's always ready for a party, that's true enough, and everyone's wanting to meet the Italian stallions. There are a million rumors out there. Everyone wants a look-see at the morgue, and why in the world do you have a picture of JLo on your desk?"

Prissy smacked her palm to her forehead and looked at Charlotte. "I almost forgot the most important thing of all," she said to Charlotte. "What were you doing in the Biscuit's room that would get Camilla in a huff and wanting you out of town? That woman is downright scary."

Charlotte pursed her lips in an innocent expression that didn't quite carry over to her eyes. "I was just looking at a bowl, and if that's what's got Camilla in such a state, just think where she'd be if she knew that I knew she didn't *own* a restaurant in Columbia, like we all thought she did thirty years ago. She was a *waitress* at the restaurant. I talked to Brie's friend last night, and Camilla's husband was killed in a train accident and got a huge settlement. She came here and married Otis a month later. She had high-faluting aspirations for herself and mostly for her son. The marriage was more of a social move than an all-consuming-love move."

"But what was in it for Otis? Why would he marry Camilla? Why would anyone?"

"Money for his hotel. William's death was very convenient for Camilla. Very, very convenient."

Prissy's brow furrowed. "But why would Camilla care if you knew that now? She's got the husband and the money and the status."

Charlotte pushed herself back from the desk and paced the office, then turned suddenly. "Unless she found out Griff hired me to find Jaden and she doesn't like me poking around in her business. There's something going on with Camilla and Magnolia House and Griff and the missing Jaden Carswell and Griff won't give me a straight answer when I ask questions. What's that all about? He hired me!"

BrieAnna stood and held out her hands. "What if he's playing you like Aunt Wilkes's parlor piano. You're new at this PI thing, so maybe he hopes you'll find nothing on Jaden and that will be good enough for the courts and he can have her declared legally dead. Ta-da, case closed, and Griff gets the hotel fair and square."

Charlotte growled. Her eyes thin slits. "Why, that scum-sucking, low-life Yankee varmint. He's counting on me being rotten at what I do. I'm just guessing now. There's no proof but it sounds mighty interesting. There's only one way to find out for sure what that toad's got brewing in that conniving brain of his. I need to sneak into his office and take a look around. I bet there's information there and I'm missing something important."

"Like your ever-loving brain," Prissy said. "Have you gone completely daffy? That's breaking and entering, and Bebe's going to be totally honked-off if she finds out about it. You can't do this. I . . . I forbid it. What if Bebe has to lock you up, fingerprint you, take one of those totally unflattering pictures and . . . and . . . and teach you the words to "Chain Gang"? Prissy blushed. "Hey, it's all I could think of. You got me rattled here."

"I can't let Griff Parish make a fool of me because he thinks I'm a bungling PI." Charlotte held up her scarred pinky and wiggled it. "And I need help."

BrieAnna sighed. "Oh no, here we go. She's playing the blood-sisters card. That is such a cheap shot. We need to put limits. Only two per year."

"Camilla wants me gone, Griff wants me stupid, and my dad wants me to sell carpet. I'm desperate here and need to get into Griff's office. So, are you guys gonna help me, or what?"

Chapter 5

Charlotte hurried up to Prissy, sitting at a cozy table in the Magnolia House bar. "Where have you been?" she whispered over the subtle piano music and low chatter. "I should have gone with the *or what* part of your little speech yesterday."

"Hey, that was some of my very best guilt-tripping to get you and Brie to help me out tonight." Charlotte sat down in one of the padded club chairs and finger-waved to BrieAnna at another table, littered with glasses and surrounded by ladies in floral print dresses. Brie scowled back.

"Big Al's been showing me carpet samples all afternoon. I love the man, I truly do, but carpet? Only thing I can remember is buy wool. And what in the world is virgin wool? Wool that hasn't had sex? A carpet that hasn't had sex on it? I sure couldn't ask Al. I really have to make this PI thing work."

"Well, I think liquoring up the garden club to supply you with a distraction so you can get into the Biscuit's office is not going down in investigative history as an all-time great moment."

"Okay, it's not *The Da Vinci Code*, but with Mrs. O'Hara and her bar-dancing reputation, we should get what we need. It's Griff's night off and Daemon's overseeing a dinner party, and even if they do show up, everyone getting Mrs. O'Hara off the table and discreetly herding inebriated ladies into cabs will keep the staff busy. How far along are my decoys?"

"Four rounds of dirty double martinis and counting. Brie told the bartender to put it on your tab."

"Do you know how much they get for a martini? And I don't have a tab."

She took Charlotte's hand. "Well, you sure do now. Brie got the garden club ladies here on the pretense of discussing renovations to the gardens at the morgue. Ladies can't just go out on the town and drink in Savannah, but if there's a pressing social cause, imbibing's perfectly acceptable, especially if someone else is picking up the tab. I hope all this effort is worth it."

"A baby doesn't disappear off the planet earth, and I can't see Otis just forgetting about a baby his best friend entrusted to him. Otis was a good man, honorable, did a lot to make Savannah what it is today. I'm betting he kept up with that child, least for a while. Heck, he left her the hotel. Getting into his office is the only way I'm going to figure out what's going on and why Griff's not leveling with me. Why would he hire me to find Jaden and not give me all the facts about her? He wants me to blow this case, and it's not going to happen."

Charlotte pulled in a quick breath. "Uh-oh. I just heard Mrs. O'Hara order *tee more martunies* . . . that's under-the-influence talk for two more martinis. It's showtime."

Mrs. O'Hara gulped her drink, tossed the olive in the air and caught it between her teeth. Thank goodness she'd removed the toothpick. Guess she did olive-tossing before. When she stood on the chair, twirled her purse over her head and yelled to the piano player, "Give me 'Dixie,' sweet buns, and make it snappy," Charlotte took off for Griff's office.

With women clapping, singing and now dancing and waiters freaking out and other guests wondering what in heaven's name was going on, no one noticed that Charlotte bypassed the restrooms, took a quick turn, then made for the hallway. Griff's door was locked, and thanks to one week of student teaching at Riverside Jr. High, she was in. Who said there was no learning going on in schools today?

She closed the drapes on the window that overlooked the dining courtyard, then clicked on a pen flashlight. She held it in her teeth and gazed around. She could have held it in her hand but in the movies the light was always clamped in the teeth. The last time she was in this office, she had something else in her mouth . . . like Griff's tongue.

She sat in Griff's big leather chair behind his desk, his scent of sea and leather wrapping around her, making her all tingly inside. Forget Griff; the tingle was newbee-PI jitters. The left drawer held business cards, stationery, wintergreen mints. She crunched into one and watched the sparkle in the dark. The middle drawer held keys—little ones, like for a diary or jewelry box or file cabinet. Using PI intuition, she went with the cabinet idea. Opening the first file drawer, she spied a folder with "Carswell" written in big black letters right in front. Well, dang, skippy, this PI stuff wasn't so tough. This was just what she was looking for.

Taking RL's tiny camera, she snapped a picture of one page, then the next, when the office door opened, giving her a heart attack right there on the spot. A flashlight blinded her as the door closed with a solid click. She held up her hand to block the beam. "All right, all right. You caught me." Least that's what she wanted to say, but her mouth was full of flashlight till she took it out. "Griff?" Except why wouldn't Griff just turn on the light?

The light became even more blinding, and when she aimed her flashlight back trying for a little blinding of her own, she got pushed against the wall. "Ouch!" She stumbled and fell, camera and flashlight skidding across the floor. She grabbed for a leg, definitely a *he* leg, which yanked free and ran out of the room. Rubbing her head, Charlotte pushed herself up and caught her breath, hoping her racing heart wouldn't beat right out of her chest as the door slammed shut. How'd someone know she was in here? Why would they care? Unless they were watching her. And why would they be doing that? So much for the easy life of a PI.

Charlotte retrieved the flashlight, then parked herself on the edge of the desk to try to stop from shaking all over. The blasted file was gone, she was scared spitless and "Stainmaster Carpet Employee of the Month" looked like a very real possibility in her future. She locked up the file cabinet and tossed the key into the desk drawer. She wasn't the only one looking for Jaden Carswell . . . or maybe someone wanted to make sure Jaden wasn't found. Someone like Camilla, to ensure Griff was sole heir of the hotel, or maybe Griff, so Jaden would be declared legally dead.

RL was right about one thing, she was so not up to speed on this PI stuff. After visualizing JLo and a size four, she needed to do Arnie and *The Terminator*. Least she had some information on the camera . . . wherever it was. Searching, she ran the beam over the carpet, the lock clicked and the door opened, making every hair on her body stand straight up. This place was busier than a freaking shopping mall. This time the overhead light flipped on and Griff stood in the doorway. "What are you doing in here?"

Getting my PI butt kicked. But instead of saying that, she needed to stall and find the blasted camera. Crossing her legs, she gave a coquettish wink. "Waiting for you, of course."

"How'd you get in?"

"The door was open, so I figured you were around and decided to wait."

He wore a tux, the expensive kind that fit perfectly. Collar open, bow tie undone, the hottest hunk of maleness on earth. Too bad he was also the slimeball who was using her. She had to really concentrate on the slimeball part because the hunky part looked really good.

"Want something?"

She crooked her finger in a come-to-mama way. How could that pop into her brain when she was supposed to be concentrating on the slimeball part?

"Last time we were together in here we weren't exactly seeing eye to eye." Griff's closed the door. "Fact is, you left in a huff."

"Guess what, I'm unhuffed." She tilted her head like Prissy did. She could do with some cute right now, to make this convincing.

"Something wrong with your neck?"

So much for cute.

"What's with the flashlight?"

"Safer than candles."

He leaned against the door, folded his arms and gave her a half-smile that was a lot sexy and a little mysterious. "You want to tell me what this is really all about?"

"Reconnecting. The flashlight is to get home through the back alley. We don't want everyone in town seeing me leave here. People talk, and that's the one thing we don't want. We have a case to protect, right?"

Where was the darn camera? She undid the top button of her blouse. Head-tilting may be beyond her but even she couldn't mess up an open-blouse message. She'd look around for the camera while performing kissy-face with Griff. All in the line of work, of course.

He let out a long, slow breath and raked back his dark hair. "When I'm least expecting it, you show up."

She could relate to that.

He turned off the light, plunging the room into darkness, the only sounds the last of the dinner guests in the courtyard and Griff's footsteps soft on the thick carpet, sensual, promising. Promising what? What if he tripped on the camera? What if he strangled her to keep her quiet about Jade . . . except she didn't know anything about Jade and Griff wasn't the strangling type. Crimany, there had to be an easier way to make a buck!

He clicked on the desk light, casting a warm golden glow over the polished cherry surface. "You being here is not about me, but I'm not in the mood to argue."

And just when she was about to insist that of course this was all about him and her and them together and him being irresistible, his mouth landed on hers and made that big fat lie the God's honest truth. And she so did not need it to be true. What she needed was the blasted camera, getting the job done and Griff not mixing up her life!

Except no one kissed like Griff Parish, and every darn time their lips met, she was reminded of it. No one knew how to hold her like he did, making her feel special and cherished and protected. After getting pushed around, she could do with a little cherishing and protection. Her legs went to jelly and she dropped the flashlight, then wrapped her arms around his shoulders. He tasted of brandy and all things warm and wonderful . . . except he was a slimeball . . . remember? Slimeball! He was playing her and . . . and . . . then he wedged himself between her legs, his hands cupping her derriere, sliding her close as their tongues got reacquainted.

"You have a really clean desk." She tried to think of something besides the kiss and her legs and his hands on her butt. "Always ready for action?"

"This is where I work." His eyes were as black as his

jacket, and his lips found hers again. "I like that you wear skirts."

"I like that you don't." Okay, her brain was officially fried.

"You know what the trouble with us is?" He found the soft place behind her ear, his breath on her neck, her insides liquefied.

"How long a list do you have time for?"

His lips smiled against her hot flesh as he said, "We, as in you and I, are pleasers. We want to keep peace in our families because our parents haven't always had it easy. They've put us first, want the best for us, and now we feel obligated to take care of them and put them first. But sometimes"—his mouth molded to hers, making her whole body quiver—"obligation wears thin. Sometimes we have to take a chance and find out what we really want." His gaze met hers. "What do you really want, Charlotte deShawn?"

Her brain wanted the camera, her pride wanted to beat him over the head for using her, but her body wanted sex. And being in Griff's arms, her body was winning by a landslide. "You should get a couch in here."

His hands ran up the length of her back and he framed her face. "Maybe we won't be any good together."

Together? Together! He kissed her firmly, like a brand, like you're mine, babe, least right now. Oh God, together! He took off his jacket and dropped it onto the chair, then slid off his tie, his crisp white shirt open at the neck. He had a great neck.

He undid her blouse, button by button, his fingers not soft and smooth like those of a maître d' or man of leisure, but hard like a working man's. There was a cut across his left knuckle. He touched her naked chest, her cleavage, lingering at the softness there.

"How about you undo my shirt so I know this is what you want, too."

She started at the little pleats and the buttons. Except they weren't buttons but those stud things men used for formal wear. She pushed the first one through one side of the shirt, then the other, and when he undid her bra, she nearly slid to the floor. "You're awfully good at that. Lots of practice?"

He looked deep into her eyes, his eyes smoky and intense. "Incentive. I've wanted you for so damn long, Charlotte. Since I knew what it was to really want a girl, you were the girl."

She fumbled with the third stud and dropped it beside the other two on the desk. She stared at his firm broad chest, sprinkled with tiny black hairs and sporting a nice tan. If she looked into his eyes again, she'd combust. Then his hands cupped her breasts and she combusted anyway. Closing her eyes she rested her forehead against his chin, her hands on his pecs, feeling his heart and his heat. "I . . . I can't do this. I can't see the buttons. I have sex blindness. You're driving me crazy. Was I really *the girl*?"

He kissed the top of her head. "Yeah." His voice was shaky, his hands not so steady, and that made her feel better. He was on fire for her as much as she was for him, and it wasn't all just a bunch of words. He meant it. His fingers helped hers, and his shirt fell open.

"Do you know how much of a really bad idea this is? I'm working for you, our families make those families in *Romeo and Juliet* look like best friends."

"Maybe after we do this"—he ran his thumb over her left nipple—"we'll be done with each other, least in this way. Like climbing Everest. Get it out of our systems and then go on with our lives."

"So every time we see each other, we won't be thinking . . .

sex, like I have since you walked into the office? It didn't work with the kiss."

"What kiss?" He stroked her other nipple.

"The one in the carriage house that I thought would satisfy my kissing cravings for you."

He tipped her chin so her gaze met his. He grinned, his eyes twinkling, and that was a welcome respite from the smoldering. "You have cravings for me? Look at me and think sex?"

And sometimes slimeballs. "Half the population of Savannah looks at you and thinks sex. The other half is men, and probably some of them are thinking sex, too."

"We've been in foreplay mode for years."

Just foreplay. That's what he said, right? Nothing between them but sex. Nothing . . . involved. "Like scratching an itch."

He laid her back on the desk. Some itch! Then he kissed her until she pushed him away, landing him sprawled out in the chair, the little wheels sliding him across the carpet. Panting, she sat up.

"You're calling this off?"

"You look really good in that chair with your shirt open, all yummy, but I want more. I need more."

He held out his arms, suddenly looking totally comfortable and at ease with himself. "Honey, I hate to break it to you, but this is it. This is all there is."

"Yeah, well, I want it naked. If this is a one-time deal and we've been building up to it for years, we need to make it count. No clothes in the way."

A sly smile pushed at his lips, but he didn't move. "Is it going to be a two-way street?"

Getting up all her courage, she pulled off her blouse, twirled it over her head and let it fly off into the room, landing on the floor where she'd have to pick it up and could look for the blasted camera. Amazing that she could even think of the camera right now. She flipped her bra in the other direction in case the camera was there. That was the real reason she was behaving like this—work. Sex and work, gave a whole new meaning to multitasking.

His eyes widened. "I didn't figure on this."

She came here for info on Jaden, but now that the opportunity presented itself—himself—she was taking advantage. She stood, unzipped her skirt, rounded up all her courage, then stopped.

"Things were just getting real interesting." His voice was low and husky.

"You go out with a lot of skinny girls."

"Meaning?"

"Oh, for heavens sake, Griff, don't be obtuse. I'm a full-figured gal. Not exactly made for stripping."

He stood, took her skirt and let it drop to the floor at her ankles in a soft swoosh. That left her in panties. "Oh, honey," he said in an appreciative voice. "You are so made for stripping. You're made for me."

She inhaled a quick breath, and he looked as surprised as she felt at the words. "You are delicious, and this is getting too close to the quickie you don't want."

Then he pulled off his pants too . . . "Red and pink kissing-lip boxers?"

"All I had clean. Rough week." Then he stepped out of the boxers, revealing something not funny at all. An old friend, a rather large old friend, though they never got acquainted. "Oh . . . my."

"Sweetheart, we haven't even gotten to the *oh my* part." He took a condom from his middle drawer.

"Good gravy, Griff. You've done this here before?"

He pulled her into his arms. "Do we have to talk so much?"

With his erection pulsing against her bare abdomen,

talking did seem like a total waste of time. How long had she been wanting this? Dreaming of this? Mentally orgasming over this? "Just making conversation." Then he kissed her and set her back up on the desk. "You have done this before."

He leaned her back again, this time his face to hers, his eyes dark, smoldering and mysterious, her body stretched out like a corpse.

"I'm feeling a little self-conscious here."

"I'm feeling a lot turned-on here. And I want you to feel that way, too." He kissed her, slowly, deliberately, his lips taking hers on an extended sensual adventure of kissing and nibbling and tasting. His calloused hand cupped the underside of her left breast, his thumb pad stroking her nipple, the cherry desk reduced to ashes.

She gasped, drawing his tongue deep into her mouth, his thumb making firmer strokes, now playing with her sensitive flesh, making her blood flow fast and hot. She laced her fingers in his clean, soft hair, his lips devouring hers, and he slid on top, bracing his weight with his forearms. His thighs straddled hers, his firm, bare legs next to hers . . . a real turn-on. Like she could be turned on any more. Then he kissed her chin, her neck, the indent of her cleavage.

Lust made her insides wet for wanting him. And when his lips closed over her left nipple, she nearly evaporated in a gush of steam. Surprise, surprise, she could be turned on more. He suckled the hardening tip, then the other, his hand fondling. He sat up, his gaze feasting on her in the dim light, making her feel beautiful. "I knew we'd be good together, but I didn't know it would be this good." He scooted back, planting kisses at the notch of her navel, then tracing a scorching path with his tongue all the way . . . down.

"Griff?" She raised her head up in time to see him fix a kiss at the apex of her legs. "Oh, Griff!"

"Oh, honey." He climbed off the end of the desk and spread her legs wide, and before she could catch her breath, he pulled her in one long stroke toward him, sending desk stuff crashing to the floor. He draped one leg and then the other over his shoulders, opening her wider. Cupping her bottom, he lifted her hips from the desk, his hot gaze fusing with hers. "You're incredible."

He kissed the soft inside of her left thigh, the heat of his mouth radiating through every inch of her. Deliberately, he inched wet kisses upward, his strong rough hands holding her firm, claiming her, giving her pleasure, and when he bent his head, his tongue touching, stroking her intimately, it was more than she could stand.

She gasped. "I . . . I . . ." Her body shifted from hot to cold and back again, and her fingers fisted a handful of papers from the desktop, her legs stiffening as an orgasm of earthquake proportions shook her from head to toe. "Ohmygod, Griff!"

And suddenly he was inside her, her body opening to him as he filled her completely, her legs now at his waist as he stood at the end of the desk taking her again, then again!

"God, Charlotte!" His head arched back while thrusting into her once more as desire, passion and just plain old lust unlike any other consumed her. She clung to him, feeling him a part of her.

Sounds of their breathing filled the room along with the heavy sweet aroma of sizzling intimacy. His hands cupped her sides and he pulled her up, enfolding her in his arms, his heart beating wildly against hers. "I'm going to need a new desk."

"Think we ruined it?"

He looked her in the eyes, his nose touching hers, his voice uneven. "Like I could ever get any work done here after this? Takes distraction to a whole new level."

"Go through a lot of desks?"

He paused, then closed his eyes for a second before he said, "I've had this one for fifteen years. It's you, Charlotte. There's no one like you." He licked his lips, then hers, and she returned the favor. "I don't know why the hell you're here, but I'm damn glad you are."

He smoothed back her hair, then kissed her temple. His strong hands on her cheeks were caring, loving, his kiss touching her heart. "You are an incredible woman."

She'd never felt so close to a man, and it went beyond a sexual kind of closeness. There was more, something meaningful, something mutual. "I'll thank Jaden Carswell for bringing us together."

His eyes suddenly cleared and his shoulders stiffened a fraction, nothing that could be seen even if the lights were bright. He changed somehow. "You are the best sex I've ever had. Incredible sex. You should give lessons."

"Lessons?"

"Yeah, how-to-please-a-man kind of lessons."

A chill replaced the warmth that had touched her heart. "I think it was the other way around."

"You're a good partner, Charlotte." He winked, and it was one of those cheap winks, the kind that said "Thanks, now I have to go." He took himself from her, and she felt used and a damn fool.

Turning away he wrapped the condom in one of the papers she'd crinkled, then tossed them into the trash can. Without looking back, he snagged her skirt from the floor and tossed it to her. "Now we don't have to be curious about each other. It's over and done with."

Blast his no-good hide! Okay, she thought, it was just going to be sex to her, too, least at the beginning, but then . . . Then what? "You went overboard to please me."

He stopped scooping clothes and stared at her, his eyes unreadable, not like before, when they were on fire for her. "Guess I was trying to impress you with my technique."

He went back to his clothes collecting, and if he flung any more of her garments at her, she'd scream in frustration and strangle him with her bra. It was more than sex to her, and no matter what he said, this was not just about him getting his rocks off with someone he'd wondered about.

He tossed her a shoe and she threw it back, hitting him square in the back.

"Hey!" He turned and faced her.

"I don't believe you. This was more than a quick roll in the hay . . . or on the desk. You were good to me, for me."

"Technique, remember."

"You could have techniqued yourself into your own orgasm, or found someone else and to hell with me, but you didn't do that tonight. You made a point of us being together." She slid from the desk as he stepped into his pants and shrugged on his shirt. She poked him in the chest, her body close to his, and she wished it was for something other than pitching a fit. "You want me to believe that *just sex* stuff, but it's a lie."

He turned away and strolled to the door. "Suit yourself, Charlotte. But trust me, this was all about the sex and us speculating for a really long time." He glanced back. "It was good, sugar, damn good. Not the best but—"

"You said it was the best."

"Isn't that what every woman wants to hear? But right now you need the truth so you don't think this little encounter is more than it is. I don't want you hurt, Charlotte, but there is nothing between us and there never will be. That's a fact I can promise you. Now be a good girl and turn off the light when you leave. The door locks automatically, so you don't have to fuss with it like you did when you let yourself in."

"Good girl? I'm a good girl?" She threw her other shoe as he closed the door behind him. "Damn you," she hissed into the empty, dark room. How could she read so much into a bad case of curiosity? She cared about him, he cared about her, least that's the way it felt, because they made love, gave pleasure and took it. And even if she was wrong about that, how in blazes could sex be better than what just happened between them?

She was no pro on the subject, *but not great?* Not the best? She put her fingers over her mouth to keep from laughing. For the first time in her life, she wanted to be the best at something.

She retrieved the camera and the flashlight and her shoe by the door, then closed it behind her, the lock clicking into place and snapping her thoughts away from Griff and sex. That was some big snap.

Think, Charlotte, think. She'd gotten into this office by jimmying the lock, which means the guy who pushed her did the same or he had a key . . . like Griff. If he really intended for Jaden to be declared dead and Charlotte not find her, Griff could have seen her enter, come in and grabbed the file, then reappeared a few minutes later to make himself look innocent. The pant leg she grabbed was fine material, light wool, not the cheap poly stuff. Good grief, she was picking up more from Al and carpet class than she realized.

So, was the intruder Griff or not? She pictured him in his tux, then without his tux, and that led to totally naked and suddenly she felt all warm and wanting and disgusted with herself for having the hots for him again. "What a mess," she whispered.

"Who in the world are you talking to?" Prissy said from behind. "Did you get what you needed? Find anything out? You were gone ages. What in the world happened? I was worried sick about you. You're a mess."

She pulled Priss through the door that lead to the now nearly deserted courtyard with only a few diners remaining. They ducked behind a magnolia tree. "Someone came in and pushed me to the floor, then stole the papers I needed. I had them in my hand, Priss. Right here." She made a fist, then remembered the fist she made when she was having the orgasm-to-end-all-orgasms. "I'm not the only one after Jaden Carswell."

"Or someone wants to make sure you don't find her, and that's not just Griff. Someone's watching you real close, girl."

"Gee, I feel so much better now."

"Maybe you should forget all this, Char. Things are getting dangerous and someone's not liking what you're up to. What are you going to do?"

"Go visit Ray Cleveland."

"Oh yeah, great answer. Let's go see the local mob guy. That's so much safer."

"He's the only one left from the original deal who had a vested interest. Maybe he remembers something about Jaden. Everyone else is dead."

"Except the killer, and Cleveland could be that person. You need to take Bebe with you."

"Like he's going to tell me anything with the police around. But you're right, I should take someone. It'll look more casual, friendly. Always good to keep the local mob boss guy friendly." She flashed Prissy a sweet, innocent smile and batted her eyes.

"No way. I did my blood-sister duty tonight. I'm resigning my pinky. And you left me high and dry at the morgue. I'm still mad at you for that."

"I had a good reason for leaving, and I'm not after the necklace or the murderer, just Jaden, and I'll tell Cleveland that. If he knows anything, he'll give us the information just to shut us up and keep us from digging any further. And consider this: Beau might be there. What about that, hmm? You have to admit, Beau Cleveland is the finest young gun in Savannah."

"What about Griff?"

"Griff's thirty-three. He's fast approaching middle-aged gun."

"Beau's a little young for me."

"Twenty-eight isn't young. It's prime, grade-A Southern beef."

Prissy bit her thumbnail because Beau Cleveland was enough to make any woman bite every nail she had clean off. "Then you have to help me with my morgue party. Set things up, get the place in shape. I can't get any workers till we get money. And you can't leave me this time."

"So it's a party for Ray Cleveland?"

"Okay. It's a deal." Priss let out a long breath. "With all this ruckus over a missing baby, do you ever wonder about who you really are? Where you came from? Sometimes when I get these feelings like I did with Griff's check and now with the morgue, I wonder where they come from. You know that saying about the apple not falling far from the tree? Though this is Georgia, so we think peach. Don't you wonder about your tree? Like why Bebe knows how bad guys think, can shoot a fly off a donkey's behind and always wins at poker? Why Brie is neat and perfectly dressed, and why you built your cottage, can fix a leaky faucet and always know which is the best paint, even if you do screw up picking the color?"

"Bebe's stepmom is enough to make anyone carry a gun. She nearly ruined that girl. I'd like to shoot her myself. Brie was raised with a silver spoon in her dainty little mouth, you were raised by nuns who really get that spiritual stuff and I read that how-to book from Home Depot. You bought it for me, remember?"

"I bought it for me, didn't understand a word and gave it to you. You built yourself a flipping house."

"RL helped. I'm not too good at the electrical stuff. We swore at the cemetery not to look back, Priss. Parents didn't want us, so we don't want them. RL never talks about his sister, and I never ask. She left me and took off, and that's the end of it. Pretty much the same thing for Bebe, and you got left in a basket on the church steps and Brie was adopted outright. The four of us are family through and through. We've been there for each other since grade school, when kids made fun of the four little orphans. Who else do we need?"

Prissy threw her arms around her. "You're right as rain. It's us, just us, and we're doing fine and dandy the way we are. And there's no reason to look any further."

Chapter 6

Griff cut through the dark alley and made for the carriage house. He stripped out of his tux and thought of another strip . . . Charlotte's, fifteen minutes ago, right there in his damn office. This was screwing up his plans big-time—mostly because he was screwing her!

Disgusted with himself, he yanked on jeans and T-shirt. In his truck, he headed for the row houses. After his latest blunder, he'd never get to sleep, and pounding the shit out of concrete and bricks was just the thing. Finding temporary homes for the tenants had been a good idea or they'd string him up by his balls for all the racket.

He took Drayton to avoid driving around the squares that were little parks all over the city. With twenty-one of them no one ever got anywhere fast, though it sure enough made Savannah one beautiful place. He couldn't imagine living anywhere else. The possibility never crossed his mind. He turned onto Pearl and killed the engine in front of the row houses. Rotting, cracked, peeling now, but in a year or so they'd be showplaces, and that the residents were willing to put in sweat equity to keep their rents low helped a lot.

He hoisted his toolbox from the truck bed, went inside, hit the lights and started prying up floorboards. Not that tough a job, but since he aimed to use the good pieces of pre–Civil War pine to keep the place authentic, he couldn't just rip away like a bulldozer.

"What the freaking hell are you doing?" came a familiar male voice behind him.

"And what the hell is Beau Cleveland doing on Pearl Street at midnight, though I'm sure it's something female-related."

Beau leaned against the doorjamb, sun-streaked hair mussed, tie hanging at his neck. "Saw your rusted heap of a pickup when I was returning a little lovely to her place over on the next block." Beau let out an appreciative sigh. "Griff, I've got to tell you, the woman's dynamite."

"Hell, you say that about every woman."

He grinned. It was the shy-boy one that sent every woman in Savannah into sexual meltdown. "I love 'em all, man, I truly do. Short, tall, fat, thin. Women are phenomenal. Their hair, that skin, the way they smell and their eyes. God, they have great eyes and hips. Gotta love the hips." He put his hand to his heart. "Women are my damn weakness."

"And the feeling's mutual," Griff chuckled. Nodding at Beau's duds, he asked, "A tux kind of night out at the Cove?"

"Dad had an all-day shindig on the island. Dynamite's our new hostess. Some congressman flew in from Atlanta and rented out the whole damn place for his friends. Always nice to see our tax dollars at work."

Griff laughed. "He rented all of it?"

"Till he lost his shirt. Some people do not understand the science of blackjack and that craps is a sucker's game. What a total dick. How the hell does someone like that get elected?"

Beau walked across the empty room, his footsteps echoing against the bare plaster walls and high ceilings. He sat down on Griff's toolbox, resting his elbows on his knees.

"Woman problems? That's the only thing that'll get a man doing demolition in the middle of the night."

Griff sat on the floor and leaned back against the brick fireplace, feeling tired clear through to his soul. "It's that damn will."

"Jaden?"

"I've got Charlotte deShawn trying to find her."

Beau's mouth gaped. "Holy shit. Now there's a twist for you. When did you come up with that idea?"

"Couldn't think of another way to handle it."

"Well, you sure as hell got the ball rolling now. Going to be interesting to see where it stops. You know, if you're having cash problems, Ray can lend you what you need." Beau laughed. "Seems to me we've been bailing each other out of one mess or another since that bar fight over in Garden City a million years ago."

"You were seventeen, getting ready to ship out to Afghanistan, full of piss and vinegar and picking fights with the redneck boys. Did it have to be the rednecks? That was about as smart as what I've got going."

"Got your dicky in a twist?"

Griff puffed out a lungful of air. "Hell, I got it in Charlotte."

Beau laughed full-out. "Oh fuck."

"Yep, that's the problem all right. Of all the women in Savannah . . ."

Beau stood. "Charlotte's a good person, and she's got some mighty fine female friends. That BrieAnna's something else." Beau swiped his forehead. "Every time I lay eyes on that woman, I break a sweat."

"You better come on out to the island tomorrow. We'll fish, get drunk, eat fried stuff. You need a break while you can get it. I got a feeling your life is about to take a head-first dive straight into the crapper."

"Nice way of putting it."

"Hey, what are friends for if not to cheer you up?"

And the next morning, as Griff headed out to Thunderbolt Island, he agreed that the crapper looked like his obvious destination. Turning off 80 a little too fast, he skidded onto a part crushed shell, part sandy road. For a long time, Griff couldn't understand why Ray didn't blacktop the road, then he realized you could hear a car coming from a mile away. The good thing was, there weren't any cars to kick up a cloud of dust till the lunch crowd start arriving hours from now.

The beating sun baked Griff's bones as the island sprung up around him. Palms gave way to marsh grass and swaying sea oats. How many places had an actual turtle-crossing sign? He felt carefree, with no Charlotte worries . . . until he spotted her blue Chevy off the side of the road and Charlotte flagging him down. When the gods plotted against you, there was no escaping, even out to Thunderbolt Island.

He pulled off to the side, careful not to get his car stuck in the sand like Charlotte's. Killing the engine, he wished he could do the same to his sex drive. Every time he saw her, his heart jumped. The worst part was, so did his damn dick. He ambled over, hands in his pockets to keep from snatching her and kissing her and God knows what else. Shit.

She had on another one of those skirts he liked, this one blue and full and catching the ocean breezes. And a yellow blouse with a teasing scoop in front that stopped just at her cleavage. Hair pulled back, soft and fresh and tumbling to her neck. Shoving his hands deeper into his pockets, he leaned against her car and gazed out over the marshlands, wild and untamed . . . like Charlotte. "Lost?"

"And then I tried to turn around and got stuck in the sand, and before you get all uppity with the 'You're always lost, Charlotte' comments, I'm out here on business for you. Ray Cleveland may remember something about

Jaden. I'm surprised you didn't ask him right off, before you contacted me."

That damn well got his attention, and this time it wasn't Charlotte and sex. "Cleveland's not going to appreciate your stirring the pot with a game of twenty questions about a murder he was a suspect in."

"So, you haven't asked him? Is it because you're friends and didn't want to be rude?"

"You don't poke friends in the eye with a stick. And didn't you get all that you needed last . . ." The sentence hung like a waiting noose. He was going to say *last night*. But then Charlotte didn't know he knew why she was really there in his office. If this got any more confusing, he'd have to get a scorecard to keep track of the players. "Last time we met," he rushed on.

"Last time we met, we were more intent on scratching an itch than you telling me anything about the case. 'Course you didn't have any trouble telling me I wasn't good in the sack—make that the desk—but I'm sure I'll survive."

But, would he? He couldn't get Charlotte out of his mind. "I'm sure you'll be fine, and you're not lost. The Cove is around the bend, and Ray's probably there, but leave him out of this, Charlotte. I mean it. He went through enough with that murder case. His wife left him and took his kid. He never saw her again. He lost all his money to legal fees and had to start over from scratch."

"I'm running out of people who remember that baby. I have to ask him. Maybe he'll give me a straight answer, because you're sure not."

"Why would I keep something back?"

"Now that is the sixty-four-dollar question. What is going on with you and this case and me?"

A cloud of dust approached and Charlotte said, "That's BrieAnna's Beemer."

Thank God, Griff thought as the Z4 skidded to a stop.

Least that would put an end to the questions he couldn't answer. BrieAnna slid from behind the wheel, hair perfect in spite of riding in a convertible. No wonder Beau was a little intimidated.

Her forehead furrowed, and she waved one hand over the road and parked the other on her hip. "Well now, there's dust all over my car." She looked at Griff, good manners winning over a good detail job, and she flipped into Southern-belle mode befitting a tiara on head and baton in hand. She smiled. "Why hello there, Griff. And how is your mama these days?"

Before he could answer, Charlotte said, "Prissy sent you?"

"Well of course she did, because she's meeting up with the hottie brothers. That is some job; having Prissy at the morgue gives me the heebie-jeebies."

Charlotte said, "The Cove is right around the bend, and you can give me a lift and maybe Mr. Cleveland can get my car out of the sand."

"Before or after you piss him off?" Griff asked.

"I don't think we should be upsetting Mr. Cleveland," Brie chimed in.

"For crying in a bucket, you two. I'm just asking about Jaden, that's it." Charlotte turned to Griff. "And you're here because . . ."

"Fishing, same as you." He followed Charlotte and Brie-Anna to the rambling white clapboard with green awnings perched on the shoreline against a bright blue sky. No cars in the lot at this hour, but cruisers, sailboats and runabouts bobbing at the dock along with Ray's Donzi, which could outgun anything on the water. The girls started for the main entrance, the sea breezes playing in Charlotte's hair. Hell, that's exactly what he wanted to do! He took her arm, letting BrieAnna go on ahead. "What if I call you off the case?"

"Too late, Skippy. Already spent the money." Her expression turned thoughtful. "Besides, it's getting personal, beyond a job. I want to let Jaden know that people cared about her, who her family was, that she wasn't just kicked to the curb for convenience's sake."

Crap! There was no turning back the clock now. Where this would all end was anyone's guess. Catching up with BrieAnna, they took the crushed-shell walkway at the side of the house that led to the back screen door and caught the aroma of sausage and onions and crab wafting out. Ray, in shorts with no shirt or shoes, stood at the big stove cooking. Griff knocked, and Ray bellowed, "If you're horny and handsome, this is the place to be." He looked up, smiling at Griff, till a flash of caution dimmed his eyes when he spied BrieAnna and Charlotte.

He turned off the stove and set the pan to the side. Wiping his hands on the towel tied at his waist, he smiled genuinely as he let them in and shook hands with Griff. "Long time no see, boy. How's your mama? Give her my best now, you hear."

He turned his attention to the girls, restaurant-owner smile in place. "Welcome to the Cove, ladies. What brings you out my way this lovely spring morning?" He studied BrieAnna across the stainless counter. "A donation for your house projects? You do mighty good work there, Miss Montgomery. All of Savannah is in your debt."

Beau strolled into the kitchen, smiled at Charlotte, then stopped dead when his gaze landed on BrieAnna. "H-Hi."

"Hello, Beau. How have you been?"

"Uh . . ."

Well dang. Who was *this* Beau Cleveland? The one Griff knew never said *uh* to a girl in his life. Usually he sallied up next to her, slid his arm around her easy like and whispered something sweet and sexy and charming that had her giggling, blushing and falling into his arms.

Ray said, "I'll get my checkbook and—"

"No need, Mr. Cleveland," Charlotte rushed in. "This isn't about a fundraiser."

Griff gritted his teeth. "Charlotte, this is a bad idea and—"

"I know it was a long time ago," Charlotte cut in, completely ignoring Griff. "But do you remember Jaden Carswell, William's daughter? And I'm not here to cause you any unpleasantness. I'm just hoping you remember something that will help me find her for a client."

Ray gave Griff the expected are-you-out-of-your-mind look. "Let me guess, you're the client?"

Fuck! "Well, I can promise you that this part sure as hell wasn't my idea."

Ray laughed and ran his hand over his buzzed hair, which was equal parts gray and bleached blonde. "Oh, this is rich. Just when you think you've seen it all, something else rolls in."

He said to Charlotte, "I don't know much. I had my own situation at that time. But I do recall seeing Otis stroll that baby in the park on occasion. Mostly the nanny had the babe, but now and then Otis took her out. Touched my heart, him doing that, with everything going on in his life."

Ray looked Charlotte square in her eyes. "I'd say the man had a true affection for the child, he truly did. And when you find her, you need to make her believe that. Otis did what he thought was best at the time."

Charlotte felt her stomach flip. She didn't know what to think and was totally surprised when Ray Cleveland took her hand. She didn't know him all that well, more by reputation than anything else, but to her he seemed genuine and sincere. She asked, "Why did he send her away?"

"Sometimes people get caught between the devil and the deep blue sea, and have to make choices that they know aren't right but have to be done. I think that's what happened to Otis and Jaden."

Charlotte didn't have a clue what that was all about but nodded as if she understood perfectly. Ray was doing his best to be cordial, and there was nothing to be gained from her pressing the point. Maybe when she thought about it more it would all make sense. "Thanks for your time, Mr. Cleveland. I appreciate it."

She started for the door when Beau blurted, "I'll take a hundred chances or tables or . . . whatever it is you have going on." Beau stared at BrieAnna as if he'd never seen a woman before. Everyone else stared at Beau as if he had grown another head. That was a lot of staring.

"Excuse me?" BrieAnna pinked top to toe.

"And . . . and you can raffle off a private party at the Cove."

"For?" Brie whispered, looking as befuddled as Beau.

"For . . . For . . . You're always having events for restoration projects. I thought . . . if you needed to . . . I . . . we'd be happy to . . ."

Ray bit back a grin at his usually very suave, sophisticated son. "I think what Beau is trying to say is, we'd be happy to donate or give something to whatever your most recent cause happens to be, Miss Montgomery."

BrieAnna beamed. "Why, aren't you both the very best." The girl could write a book, *Southern Belles-R-Me*. "You are too kind. As a matter of fact, we are having an event at the old morgue on Saturday and we'd be honored to have you and your father attend. Reserve a table perhaps?"

"Two," Beau rushed in.

Ray held up his hand. "We have a packed house here on Saturday nights, but I don't think an army of wolves could keep Beau from your event."

"Why, any time you all have would be just wonderful."

Charlotte led Brie out of the kitchen because the stars in her eyes would probably make her walk right off the dock and straight into the water, and having a lovesick friend drown would be downright horrible.

"Mercy! I think I just made a complete fool of myself," Brie stammered, fanning herself with her hand. "What's wrong with me? Beau's just another boy and—"

"And except this time it's boy-o-boy! You've known each other exists, but mob-boss son and pillar-of-the-community daughter don't run in the same circles." Charlotte chuckled. "This is going to be very interesting."

"When you're around, everything's interesting," Griff said from behind her. She stopped, letting him catch up as Brie said, "I'll meet you at the car. I have some thinking to do."

"And you can do me a favor and get Beau to fish my car out of that sand trap."

Brie wrung her hands. "Well, I suppose I could do that. Talk to Beau, I mean." She nodded as she headed back to the screen door. "Yes, as a matter of fact I think I'd like that very much."

The door banged shut, and Griff said, "See, you came all this way for nothing. Ray didn't know zilch about Jaden or her parents."

"He knew Otis cared for Jaden, and that's a lot." Griff had on docksiders with no socks, baggy shorts, and an old gray T-shirt. He looked mussed and sexy. "What was your nanny's name? The lady who took care of you when Camilla was off playing cards or having tea or shopping, or having her claws sharpened."

Griff sat on the top rung of the sidewalk railing. Resting his arms on his thighs. His eyes matched the sea and sky at his back, his personality the snake in the grass.

"Mrs. Wellington watched me, and I'm guessing you think that she could have also been Jaden's nanny." He put his hands on Charlotte's shoulders, his gaze holding hers as he brought her near, his lips getting closer, but instead of kissing her he said, "I thought you finding Jaden was a great idea, but I was wrong. You're dredging up a lot of memories for people I care about."

She stepped back and peered out at the water, getting her mind off Griff and focusing on the situation. "I swore I never wanted to know who my real parents were, mostly because they abandoned me, and that's not a great feeling. It makes you feel unwanted, unloved and a whole lot of other crappy stuff. So I decided, along with Brie and Priss and Bebe, that that part of my life was over and I wouldn't go there again, ever."

She faced Griff. "But Otis tried to made amends for sending Jaden away, and she has a right to know that she isn't completely dumped. Actually she *needs* to know that. It will fill a hole in her life, save her hours of therapy and tons of money. It's not just about you having complete control of Magnolia House anymore, Griff."

"What if Jaden's doing fine wherever she is, just like you are, and this will just upset things for her? Is it worth the risk?"

"I think the risk is in finding Jaden. Wouldn't things be better for you if she's not found?" Griff looked as if he'd been smacked with a dead fish. "Brie and Prissy and I have talked this over."

"What the hell ever happened to privileged information? Isn't that part of the PI code or something?"

"It is privileged with me and Brie and Prissy, and the way we see this is, if I can't find Jaden, you can have her declared legally dead and you get Magnolia House free and clear."

"When have I ever said that?"

"When you dumped this case in my lap instead of hiring some big firm in town. It didn't make sense, but now it does. I'm getting close to finding her and I'm not quite as dim-witted as you think, and here you are, calling me off the case. You're not concerned about dredging up old memories. You're concerned that I'm homing in on finding Jaden."

He raked back his hair. "You are way off base on this one, Charlotte."

"Guess that depends on your point of view, because I think I'm right on the money. You're using me and my inexperience. Well, I may not be that great at what I do, but I'm getting better, and I am not giving up till I find Jaden Carswell." She walked across the parking lot and down the road, hoping her Chevy was up on the road by now. Or not. Maybe Brie and Beau were necking in the bushes instead. But whatever happened between them had to be better than where she and Griff were, because that was nowhere!

"Well, how was Beau?" Charlotte asked Brie, a black Jeep fading down the road.

"He kissed me." Brie didn't move and stared at the cloud of retreating dust.

"That's a good start."

"Bad start." Brie turned to her, her expression one of misery. "The kiss sucked. Well, it didn't suck, and I'm thinking that was the trouble, or something sure was. I don't know," she wailed, and buried her face in her hands. "He's a really pitiful kisser, Charlotte. The worst kisser on the planet." She peeked between her fingers. "And we were off to such a great start with this instant magnetic attraction in the kitchen, and I felt myself falling head over heels and anticipating one of those kisses I'd heard about, and then . . . this! My cat gives better kisses, Char."

"Least he got my car back on the road. Guess he can do something right. Maybe he needs kissing lessons."

"This is Beau Cleveland we're talking about here. That's

like saying that Woods person needs golf lessons. And just how do you go about telling someone they aren't good at sexy stuff? Mighty touchy subject."

Amen to that, Charlotte said to herself, then said out loud, "But if you don't do something, you'll spend the summer with that guy your mama fixed you up with at the garden party—hairy mustache, comb-over, chief of staff at Provident Hospital? Think about it, Brie. It's that, or sun-streaked hair, a body to swoon over, the local mobster's son. Is there really any contest here on which you want?"

"Mama's never going to understand, I can tell you that much. She'll pitch a royal fit. We're dealing with the president of the Oglethorpe Society Auxiliary, the Women's Afternoon Card Club and the Historical Preservation Association. Mama's wonderful and precious and I love her to pieces, but I'm afraid the woman's a dreadful snob, and me going out with Ray Cleveland's son . . . Oh my."

"Focus on the *oh my* part. Beau's delish!"

Charlotte followed Brie's Z4 back over the bridge spanning the Intracoastal Waterway, dotted with fishing and shrimp boats motoring out to sea. She needed to talk to Mrs. Wellington—wherever she was—to see if she remembered Jaden. But first Charlotte had to stop off at the morgue, to see how Priss was doing.

Charlotte pulled around to the back of the morgue, the courtyard quiet as a . . . she needed another word besides *tomb*. That was much too close to home. A rambling live oak with swaying moss towered over the courtyard, shrubs grew out of control, weeds littered the grounds, pavers were cracked and missing, the wrought-iron fence was broken in two places.

Charlotte headed for the side entrance under the portico, where they undoubtedly hauled the dead into the hearse. Next time Priss took a job, it should be an old candy factory. Visions of loading chocolate she could deal with.

Charlotte yanked open one of the double doors and Prissy jumped a foot. "Holy moly, you scared me to death."

"Well, you're at the right place." She eyed the peeling wallpaper and stained floors. "And this is party central in three days? You've got to be kidding."

"The party will be outside, in the garden. We have a tent coming. But get this, the nuns are helping by doing the catering. And four of them are fixing up the downstairs bathroom right now." Prissy beamed. "It's a family business. St. James and Sisters. You know, like Bubba and Sons."

"Thanks for sending Brie out to the Cove. Moral support is always good, and she's decided Beau Cleveland needs kissing lessons."

Prissy smacked her hand to her forehead. "I always miss the good stuff." She took Charlotte's elbow and ushered her back outside to the courtyard. "Okay, do-it-yourself whiz kid, I need you to make this place perfect. You promised, remember?" Then Priss held up her wounded pinky and smiled sweetly.

Chapter 7

Sam parked in front of the morgue under one of the old black iron streetlights with the frosted globes that turned the city into one of those Thomas Kinkade paintings his grandmamma had over the mantel. He missed Atlanta—it was home, there was family—but Savannah . . . Savannah was the Mona Lisa of the South—small, charming, mysterious and . . .

Christ almighty! What the hell was he doing, waxing poetic about a stupid damn streetlight! He was procrastinating. The last thing he wanted to do tonight was attend this blasted party and meet up with Pricilla St. James. It was one of those keep-away-but-got-to-have-her situations and not bank president–like at all.

So why did he want her? It made no sense. The woman slept with him to get a loan. He couldn't be attracted to that . . . but he was definitely attracted to soft brown eyes, a great shape and incredible hair. Hot flashes did not happen only to women, because thinking about all those curls made him hot as hell right now. He'd give a month's salary to be running his fingers through her hair, and maybe he and Priss would wind up in bed and . . . Dammmit all!

"Party's around back, big boy," came a too-familiar voice from beside his car, making his insides jump and his dick hard, proving why his procrastination was justified. He slid from the car, taking his time, trying to will away his obvious condition. She looked even more fabulous than she did five nights ago in the Magnolia House bar. Shit! Maybe if she dyed her hair he wouldn't care so much. "Ever think about cutting your hair? Being a blonde?"

"That would almost be as much of a shock as finding you here."

"Half the town heard you invite me at the bank. How could I not come?" He leaned against the lamppost, trying for the cool approach, until she took his chin between her thumb and forefinger, turned his head from side to side, her touch mesmerizing and erotic. Double shit.

"No physical evidence of my handprint on your face. You had that slap coming, you know. Are you going to apologize?"

"Hey, you hit me, and I still don't know what you're up to. And there's more going on here than a pick-up line at the local bar."

"And you did the picking up."

"With you dressed the way you were, every man in that bar was watching you."

"Not likely they weren't. A skirt from the Gap and blouse from Old Navy are not exactly Paris Hilton attire."

He eyed her midnight-blue dress, which shimmered. Silk maybe. It swayed when she moved.

She nodded at the morgue, A fine piece of Georgian architecture and a whole lot of falling apart. "We cleaned the windows just for you."

"And my bank's money. Nice chandelier."

"Italian amber, but there are fine original chandeliers all over the house. The place is a real gem."

"Not to mention money pit." He knew all about gems . . . Prissy's sparkling eyes, her laughter, her walk.

"Let me escort you around back to the party." She took

his hand, her touch electrifying, and he pulled her to him. Her brown eyes lit with the same gnawing hunger that would not leave him no matter what he did. Drinking bourbon, running, burying his head under a damn pillow, singing "100 Bottles of Beer on the Wall" till two AM had no effect at all. He wanted her. "You're stunning."

Her lips parted, eyes dreamy, and he nearly blacked out as lust shot through him.

Her expression turned vulnerable, and he never wanted to let her go again. "I give myself these pep talks, Sam. That you're just another man hell-bent on making my life miserable. And then . . . then we end up like this. We don't like each other, remember? We're enemies. This isn't making any sense."

Loretta Mae Johnson giggled as she walked up the drive toward the party. "You two sure don't look like enemies to me, honey. You all seem real friendly-like."

"We need to get out of here," Sam said, a breeze ruffling the tree. He led Prissy into the shadows beside the front porch, a gnarled mulberry bush and a stone fountain overgrown with ivy concealing them.

He stroked her cheek; his heart raced. "I could eat you up. You know that. Every time I see you, it's the same." Then he kissed her just like he'd been dreaming about for days. His body tensed, his damn dick went from hard to throb and her mouth opened for him. Why couldn't it just stay shut and she give him a karate chop to the gut? Then this attraction would be done with . . . maybe. Probably not.

Instead her hands clawed their way under his sport coat, then held on to him as he pressed against her pelvis, hers pressing in return. The heat from her body penetrated clear through her dress. "I want you," he blew in her ear. "Now, here, any way I can have you."

She stilled for a moment, as if deciding what to do—go,

stay, beat him over the head with a branch from the mulberry tree. Just when he thought she might cut and run, her mouth captured his, her tongue doing some incredible thing that was downright obscene. Damn, he liked obscene, least with Prissy St. James. He hiked up her skirt, she unzipped his fly and, without asking, she fumbled for his wallet and covered him with the condom. Breathing labored, he whispered, "This is a bad idea."

"I agree. Do you want to stop?"

He backed her against the latticework at the side of the porch. She leaned back and wrapped her legs around his waist the way she'd done in the elevator. They were getting pretty good at this. Too good. Cupping her sweet bottom in his palms and holding her tight, he held her to him while he entered her with an instant mind-blowing orgasm unlike any he'd ever experienced . . . except in that damn elevator. His body roared with release and he swallowed her desperate groans of raw pleasure as she trembled, then nearly sucked his lips off.

"Holy mother," he breathed, his brain spinning at warp speed and beyond.

"I'm going straight to hell," she whimpered, the breeze stirring the leaves again, harder this time, and helping to muffle their voices. "The dear sisters, the ladies who raised me to be a good Catholic girl and taught me to mind my manners and how to set the table proper-like, are inside this very house doing up heavenly mushroom canapés and I'm in the front yard doing up you."

"I think we're doing each other." His fingers pressed into her bottom and he wanted her all over again, nuns or no nuns, mushrooms or no mushrooms, right now, his damn dick swelling and gearing up for action . . . again.

Her eyes narrowed. "You're taking that Viagra stuff? Is that what's wrong with you?"

"What's wrong with me is you. The way you look, smell,

feel, the whole damn package. Why couldn't you be a guy? Hell, I'd fall for you no matter who or what you were, and trust me, I sure as hell don't go around saying that to just anyone."

The sound of conversation and footsteps on the sidewalk came their way and they froze in place, her smoldering eyes and full delicious lips an inch from his. He wanted her hot and ready for him, not just tonight or in some damn elevator, but all the time, every day. He wanted to know she was his, only his, and he wanted nothing more than to please her in a real bed and not in some damn bushes. The thought of him not being the only man in her life made him a little nuts.

When the group passed, he set her down, and she took a step back and held up her hands and shook her head. This did not bode well for being only his.

"Okay, that's it. I quit. I can't do this anymore."

Well, fuck. Though it didn't look as if that would be happening again anytime soon.

"No more fooling around like this. It's juvenile, and it's getting in the way of our business together and I can't have that."

"Sweet stuff, we have no business together. I'm not giving you the loan. It's not personal. It's common sense. Let's forget about business and concentrate on us."

She straightened her hair and dress; he zipped his fly, then followed her out onto the cobblestone drive of Savannah-gray pavers that cost about a hundred bucks a piece now. She paused by the black iron urn overflowing with yellow and white flowers and surrounded by more baskets of the same flowers. Partygoers strolled by, greeted Sam and commented on the flowers. Prissy had worked her ass off to turn the place into a garden party. He had to give her that.

She peered up at him. "You know . . ."

"Any sentence that begins with *you know* is never ever good."

Ignoring him, she went on, "The press is here and tomorrow there will be pictures in the *Herald* of this event, and if word gets out that the bank doesn't support rehabbing an historical building, the folks wining and dining in back won't like it one bit. In fact, they'll consider it a snub, and they're all probably big customers of yours."

"You're blackmailing me again? You already ran that scene when you were at the bank."

"Ah, but this time the scene has real live pictures." She patted his cheek and nodded at the crowd spilling out of the white party tent. "Hospital trustees, president and treasurer of the Oglethorpe Society—you get the picture. And it's not personal between us because there is no us. There's just business."

"How about just sex?"

Her forehead furrowed. "Is that all you think about?"

He considered the question. "Since I met you, yeah, that's about it. Not doing my career a world of good."

She stepped around him, then paused and turned back. "What exactly is your problem with this place? Barring divine intervention, what would it take for the bank, for you, to okay the loan?"

"For God's sake, woman, Vince and Anthony aren't this relentless in securing a loan for the morgue. Why the hell are you?"

"I want this job. I need this job. I have plans for the money from this job. Are you following me here?"

"Money for more sexy dresses to drive men nuts?"

"A Viking stove, a Sub-Zero fridge. All clad!"

"If you need money, I'll get you a job at the bank." Though that was a really bad idea, since he'd never get any work done and just be sniffing around Prissy all day."

"I don't even balance my own checkbook, Sam. The bank tellers weep when they see me come through the door."

He ran his hand through his hair, though he felt more like pulling it out. "Here's how it works. First, you need a contractor and you need to get prices for labor and materials and a guarantee that the workers won't walk off the job. That means you have to assure them somehow that this place is sound and not haunted or whatever the hell else they think is going on. Not that I believe in such crap, but others do. I need a timetable for when the work will get done and the doors will open for business. That's a business plan in a nutshell. You have to do a lot more than balance a checkbook. You have to deal with construction, rehabbing, random ghosts. Any idea how to handle any of those things?"

"After tonight and all the good press, the idea of something sinister going on will fade. The nuns are in there now. That should be enough to unhaunt the place. And I got the money together to throw this shindig, didn't I?"

"How exactly did you finance it?"

"Mr. Visa and Mr. MasterCard, and don't give me that 'you did credit card debt' speech because it's all your fault." She folded her arms. "I wouldn't have to max out my cards if you lent the Biscotti brothers the money in the first place."

"Have you ever taken a finance course?"

"Isn't that what this is?" Sam groaned and Prissy waved her hand at the tent and string quartet and plates of food and all having a good time. "See, everything's just fine and dandy, and I'll have one of those business-plan things on your desk by Wednesday."

Prissy trotted away from Sam Pate knowing full well he was standing there growling and snarling—though he probably looked yummy as all get out while doing it—at her naive declaration of having a business plan. So she was a tad optimistic, but right now she needed a boatload of the stuff to get this project off the ground and make it work. And by golly, it was going to work!

She caught up with Griff and Camilla and thanked them for coming, though Camilla's ice-cold stare suggested Prissy St. James was the last person on earth Camilla came here to see. But that was okay. Camilla—grande dame of Savannah society—came all the same even if it was out of blatant curiosity.

Another gust of wind ruffled the trees, sweeping the dark branches across an even darker sky. The purple and white rhododendron and pink azaleas they'd all stuffed in the ground a half hour before guests arrived danced and swayed, the white tent fluttered, torch lights flickered. No rain! Oh God, please no rain tonight. Think drought.

Brie bustled up beside her. "Guess what, girly-girl. I have a new client for you. Said if you can pull off rehabbing this place, he'd like to talk to you about an old theater he bought over in Beaufort."

Prissy's heart stopped. "Really? You wouldn't kid about that? Another job already?"

"Free movie tickets instead of free caskets. I'm a fan." She glanced around. "Weren't you just talking to Sam Pate, the key ingredient in this little plan?"

Prissy glanced back. "I thought he was right behind me. How am I supposed to blackmail him if he's not around to get blackmailed. Blast the man."

"Can we blast Beau Cleveland, too?" Brie's socially perfect smile dropped to a frown. "He's not coming. I just know it. He's going to dump me before I get a chance to give him kissing lessons, and it'll be another failed relationship in the diary of BrieAnna Montgomery and I'll end up spending the entire summer with—"

"With me, I hope," came Lamont Laskin's voice out of

the crowd. "How are the good nuns these days?" Lamont greeted Prissy without taking his eyes from Brie. "I've been searching all over for you, Ms. Montgomery." His gray eyes twinkled, his mustache twitched. "You see, I have a medical convention in Milwaukee next month that I know you'd enjoy. You could come with me. We can see the sights. I'm told they have wonderful jazz clubs. We can get acquainted."

"But we've known each other for years," Brie offered, her social smile plastered in place, though cracking a little at the edges. "We're already acquainted."

"And I want us to be very special friends." He winked and Brie shivered. "Cold, my dear? Let me lend you my coat."

Brie held out her hand and took a step back. Seemed this was the night for back-stepping from men. "I'm doing quite well, thank you, and you need to get back to the party, Lamont." She nodded toward the big white tent. "The sisters just brought out their tomato sandwiches. I'm sure you love tomato sandwiches, and these are the very best and not the least bit soggy. Perfection."

"Just like you, my dear." Lamont's eyes brightened. "Just like you, indeed. I'll be saving a place, so don't you be gone long now, you hear." He winked again and strolled off, hands in pockets, whistling a little off-key.

"Oh Lord, have mercy and shoot me now," Brie whimpered. "What am I to do? If I don't spend time with Lamont tonight, Mama will get wind of it and have a coronary right on the spot."

"We have a cardiac specialist handy." Prissy nodded at Lamont, meandering up to one of the tables lit with candles and holding spring flowers and a little fountain and a chocolate hazelnut cake and a platter of tiramisu that Vince had whipped up for the occasion.

"This is not one bit funny, Prissy St. James. The Laskins

are trustees for the Telfair Museum, on the advisory board for Colonial Park Cemetery, Lucas Theater and Savannah College of Art and Design. Mama drools just reciting the list. The very thought of me being connected in any way to all that qualifies me for sainthood in her eyes. Why can't Lamont connect to someone else? Why me?"

"Girl, you had your hair done, you wearing a strapless Vera Wang and strappy Jimmy Choos and you're a perfect size four. No other woman has a chance against that. I considered tripping you myself."

Brie stomped her foot. "This is where Beau Cleveland is supposed to drive up in that big red phallic-symbol Jag of his and whisk me off to his island for a weekend of kissing till our lips turn blue." She glanced around. "So where in blazes is that no-good scalawag?"

Prissy said in a singsong voice, "You want the bad boy."

Brie stood tall. "Yes, I do. I'm entitled to a . . . fling."

"So we'll just find Lamont someone else for his convention. Make him fall in love, get you off the hook with your mama." A big raindrop smacked Prissy's nose, then three more fell on her head. This is what happened when you did the deed in the front yard and fifteen of your own mamas were ten feet away making dinner.

Anthony came up beside her, drops marking his black shirt, his eyes big. "What are we to do? There are all these people getting wet and they cannot fit into the tent. We'll tell them to go home, yes?"

"No," Brie said, "we'll take the party inside and we have an excuse for it not being up to snuff. Everyone's dying to see the place." She grinned. "A little morgue humor. This is so perfect."

"Inside?" Vince put his hand to his chest and shook his head, looking frazzled in his dark plum shirt and charcoal pants. The man had impeccable taste. "But that is impossible. It is not safe inside. It is . . . demolished. Someone will get hurt."

Wind caught the underside of the tent, puffing it out like a giant marshmallow. Tablecloths rippled and more drops fell. Brie held up a champagne flute and tapped it with a sugar spoon to get the crowd's attention. "Yoo-hoo, everyone. The Biscotti brothers and I thank you for coming to this wonderful event, and now that it's raining we're taking the party inside right quick, so don't you all go and leave. Come get an up-close view of the Anna Colquitt Hunter mural Anthony and Vince discovered when stripping wallpaper the other day. Isn't that exciting? It's in the music room, and so lovely, it'll make you cry. Just follow . . . Mr. Griff Parish." She waved to him. "He's standing by the doorway and will show you inside. But mind where you walk—this fine old place is a work-in-progress that the Low Country Bank is financing." She put her hand to her bosom in perfect Southern-belle style. "Aren't they simply the very best? Savannah is indeed lucky to have Mr. Sam Pate as a patron of our restoration efforts."

Everyone nodded and smiled, adding a lot more nails to Sam's coffin. Morgue humor was catching. He'd have to give her the loan after this. Mrs. O'Hara grabbed the nearest bottle of champagne, Lamont the tomato sandwiches. The others did likewise, all starting for the side entrance. Camilla tried for the exasperated dignified look that was her trademark, but it seemed that getting a firsthand view of the morgue was too much temptation for her. She tucked her pocketbook under her arm, harrumphed and hustled for the door as well.

Vince fidgeted and Anthony muttered as the crowd streamed by. "We agreed to a garden party, a simple garden party, not this, not all these people in our place. This will never do!"

But mostly it sounded like he didn't want a party at all, Prissy realized. Neither brother was excited about the event, never had been. In fact, Sam Pate was right as rain about one thing. She was considerably more persistent in securing a loan to rehab the morgue than either of the brothers. At first she owed it up to shyness and being in a new city, but now . . . why would they still not welcome help, money, support and her expert services? This was a business and they were businessmen, right? What was really going on here?

The rain fell harder and Prissy snatched up the salmon mousse platter, Brie grabbed the chocolate cannoli cake and Charlotte took the plate of chocolate-covered strawberries. Vince and the sisters had outdone themselves for the event.

The crowd flowed inside through the dingy hallway, everyone chatting, not caring about stepping over drop cloths, paint cans, chunks of plaster and all the rest. Only in Savannah did people gush over dilapidated buildings. The crowd wandered through dusty rooms, drinks in hand, oohing and ahing over the potential of the place, the intricate moldings, the chandelier in the entrance foyer and especially the mural. Sister Roberta and Sister June set out coffee and Sweet Sister pralines on the paint-spattered scaffolding and passed the rest around. Prissy grabbed Vince's hand. "Oh, this is marvelous. Everyone's having a mighty fine time."

Vincent exchanged concerned looks with Anthony, then said, "Except we now have people everywhere in our house. They are like ants at a picnic."

"But everyone will be talking about this place tomorrow, over their morning coffee, on the phone, at the hairdressers and everywhere else in town. People are excited, and with all that support from the community, how can the bank turn you down for a loan?" She kissed him on the cheek. "We're in, Anthony. We went and did it."

A clap of thunder shook the place and jags of lightning glared through the windows as the wind kicked up. Charlotte rounded the corner. She looked great tonight in a long black dress, spaghetti straps, stilettos—so not Charlotte at all—which translated into Griff on the brain. She said, "I'm going outside for some chairs."

"Honey, there's lightning. We don't need you being a crispy critter," Prissy said, and Vince added, "I can get the chairs if you feel it is necessary, though I'm not sure all these people here are necessary."

"You need to socialize and schmooze," Charlotte whispered. "This is your big night. Be your charming Italian self. Drum up business. Go pinch a few fannies."

"Wish it was my big night," pouted Brie. "Just wait till I see that Beau Cleveland again."

Lightning sounded again, making everyone jump. "Some storm," Lamont said as he passed by, sliding his arm around Brie, sniffing her hair. Ick! "But I have to admit, this is a most fascinating place, and so are you. I should tell you there's an opening on the board of trustees at the Telfair. I could recommend you for the position. We could work together. Isn't that grand?" He smiled and strolled off.

Brie looked ill. "If Mama finds out, she'll have me engaged to Lamont before week's end. How am I going to get out of this? What should I do?" She pointed out the window. "And what's wrong with that tree?"

From the corner of her eye, Prissy caught sight of the big oak swaying—a lot—straight for the house. "Sweet mother," Prissy gasped, clutching Brie's arm as a loud cracking sound filled the whole house. Someone screamed, lights went out, more screams as the tree smashed into the side portico with a deafening thud that quaked the whole house.

"Holy shit." Was that Camilla's voice?

Griff stood on the scaffolding in the central hall and held up his cell phone, offering a bit of light. "Is everyone okay?"

"Oh my stars and garters," screeched Mrs. O'Hara from the next room. "What has happened? Where are my children, my babies? What's going on? This place is truly haunted."

"Your kids are married and living in Biloxi, Hillie. Give it a rest," someone groused.

But that left the ghost issue. So much for unhaunting. Griff said to the crowd, "I'm calling the fire department now. No one move; you could trip. There could be live wires down outside the house, so sit tight."

"We're trapped in a haunted house with vampires," Loretta Mae yelped, wind and rain hammering the windows.

"Was that a bat?" someone added.

Prissy's hair fried. "There are no such things as vampires, even in Savannah."

Mrs. O'Hara said, "We need something more than champagne. I brought my own fortification." She took a silver flask from her purse, took a gulp from it, then passed it to the lady beside her, who did the same.

Sister June held up a lit candelabra and led the group from the music room into the main hall. Sister Roberta held another candelabra and a tray of pralines, passing them out as she made her way through the crowd. Whiskey, butter, sugar, chocolate . . . Prozac Southern-style.

Sirens sounded, and Anthony used a flashlight to make his way to the front door. He opened it to rain, wind, more lightning, a firefighter, Bebe in a raincoat even uglier than those suits she wore and . . . "Sam Pate? What is he doing here?" Prissy said in a low voice to Brie.

"Honey, he's looking right smart, and I know you agree

because you're squeezing my hand tight enough to stop circulation. Think maybe he has a sister and I can fix her up with Lamont?"

"What about fixing him up with Bebe? She's one of those cerebral people and she likes jazz."

"I don't fix up anyone who totes a gun. Things don't always go well."

Bebe called out, "Everyone okay? I'm Detective Fitzgerald and this is Fire Chief Howard. The tree took out the electricity to the house, is all. We'll have everyone on their way as soon as the fire department finds the main circuit and cuts the power."

"Hi, Bebe," Brie called over the crowd, doing a finger-wave. "And how's your mama these days?" Brie added, though Prissy knew she asked out of courtesy more than caring. Bebe's mama was a first-class witch who needed to burn in hell for all eternity and everyone knew it.

"Those damn ghosts made that tree fall, if you're asking me," Mrs.O'Hara declared, then hiccupped. "They never did like people nosing around the premises. Everyone in town is aware of that."

Prissy said to Brie, "There can be no talk of ghosts or vampires. I'll never get workers here and Sam will never give me that blasted loan and—"

Sam jumped up on the scaffolding where Griff had been and took the candelabra from Sister Roberta. "Hello, everyone." He flashed that dazzling smile that stopped women in their tracks and made their hearts bounce around in their chests like ping-pong balls. "I'm sure you all had the best of times tonight. Some great food and good champagne, visiting with each other and then a chance to see the inside of this fine old place. It's been a real adventure."

Tension subsided a bit and everyone nodded as Sam moved past the talk of ghosts. Bebe interrupted. "Okay, folks. The fire marshal said it's safe for you all to leave now." And Sam added, "I left the headlights on in my car and it's aimed right at the front door so you all can take the steps without falling." Sam made his way toward Prissy against the crowd heading for the front door. "Hi. Are we having fun yet?"

He did look sort of knight-like in his gray suit. "Why'd you come back?"

"Heard the sirens heading up Drayton and there was a storm, and I just put two and two together. I figured you might need some help."

"That's a mighty impressive two-plus-two. Then again, you are a banker." Prissy stood on her tiptoes, her eyes to his incredible ones, and kissed him on the lips right there in front of everyone and not caring who saw it. Kissing Sam Pate was always pure magic, making her quiver and sweat and get the chills all at once. Kind of flulike except so much better. She framed his face with her hands. "I thought you didn't want me to get the loan, and here you are telling everyone what a great time they had and making them forget all about this here place being h-a-u-n-t-e-d."

He looked apprehensive. "I didn't want folks to freak out. I thought maybe I could help." He glanced around, frowned and raked his hair. "Everyone's okay, right? Are you sure? Is there anyone missing or strayed off?"

Prissy's gaze followed Sam's. "No one's complaining. Enough booze has that effect on people."

Bebe helped the last of the partygoers out the door and down the front steps and Griff sent Camilla home with friends who were probably headed for the nearest bar. A sense of peace settled over the house and Anthony got out a bottle of Jack Daniels black label, Sister Roberta brought glasses for everyone, Griff poured a round. Vince said, "*Cento anni di slute e felicita.* A hundred years of health and happiness."

Prissy added, "To new friends; to my sister family, who always help me out, even when I ask them to do crazy things; and to old fiends, Brie and Bebe and . . . and . . . Where's Charlotte?" Prissy shivered, and this time it had nothing to do with sex and Sam Pate, but a feeling, a really terrible one.

Her gaze met Griff's, and he shook his head in an I-don't-have-a–clue way.

Brie put down her glass. "Do you think she really went after those chairs? She wouldn't do that, would she?" Everyone's gaze cut to the double doors.

"Ohmygod! Ohmygod!" Brie gasped, and Prissy rushed to the doors and shoved against them, the tree and smashed portico holding it closed. "Charlotte! Charlotte!"

"She's okay," Sam said in a rush as he came up behind her. He turned her around and kept his hands on her shoulders and looked her in the eyes, his face pinched and drawn but determined. "I mean, this is a big house. There are plenty of places Charlotte could be. And I'm thinking she ducked in somewhere to keep dry and get away from the storm. Don't panic. She's okay."

Prissy shoved at his chest, sending him backwards. "She's a best friend. I'm going to panic plenty till I find her. Charlotte!" she yelled, hysteria creeping up her spine as she pounded on the doors.

She turned around, an idea niggling around in her brain. A sense of calm somewhere deep inside fought its way into her brain. "The very back rooms?" she said in a breathy voice that wasn't her normal tone at all. "She . . . she . . . Charlotte could be there, looking for chairs or trying to find another way into the house."

"She came in through one of the back doors," Sam offered, his gaze meeting hers, their brains following the same path . . . or following something.

Bebe had her cop face in place, never a good sign, the dark worried look in her eyes an even worse sign. She pulled out her cell and punched numbers. "I'm getting the fire department back here."

Griff started for the front door. "Where the hell is that girl?"

Chapter 8

It wasn't a rainstorm. It was a freaking rock storm, least that's what the heavy raindrops felt like hitting Charlotte's head and shoulders. She hauled chairs across the courtyard and they banged against her legs as she tottered along as fast as possible in heels high enough to warrant a nosebleed. "Ouch, ouch, ouch!"

Lightning flashed and she felt a charge tingle up her legs and arms. So this was what was meant by an electrifying experience. Her hair felt like it was standing on end because she was sure it was. "Cripes' sake! People will just have to stand."

Dropping the chairs with a clatter, she ran for the portico and the double doors when a powerful cracking sound came from behind. Cracking was never good unless associated with pecans and making pies, and that was never this loud!

She turned. A live oak that looked more like a live dragon swayed wildly, then started . . . "Falling?" Dear Lord, it really was falling, and straight at her.

"Oh shit! Oh shit! All this for chairs!" She ran, slipping on the wet pavers, then tripped and landed on all fours. She looked back over her shoulder at the tree . . . never look back, or maybe that was down? She scrambled to her feet, swearing to wear Nikes instead of stilettos for the rest of her life even if she was trying to impress Griff. A limb whacked her on the back and sent her sprawling facedown on the drive, cheek to pavers, a two-hundred-dollar dress shot to heck.

She couldn't breathe; the weight crushing. She really did see stars like in the comics. Did that mean she was dead and in heaven and hallucinating? Except she still felt the rain on her face and was nose-to-nose with a bird's nest. Not heaven material. She wiggled her fingers, then her toes, giving thanks that everything worked. Then she squirmed from under the limb, the bark tearing at her dress and skin and hair.

Standing, she held on to a limb for support, rain falling in torrents. The portico was a pancake, the side double doors blocked, lightning zagging again. Strength she didn't know she possessed made her run for the back of the morgue, trying doors there. Locked, locked, stuck, oh crap, open. Yes, open!

She shoved in and stumbled, and this time landed on a soft rug, a dim light glowing. A warm, safe, dry room that smelled of . . . gardenias. She loved gardenias and felt instantly better. Peeking up, she spotted caskets lining the perimeter. So much for better.

"Well, if this don't beat all. We have a visitor, dear," came a woman's voice. "Look what the storm shooed in."

"Did she bring martinis?" came a man's voice. "I could really go for that right now. Been a long time between martinis."

Charlotte pushed herself up for the second time tonight and managed to slide onto a bench by a bronze coffin, brushing wet hair and leaves from her face. Her vision cleared, then settled on a man and a woman, both about her age, sitting on a rosewood Victorian settee—she on the sofa part, he on the armrest.

The woman was average size plus a little more, with a beautiful locket at her throat. She had the big hair look even for the South and the cutest black espadrilles with matching patent purse that Charlotte had ever seen. The man had great green eyes, a gardenia in his lapel, longish hair—sideburns actually—and a double-breasted suit with a wide tie and stickpin. All very chic, very retro. She was just about to ask what vintage store they shopped at when the lady asked, "And what brings you here?"

"The party. Is that flocked wallpaper?" Charlotte nodded at the walls. "Prissy's going to have heart failure. She hates flocked. I was out getting chairs when the tree fell and blocked the side door and . . . Sorry, I'm babbling. A near-death experience can do that to a person. Winding up with caskets compounds the problem." Time to change the subject. "Were you at the party, too?" Though Charlotte knew she'd remember them.

The woman shook her head. "We're just visiting."

"Friends of Anthony and Vince?"

"We run into each other from time to time."

Charlotte took a deep breath trying to keep her head from spinning. She was dizzy and unsteady; the storm still raged outside. "Nice meeting you. Guess I better get back." She nodded at a door on the other side of the room. "My friends will wonder where I am, or at least where the chairs are."

The woman said, "You have good friends. You're very lucky to have them and they you." It was a statement and not a question, and Charlotte gave a slow nod of agreement as she thought about that. "We were all adopted, and in this town, if you can't trace your roots back to Oglethorpe and his boat buddies, some Civil War general or Paula Deen, you're damned. We didn't measure up with the other kids at Blessed Sacrament, so we became friends."

"It's good that you found each other and stayed together all these years. You're family. Connected."

"Have you lived in Savannah long? You look familiar. Do you shop at Piggly Wiggly? Everyone shops the Pig. And . . . and how do you know who I am?"

The two exchanged loving looks. "Oh, we've been here for years and years," the lady said. "And I understand you may be going into the carpet business."

"Not if I can help it." Charlotte leaned her head against the bronze coffin, feeling woozy. "I'm trying to find someone." They seemed so friendly, easy to talk to.

The woman said, "Shouldn't be too hard if they want to be found. If not . . ."

"This involves an inheritance. You're not much older than me, but you seem to know this place. I didn't even know about this room. Have you ever heard about a murder or a baby or a missing jewel necklace connected with the morgue?"

"Perhaps you should go and ask your daddy."

"He doesn't want me anyplace near this missing-person case, but we need the money, so I'm on my own."

"Ask him about the baby and the adoption."

That grabbed Charlotte's attention and she fought through the fuzzy feeling to make sense of it. "The baby was adopted? Here in Savannah? And RL knows about this? You're kidding."

"I would never kid about that, dear."

"How do you know all this?"

A loud pounding sounded on the door that led to the rest of the house.

"Charlotte?" called Griff. "Are you in there? I hear you. Are you okay? Charlotte, let me in. The door's locked. What's going on?"

Charlotte sighed. "That man's cute enough, but he's sure used to getting his way."

"That he is, dear," the woman said on a lilting laugh.

Charlotte wobbled to the door with one shoe on and one . . . somewhere. She flipped the lock on the door.

"Charlotte, dammit, let me in."

"Oh for Pete's sake, Griff, what do you think I'm doing? It's stuck. The blessed thing won't . . . give . . . an . . . inch," she said, pulling with all her might. She pulled one more time, the door yielding way, flinging her back. Tripping, she landed in a heap, her head smacking the floor. She felt tired to the core, as if someone was sitting on her and she couldn't get up if she tried. Then she felt nothing at all, till someone started slapping her. Was that nice? Like she hadn't been beaten up enough today?

Griff knelt on one side. Prissy and Brie were on the other, Brie holding a candle, both looking wide-eyed and scared and not breathing. The sisters peered down, fingering their rosaries. Maybe this time she did croak and this was her funeral.

"Well, her eyes are blinking and she doesn't look too awful bad," said Sister Roberta.

"Something like a drowned rat, if you ask me," offered Sister June.

Those little white lies that made everyone feel better didn't exist in the world of the sisterhood. They needed to be told the truth wasn't all it was cracked up to be. "Doesn't she look fine" would be good right now.

"Thank heaven you're okay," Prissy whimpered. Tears filled Brie's eyes.

Griff gave her one of those relief kind of smiles, then started touching her ankles, her knees, her—

"What do you think you're doing?" she croaked in a weak voice.

"Just lay still. I'm checking to see if anything's broken."

He wasn't finding anything broken, just really turning her on. One more inch by Dr. Griff and she was a goner, probably going into some kind of orgasmic huffing and puffing right here in front of her best friend and the nuns. Scar the ladies for life. Charlotte sat up way too fast, feeling instantly nauseous, but managed to shove Griff's hand away. "I'm fine, okay. Just a little rough patch here. Nothing serious."

"You're bleeding," Brie gasped. "I hear the paramedics coming."

"No paramedics. No people I don't know pawing all over me. Besides, I'm fine. I tripped. And will you all quit looking as if I died."

Griff took a handkerchief from the inside of his perfect gray suit that didn't look all that perfect at the moment. He dabbed her head. "You're bleeding in more places than one."

"I'm leaking, not gushing. I'm okay, really. Just ask . . ." Her voice stopped dead in her throat. "Where is everyone?"

"They all went home," Prissy said. "The party's over."

"I mean, where are the two people on the settee? Where's the settee? Where the heck are the caskets? This place is a filthy mess. Did you all move me?"

Griff exchanged looks with Prissy and Brie, the worried looks back in place. Griff said, "This is where we found you—on the floor, no one else around, no settee and definitely no caskets. You need to go to the hospital and get checked out."

Brie bent closer, her eyes an inch away. "Can you see me?"

"You're right in my face."

"What's your name? When's your birthday?"

Charlotte took a handful of Griff's jacket and Brie's shoulder, and stood. Taking the candle from Prissy, she held it high to a dark musty, dusty, empty room except for an old settee in the corner with a carved rosewood back that hadn't been sat on in years. "I don't get it. There were people here. The room was . . . nice in a casket-viewing sort of way. Except for the blue flocked wallpaper." She turned to Prissy. "You would have hated the wallpaper."

Bebe stood in the doorway now. Paramedics were at her side, holding their little black bags. No one moved, everyone looking at her. "Hey, I'm serious here. There were people. A husband and wife probably. They knew me and RL, and shopped at the Pig."

Griff took her hand. "You were unconscious, Charlotte."

Prissy said, "You dreamed it. Remember how you used to dream about owning a McDonald's and having free fries anytime you wanted. Though why you didn't dream about owning Neiman Marcus is beyond me."

Charlotte rubbed her eyes. "The three of us talked about Jaden right here in this room. I'm going home, getting a bath, and me and Ben and Jerry are doing some serious damage to a pint of chocolate chip cookie dough ice cream and try and figure this out. And I am not going to the hospital."

Griff's eyes narrowed and he suddenly looked a lot less mannered swanky-hotel owner and a lot more don't-mess-with-me construction guy. "Wanna bet?"

"What are you going to do, big boy? Strap me into that ambulance?"

And before she took another breath, Griff scooped her into his arms and strode for the door, saying to the paramedics, "See you at St. Joe's emergency room." He said to Prissy, "You all finish up here, I'll take care of this little problem."

"Uh, okay," she heard Prissy say.

"What do you mean, okay? This is not okay at all." Charlotte pushed at his chest. "And I am not a *this little problem*. I am not a little anything. Put me down, you overgrown orangutan."

*   *   *

Griff paced the emergency room, figuring that in the last hour he'd crossed the blasted thing thirty times round-trip. He pulled on his tie again even though he'd loosened it a long time ago. When he paced back the other way, he saw Charlotte at the nurses' station, form in hand. She wasn't smiling as she came his way. "Sign this. It says you dragged me here against my will, and if you ever do something like this again, I get to beat you up."

She had a bandage on her forehead, scrapes on her face by her nose and on her cheek. There was a bruise over her left eye and one on her chin. His heart felt like a lump of lead. He'd give anything to make her better. Hell, she could have been killed. Her dress was ripped and she wore shoes that some patient had probably left behind for good reason. Hair . . . would she ever get the tangles out? He touched her face, his heart hurting more. "You sure that's what it says?"

"Promise."

He took the board and read. "Says here they want you to stay the night."

"My health insurance has a ten-million-dollar deductible. I can't afford to stay here overnight." She tapped the board. "Sign."

"Says you have a concussion."

"Typo. Supposed to be *confession* and just a little one. I told them about that time I stole mints from that bowl on the desk at Magnolia House."

"Those are free."

"I'm not staying here."

"If I sign, you're mine." His eyes met hers, and she looked too exhausted, nothing registering. He scribbled his name, took the board and his credit card back to the nurse, then hooked his arm through Charlotte's and ushered her to his car, still parked in the emergency area.

"I should call a cab," she said as he buckled her in.

"I'm cheaper." He headed for the hotel. "How do you feel?"

"You wouldn't happen to have a Snickers handy, would you? Life always goes better with a Snickers."

"Not the food of choice for a confession."

He took MLK then pulled to the front of Magnolia House, slid from the driver's side, then helped Charlotte.

"Good evening," Ralph greeted in perfect night-doorman fashion, not blinking an eye at Charlotte's appearance. Discretion at Magnolia House was always paramount . . . even for the owner. Using his pass key, Griff called the elevator, which they took to the third floor. "Where are we going?" Charlotte asked, her head sagging on his shoulder.

"In search of a Snickers."

"Promise?"

"Would I lie?"

"Oh fuck yes."

He laughed and ran his hand over his face. He doubted if Charlotte deShawn had ever said *fuck* in her life till tonight. Least she hadn't ever said it in public. She wasn't that kind of girl. And RL would have had a tantrum if he heard. As much as the Parishes didn't see eye to eye with single dad Robert Lee deShawn for reasons now clear as crystal, RL did a good job raising Charlotte. Griff unlocked his apartment, and Charlotte paused. "Snickers are in there?"

"Or maybe some club soda. Confessions can upset your stomach."

"Just take me home."

"I've got night duty." He ushered her into the apartment, flipped on a lamp, then took her into his bedroom, wishing it was for a more clandestine reason than keeping an eye on a concussed patient. The night lights from Broughton Street sliced into the room and he adjusted the blinds, diverting the glare. Charlotte flopped back on his bed like a landed fish and stared up at the ceiling. Her eyes drifted closed. "If you intend to compromise my virtue, you should know that after our event in your office, I don't have any virtue left. I think you took it all."

"No compromising tonight, honey." He pulled out a T-shirt and a pair of boxers with a huge dick printed on the front that he'd gotten as a gag on Valentine's Day from Cindy, or was it Sandra? He would have gotten rid of them, but how? What if a maid found them in the trash? "Your clothes are still wet. We need to get you into something . . ." She was asleep, or was it a coma? Shit! "How often am I supposed to wake you up?"

"Never . . . unless you find that Snickers."

He pulled off her shoes and dropped them in the trash can in the bathroom. He got the Nanking Cargo bowl from the hall table and filled it with water. Taking soap and a washcloth, he cleaned away the mud splatters on her feet and legs. Her left eye opened. "What are you doing?"

Getting turned on. "Wiping you off. You'll ruin my silk sheets."

"You have silk sheets?"

"Hell no. Just wanted to see if you were conscious." And he needed to have some kind of conversation as a diversion from the loveliest, softest, smoothest skin he ever touched.

"Do I get to wipe you off, too?" She giggled, then stopped and frowned. "I feel rotten." She flung her arm over her face. "Do you know that all my life—well, not all, but since like maybe when I was fifteen—I wanted to see your bedroom? Actually more than see—be in it."

He stopped washing and tried to remember to breathe, because that was pretty much what he'd wanted, too.

"And now here I am, and I'm a mess." She peeked under her arm. "Why don't you just take me now so I have something good come from this night?"

He dried her legs, willing himself to not go beyond her

knees . . . well, just a little beyond. Then he helped her sit up. "Sex is us together, sweetheart. Knowing what's going on. And with you seeing people who aren't there . . . I doubt you'll remember anything that happened tonight."

"I did see people. Two. What happened to them?" She rubbed her hand over her forehead. "I don't get it. They were there, then they weren't."

"What you got was whacked on the head." He sat on the bed behind her, brushing her long hair to the side, exposing her shoulders and nape. He wanted to kiss her there. Hell, he wanted to kiss her everywhere, but she was hurt. No kissing. His dick pulsed as he unzipped her dress, the black silk falling open, revealing her lovely back inch by inch, the black band of the strapless bra, the curve of her spine. He unclasped the bra, letting it fall to her lap, the delicious swell of her breasts and graceful bend of her head reflected in the mirror along with her injuries. Shit!

She sighed. "You are going to have sex with me. Even better than a Snickers."

He slid the T-shirt over her head, the soft cotton pooling down around her. "There. Better." Covered!

He laid her back and slid the dress down her legs, dragging the shirt along to conceal her most tempting places. Thank God. Self-control was at an all-time low . . . except for the time in his office or the time in his hallway or . . . Good God! When he was with Charlotte, he had minimal control.

She looked up at him. "Coming?"

Damn close to it. "I'll be right back. I'm going to grab a shower." And get rid of this throbbing dick in the only acceptable way that would let him sleep beside her. He needed to keep an eye and nothing else on her.

"Hurry," she said, her eyes closing again. "I'm so tired. So very tired."

He pulled up the blanket and kissed her temple, a shiver

running up his spine. What if that damn tree had . . . No, he wasn't going there. He couldn't imagine life without Charlotte deShawn . . . though maybe he should. She wasn't going to be around forever. In fact, the way things were progressing, not long at all.

And Griff was reminded of that the next morning when he awoke and Charlotte was gone . . . except for a note propped beside the dick boxers he'd left on the dresser.

> Thanks for bringing me home with you. Thanks for waking me every three hours, though there are better reasons to wake a woman in the middle of the night than ask her what her birthday is. And where in the world did you get these?

Feeling abandoned, he got out of bed and stepped into jeans. Charlotte sounded okay. Probably have the headache from hell, but she was up and moving and had enough savvy to sneak out and leave him sleeping. He missed her, dammit. One innocent night together and he missed her like mad. He wanted to wake up beside her, make sure she felt okay, but it didn't happen. The two of them together never caught a break.

Cutting off the AC, he opened the windows, letting in fresh morning air before the Savannah humidity set in. He reread the note just as someone pounded on his door. Crisis in the hotel at six AM? Good God, now what? He dropped the note on the coffee table and flung open the door to . . . "Beau? Sweet Jesus, you look like hell. What ran over you? Don't even answer. It's a woman. You got that stomped-by-a-woman look."

Beau stumbled in and flopped onto the couch. "I blew it. I blew it big-time."

"If you got some girl preg—"

"Shit. I'm not totally stupid, just mostly stupid." He

raked both hands through is stand-on-end, convertible-blasted hair.

"Where the hell were you last night? Brie must have asked me five times if I knew what happened to you. I made up some cock-and-bull story about a busy Saturday night at the Cove but . . ." He looked closely. "What *did* happen?"

"I punked out, man. I choked. And when it comes to women, I never choke, except now with BrieAnna. She's perfect, Griff. Every hair, every eyelash, every cell of her incredible body. All the way perfect. And me . . . not so damn much."

Griff sat in the leather chair next to the couch, the toll of church bells drifting in. Of course they'd be tolling all morning, from Christ Episcopal, First Bryan Baptist, First African Baptist, First Congregation, St. John's, Trinity United, Independent Presbyterian. The only thing Savannah folk liked more than fried food, a good party, and martinis was dressing for Sunday church. Maybe to undo the sins of the other three. "You think all women are perfect, Beau. The hair, the skin . . . sound familiar? BrieAnna's just another woman."

Beau looked tortured. "I couldn't even kiss her the other day. I froze up. Been driving around all night thinking about it. My lips wouldn't move, my hands wouldn't move. My damn tongue like a piece of wood stuck in my damn mouth. That was downright embarrassing. Shitfire, I kissed better than that in kindergarten."

"Kindergarten?"

"I was an early bloomer. Now I need therapy. Kissing therapy. You got to help me learn how to kiss again."

Griff felt his eyes dilate. "Uh, Beau, you and I are tight, but . . . but . . . I . . . you . . ."

"Not *you*, for Chrissake. I'm not that far gone. Give me a break. Besides, you're the ugliest son-of-a-bitch on the planet. I want you to put me in touch with someone, a real good kisser who can get me going again. Jump-start my lips. I gotta get things operating like they should. I'm all screwed up. Hell, I'm doomed. You know what this is? It's payback for all those women in my life. I always treated 'em nice, gave as good as I got and more, but there was never anyone special. Date 'em, dazzle 'em, ditch 'em . . . in a nice way, but ditching is ditching. And now the special one comes along and I can't perform. Hell, I'm probably all fucked out, too. Piss!"

Griff picked up the phone and ordered coffee and juice from the kitchen. "You want me to get you . . . what? A kissing therapist?"

"Laugh and I'll flatten your ass."

Griff chuckled. "I'm sure you'd give it your best shot." And with an ex-jarhead, Griff would have his hands full. Not that it would ever come to that.

Beau added, "I need someone to practice on, someone discreet, someone who won't spread my problem all over town. If BrieAnna found out, she'd never have anything to do with me. No woman wants some candy-ass in the bedroom. I'll pay. A business transaction. Maybe someone from your staff. They're great at keeping their mouths shut."

"Actually you don't want someone who can keep their mouth shut."

"You're enjoying this, aren't you?"

"Immensely. I'll see what I can do."

"No names, all right?"

"No names. Except everyone knows you."

"I'll think of something. Just find me a partner." Beau picked up the letter from the coffee table. "You sure have been busy for an old man. And why are you asking some gal her birthday? How old was she, Griff?"

Griff got the breakfast tray from Jerome, then poured out the coffee. "Charlotte spent the night. That storm last night knocked over a tree at the morgue shindig Camilla dragged me to. Charlotte got whacked in the head. She wouldn't go to the hospital, so I brought her here."

Beau grinned. "How good-Samaritan of you. Saint Griff right here in our midst. Glory be!"

"Closer to night-duty nurse and nothing more."

"Well, that's sure too damn bad. The way things are, Charlotte'll want your head on a platter, not your dick in bed. 'Course finding a bed partner has never been your problem, so you'll just move on to the next little filly out there, right?" Beau gave him a sideways glance. "Unless there's . . . more."

"Fuck."

Beau laughed. "Oh damn. We are a pair. I got it mighty bad for some society gal whose parents are going to blow a gasket if they ever see us together, and you . . ." He laughed harder. "You're about to get the shit kicked out of you. It's going to be an interesting summer."

"It's going to be a lot of crap neither of us ever counted on."

Beau rolled his shoulders. "Just let Charlotte go, Griff."

"Like you're letting go of BrieAnna?" He laughed. "Hell, least I remember how to make out."

Charlotte sat at one of the little white wrought-iron sidewalk café tables at Scrumptious Savannah and watched Prissy bite into Monday's special, a Morning Macaroon scone. Her eyes did a this-is-heavenly swirl, and she said around a mouthful, "We didn't know whether to follow Griff and you to the hospital or what Saturday night. He looked like a man on a mission. Bebe called the nurses' station and pulled a few strings, and they said Griff had signed you out and paid the bill. So, spill it. What the heck happened?"

"He paid the bill? I didn't ask him to do that, and how

am I going to pay that off? Maybe I can eBay stuff. I have some investigation books that are completely useless. And as far as anything happening with me and Griff . . . I slept in his bed and I distinctly remember saying something about being ready, willing and able, and he saying that was taking advantage, and me saying that was just fine and dandy."

"So . . . ?"

"So he got his way and I left before he woke up. Kind of humiliating to throw yourself at a guy and him turn you down flat, even if his reasons were honorable. I wasn't looking for honor. I was looking for sex. Though I don't think I have the same effect on Griff as he does on me. In fact, he said I wasn't a very good bed partner."

"He told you that last night?"

"Another time."

"The man who hauled your sorry self off to the emergency room was someone who cared a lot."

"I don't get it either, but that's the way it is. No sex." Charlotte set her elbow on the table and cupped her chin in her palm. "So, sweet thing, I sure hope you have better news than me. What happened with you and Sam Saturday night? Anything of a steamy nature that I should know about?"

"The storm messed up the security system at the bank and Sam left right after Griff hauled you off. Sam and I are at a strange place. I think there's an attraction but—"

"You did the deed in the elevator. Attraction left the station days ago."

"But there's more. It's like we're on the same wavelength. When I was freaking out that you were in the storm and maybe hurt, Sam knew you weren't. He knew you made your way inside and I knew you were in the casket room. We just . . . knew. Both of us together, at the same time. And what was with that wacky story about the people on the settee? Where in the world did that come from?"

"From the two people on the settee. It happened, Prissy, I'd swear to it. I went back to the morgue yesterday to look for clues. Told the brothers I lost a bracelet, but they wouldn't let me look for it. What is with them keeping that place off limits? They made up some story about storing stuff and it being too dangerous and blah, blah, blah. Bottom line is, they don't like people around."

Charlotte took a bite of Prissy's scone, feeling the carbs instantly adhere to her thighs. Like that foaming cleanser whose bubbles balloon up and stick to the bath tub. She now had carb bubbles sticking to her butt. "The mystery woman told me Jaden was adopted here in Savannah and RL knew about it. I couldn't make that up, could I? Where would information like that come from?"

"A bottle of extra dry champagne, a mighty fierce lightning storm and a crack on the head. You still have a goose egg over your eye and look like you've been in a catfight."

"Did you know the police department was so desperate to find who did the murders and what happened to that necklace that they hired a medium, a Marie Landau, a voodoo priestess right here in Savannah? I got the info from the newspaper. She was supposed to be pretty good, but she got no insightful vibes. Nothing. And why are you suddenly shivering?"

"Think about this. If Jaden suddenly shows up, she'll have to face that her own grandparents didn't want her, that her parents were murdered and that there's a missing necklace smack in the middle of it all. That could put her in a lot of danger. I'm starting to think it's not so good to find her."

"Griff said that, too, but she inherited the hotel, Priss. What if she's poor and this is her chance at something."

"Could be her chance to be a corpse. Tell Griff you ran out of leads and let him have Jaden declared legally dead. That puts an end to this."

"Would you want to know if you were Jaden?" She stared hard at Prissy.

"If people don't want you, why force yourself on them? Isn't that how we've always looked at this adoption business? I had a good life growing up with the nuns. I was loved. They took care of me when I was sick, had birthday parties, and Santa and the Easter bunny and the tooth fairy were always on time. They taught me about art and how to draw, and have always supported me. Look who cooked and served Saturday night. They're my family, Charlotte. Always will be. Just like RL is your family. Why would I want to go looking for someone who abandoned me and get hurt all over again? You never went looking for your mama. It's the same for Jaden. If she cared, she would have come looking for her parents. And . . . and I've still got that bad feeling, Char."

She took Charlotte's hand. "You've got bad karma right now, honey. This is no time to be running around with stuff that's not your concern. I was scared to death in that storm and when I saw you on the floor. Oh my gosh!" She closed her eyes for a second. "Since Griff gave you that check, it's all been wrong except for you two hooking up." She winked. "Keep that part, for what it's worth, but leave the case alone. Walk away. You go any further with this Jaden business and everything's going to change. Like throwing a skunk into the room. Once it's there, somebody's sure as heck got to deal with it."

Chapter 9

"You're scaring the daylights out of me," Charlotte said to Prissy.

"I'm scaring me, too. I want to go back to life as we know it. Except for me rehabbing a morgue—I still want to do that. And selling carpeting isn't all that dreadful bad, is it? If you open a carpet store, you could be rich. The House of Charlotte."

"Sounds like a brothel. Okay, I'll tell Griff today that I'm officially off the Jaden case. No one wants me to find her, and it doesn't sound like she even wants me to find her."

Prissy grinned. "Why not run over to Magnolia House and tell Griff, and put an end to this? I'd keep you company, but I have to get a business plan together for Sam Pate."

"Bet you'd like to be getting something else together for that man. And what exactly is a business plan?"

"Best I can tell, it's like Macy's. Build a store, buy pretty things, display them all swanky, and then women like me come and ogle and buy, and the price has to cover all those expenses. The morgue is Macy's for dead people. I thought about restoring it to its original glory till I saw pictures. Blah! Lots of flocked wallpaper."

"Blue and white? Big print?"

"Did you see pictures, too? I'm into retro and all, but I'm glad those days are over!"

Maybe she did see pictures, and maybe those plus the settee in the corner made her dream about the couple being there. But the man and woman were stuck in the eighties. Why not the fifties? "Don't know if a bank president will be impressed with your Macy's analogy, but I get it. Knock 'em dead, girl."

"I'm getting to hate morgue humor."

Charlotte hugged Prissy back and headed for Magnolia House, soaking in the great weather, because when August got here, it wasn't a matter of walking but closer to swimming through the Savannah humidity. Nature's sauna. But now it was paradise in the South and everyone knew it.

She stood on the curb of Oglethorpe Square with a cluster of tourists who asked her about the Oglethorpe Monument. She explained that for reasons she never understood, Oglethorpe was perched over in Chippewa Square, one block over and two blocks up. But that was a good thing, since it took them past the Pecan Palace, which had the best spiced pecans on earth. The group of tourists tramped off, more gathered and suddenly she was pushed hard from behind, sending her straight into the path of a big orange Savannah Tours trolley!

The driver slammed on the breaks, and some darling soul grabbed her from behind and yanked her back onto the curb. The crowd gasped, the trolley driver gave her a you-dumb-woman look and Daemon Rutledge said, "My goodness, Miss Charlotte! You surely do need to take more care now."

The crowd crossed the street, but Charlotte, still shaking, didn't budge.

"Are you all right?" Daemon asked. "Did you slip?"

"I . . . I think I was pushed."

Daemon's eyes widened. "I didn't see anyone do something like that. Then again, I was giving directions to the Pirate House and explaining the wonders of pecan chicken. I happened to look up, and suddenly there you were, stumbling straight away into the street. Scaring me half to death, I might add."

"It was probably an accident. You know how exuberant the crowds are this time of year, trying to see everything in one day."

Daemon gave her an uneasy look but then a smile. "Of course. Why would someone push you into the path of a bus? Ridiculous notion." He held her hand. "All the same, let me walk with you to your destination. Just to make sure you're feeling right well enough to go on."

She hooked her arm through Daemon's and instantly felt better. Secure. "Does Griffin Parish know what a great manager he has in you?"

Daemon grinned and patted her arm as they strolled off. "I've been part of Magnolia House now most of my life. It's my family. Griff's like a younger brother. I watched him grow up and take charge just like Otis would have wanted. And where might you be heading off to this morning?"

"Remember me asking you about Jaden? I'm giving up the search. It's simply been too long ago and no one remembers anything about that baby or what happened to her."

Daemon sobered, as if considering what she said. "A very wise idea, I think. And a safe one, considering what just transpired."

Charlotte paused in the middle of the sidewalk, feeling as if an elephant suddenly took a seat on her chest. "You think my winding up in the path of that bus was—"

He nudged Charlotte along. "I don't need to be making you fret now, but how many times have you been accosted by a trolley, my dear?" His brow quirked. "And then today, when you are on this case, you are."

They entered the hotel. "You take care of yourself," he said in a low voice. "I don't like this one little bit, Miss Charlotte. I don't like it at all."

She took the hall to Griff's office and knocked just as he opened it. He looked great in a gray suit and tie with a touch of peach, and he smelled of ginger and lime and safety. "You look like crap. Are you feeling okay? Dammit all, I knew you should have spent the night in that hospital."

She stepped in and closed the door. "I came to tell you I'm off the Jaden case, just like you wanted. I'll repay you the advance money and the hospital money." She fidgeted. "I hate being in debt."

"No debt. You did the job. Jaden's . . . gone. And I've been thinking about what you said in having her declared dead. My attorney did some research. There's no evidence of Jaden Carswell ever existing."

"There was a baby, Griff, and she was William and Adie's daughter. That is the only thing we know for sure. There must be papers somewhere."

"When a child is adopted in Georgia, a new birth certificate is issued in the adopted parents' names and the old one is sealed. Takes a court order to get to the files. I think she really is dead, Charlotte. This town is too small, too many folks into everyone's knickers. Someone would know something about her, or she would have initiated the search somewhere along the line herself. And even if she moved away or was adopted by someone outside of Savannah, people today want to know their roots, where they came from."

"Not everyone wants to know. But where are the adoption records?"

"If it was a private adoption, they're with that agency, and no one knows who or what that is."

"Otis knew, and I think you do, too. I broke into your

office and found a folder with Jaden Carswell's name on the front. Then someone shoved me and stole the folder right here in this office."

Griff paced to the window that looked out onto the terrace and the guests having a garden breakfast. "There was nothing in the folder but Jaden's birth certificate and a few baby pictures. I figured you were in here for some reason that night other than waiting for me, but I guessed that you took the folder, since it was gone. If Otis knew anything about Jaden or where she was, he never told me about it. Now that the folder is gone, so is Jaden."

"Your voice changed."

He faced her. "Excuse me?"

"Your voice got deeper. Not a lot, but I've known you a long time, and when something's up, your voice changes. You're lying, Griff."

"It's . . . stress." His gaze held to hers. "I'm afraid of losing you, and that is no lie, I swear it. I've got you in my life now, Charlotte, and I'm not about to let you go. The one good thing out of all this Jaden crap is us."

"Us?" She stared at him, not breathing, feet rooted to the floor, no muscles moving. "But you said there was no us, that I was not that great of a partner and—"

"I wanted you to give up the case and figured if I pissed you off enough, you'd quit out of spite. It was getting too dangerous for you, for everyone involved. But now it's all over and there's just us."

He dropped the window shade with one hand, his other scooping her close, bodies tight, thigh to thigh, man parts to woman parts. *Ohmygod, there was an us!*

Her insides melted warm and wet. Then his lips claimed hers, and any doubt of *us* vanished in the brush of lips and thrust of tongues. He smoothed back her hair and kissed her cheek. "Let me make it up to you for being so rotten. Let's go away. Bermuda."

"Bermuda? I was just hoping for lunch at Applebee's, maybe celebrate with a margarita."

He looked into her eyes, his eyes dark and hungry. "I've known you for a long time, too. Don't be nervous. Don't be anything but Charlotte. You're perfect the way you are." He nuzzled her neck. "We'll take off for a week, maybe two."

Her eyes closed, her head falling back, exposing her throat to kisses and a little sucking. Welcome to the I Have a Hickey Club. She'd never been a member before. Membership was good. Her brain hazed. Initiation day. "I . . . I have carpet class and I can't leave RL that long."

"Three days. You can get someone to cover for that long. You'll love the ocean, the beach, the food. God, you feel great in my arms. It's as if I've been waiting for this forever, Charlotte, and now that you're here, *we're here*, I'm not letting you go."

He nibbled her lobe and chills danced up her spine. "Doesn't it bother you that the file was stolen? Someone's looking for something. And . . . Oh my Lord, aren't we moving a little fast here?"

"We've been playing at getting together for years. I didn't plan for us to fall for each other, but it happened and I'm glad." His expression turned desperate. Griff desperate for her? That was a new one. "I really mean it, Charlotte. I want us together, and I want you to remember that, no matter what happens."

He slid her skirt down over her hips, letting it fall to the floor, and any thoughts about Jaden Carswell or moving too fast slid right along with it. Too bad it didn't take the pounding on the door with it. "You better answer that."

"It'll wait." He locked the door. "This won't." He kissed her lightly, his tongue tracing a path over her lower lip till she sucked it into her mouth. Her fingers worked his belt while he backed her toward the wall and slid her onto the bookcase there. Settling between her legs as if he belonged, he slid his fingers deep into her sex, driving the air right out of her lungs and probably out of the whole flipping room. "Oh dear Lord, Griff."

His tongue stroked her mouth; his fingers—one, then more—pushed into her, slowly, deeply, caressing her wet hot flesh there, making her whimper, her insides throb. "No," she breathed, pushing him back. "I don't want it like this. I want you inside me." She could barely speak, orgasm a hair-trigger away.

"But this is working so well." He smiled. "You're on fire for me."

She undid his fly, her fingers trembling. "You have such a great dick. Blunt but true." She closed her eyes. "I meant the statement was blunt, not your—"

He laughed and kissed her. Finding his wallet, he pulled out a condom, then his pants hit the floor.

"No dicky boxers?"

"I hate boxers."

She stroked his erection, his eyes glazing, his breathing labored. "But the dicky part's pretty terrific, I can attest to that."

He slid into her, his breath catching, his muscles tightening as he filled her in places she didn't know she had. Her legs parted wider, taking him deeper. Was there a deeper? "You are such a man."

"This is the way I want us every day," he ground out. "You, me in the sack . . . or on a bookcase or in an aisle at the Pig. I don't care. I want to make love to you all the time, anytime we get a hankering."

"Hankering?" She giggled. "How you do carry on, Mr. Parish."

"Sweetheart, you haven't seen nothing yet." He nipped the end of her nose. "And now you're here and you're mine. Remember that. Remember how much I want you right this minute and how much you want me." He looked at her hard, as if he wanted more than anything for her to believe him. Then his tongue took hers and he pumped into her, making her thankful he bought expensive furniture that held together under so much . . . enthusiasm. "Am I hurting you?"

"Only if you stop." She wound her arms around his neck and arched against him as he plunged into her again, holding her so tight, like he cared, really cared. She was Griff's, and he was hers. She knew it in every cell of her body as an orgasm poured over her, her fingers digging into his shoulders, her groans of ecstasy filling the room . . . or were those his groans?

"I want you. I need you, and I don't need anything." He nuzzled her neck. "You're real, gutsy and—"

"A good lay?"

He wound his fingers into her hair. "Honorable. Trustworthy."

"A Girl Scout?"

He kissed her forehead, then her chin. "You're bright and warm and caring, and make me feel that way, too. I can be myself with you, Charlotte. No airs. Warts and all. We're going to work this out. I swear it. You're the one for me."

"*The* one?" She studied his face, making sure he meant what he said. "Really? As in . . ."

"Like I've been saying, you and me." He laughed. It was the sincere kind of laugh that stripped away anything not real. "I think I've known it for a long time, and then I got a taste of you in my life and realized it was true. We're making it happen, Charlotte, if I have to move heaven and earth."

"Meaning Camilla? RL?" She kissed him, savoring the taste of him in her mouth and on her tongue, the feel of his hands on her face, their incredible lovemaking that was so unexpected and the fact that he wanted her as much as she wanted him. And most incredible, that this was not over when she left his office.

"I kept thinking I'd be able to shove you out of my life or be content with you on the edge of it. No more. I'm done pretending."

She held him tight. "I don't know what to say. You make me so happy, Griff." Her voice trembled, then she trembled all over. "I never thought we could be together like this. It was just a dream."

"And now it's not. We'll just have to work at it."

She looked at him. "This is the kind of work I can get used to. Bermuda?"

"Tomorrow."

"I . . . I can get LulaJean to watch Daddy. The closest I've ever been to Bermuda is buying RL a pair of Bermuda shorts for Father's Day when I was ten. They had yellow parrots. Ugliest shorts you ever saw. Bermuda?"

"We'll buy him new ones. No parrots." He took himself from her, making her appreciate that soon—very soon indeed—they wouldn't be sneaking around making love but on a beach in Bermuda doing it whenever and wherever they wanted. How'd she get so lucky? Why now? But she shouldn't think about that. She should be thinking about doing power shopping and buying new clothes and lots of sexy lingerie that would probably wind up on the floor beside the bed. How great was that!

He disposed of the condom as someone knocked again. "Griffin?" Daemon called. Griff whispered to Charlotte, "I'll pick you up at seven AM sharp. Let's keep it between us. You and me. No entanglements."

"I hate entanglements." She pulled on her skirt and smoothed out her hair. "I'll be ready. I'm ready now. I've been ready for fifteen years."

He turned to her and smiled. "Me, too, sweetheart. Me, too. Nothing's getting in our way."

Chapter 10

The knocking came again, and Griff took a deep breath, straightened his suit and remembered not to look down from this very high tightrope that he felt he was walking lately. One wrong step and he was dead meat. Charlotte gave him a quick kiss, then opened the door and left as Daemon entered. He didn't bat an eye, as if a disheveled Charlotte left his office every day. But right now, Griff didn't care. He and Charlotte together was a good thing for a lot of reasons. He just had to pull it off.

Daemon closed the door. "Camilla's looking for you. You're having visitors."

"You can handle it. I'm going to Bermuda." He grinned at the thought.

"Guess again. Jaden's grandparents are here. They just registered. I put them in room 213. Seems Charlotte contacted them about Jaden and that got them thinking the necklace may be found. Last time I saw those two lowlifes was thirty years ago when they flew down here to put a stop to Adie and William selling the necklace. Adie inherited it from her grandmother and the mother thought it should be hers. Then Adie and William were killed, the necklace vanished into thin air and the parents left without a single word, never considering that baby. I always assumed they had a change of heart when Otis had Jaden brought to them. But now it seems as if the baby just up and vanished herself."

"And I thought things were calming down. Damn it all." Griff slammed his hand against the wall.

"Don't you be using such vulgar language, Griffin. Sounds like trailer-trash talk," Camilla said as she hustled in, not bothering to knock. She said to Daemon, "There seems to be a problem in the main foyer that needs your attention right away." Which was Camilla code for "I want to speak to my son alone right now."

Camilla closed the door on Daemon and said to Griff as she paced the room, "Lord have mercy, this is not going well at all. I told you not to get Charlotte involved, but did you listen to me? Of course not, what do I know, I'm just your poor old mother who suffered through twenty hours of labor. And now we have Jaden's relatives right here on our doorstep, sniffing around and—"

"They're after the necklace, Mother, and once they see that it's still gone and nothing's changed, they'll hightail it back to Boston. And as for Jaden, I have a plan. I'm going to have her declared dead."

Camilla sat down. "We're resorting to dead, now are we. I don't see that as an improvement."

"Closer to a legal loophole. There are no clues to Jaden's whereabouts, no adoption papers, no evidence she's tried to find her birth parents, meaning we have a good chance. I'll get the hotel, and everything goes back to the way it should be. We'll have to post public notices in the papers, but if Jaden hasn't surfaced all these years, why would she now?"

Camilla's brow furrowed. "I suppose that could work, and for sure it would have a better chance if you hadn't gone and stirred the pot by hiring Charlotte. What are you going to tell her now?"

"Nothing." Griff grinned. "That's the best part. This was her idea."

"What happened to your high-and-mighty idea of doing the right thing and buying out Jaden's share of the hotel? Have a change of heart and joining the dark side?"

Griff rubbed the back of his neck. "I'm going to get things worked out once and for all."

"I'm getting things worked out once and for all," Charlotte said to Bebe as they headed up Bull toward the courthouse. Least she thought she was heading for the courthouse. After what happened in Griff's office this morning, she wasn't sure about anything. "Griff can simply have Jaden declared dead." She batted her eyes and looked dreamy. "Did I happen to mention that I'm running off to Bermuda with my man, the Biscuit, free as a bird?"

"Horny as a three-puckered Billy goat. And I think you mentioned Bermuda a hundred times, and that's just in the last block," Bebe laughed.

Charlotte took Bebe's hand. "I think it's more than just horny. I think he likes me . . . a lot."

"But why?" Bebe held up her hand. "Wait, that didn't come out right. You're terrific and Griff doesn't deserve you, but why now? Why all of a sudden?"

"Simple as pie. The Jaden case threw us together and we've gotten to know each other and things . . . progressed."

"Meaning he got into your panties and you liked it."

She pulled Bebe to the side. "Okay, that's it. No more cop questions, no more interrogations for just this once. Griff cares for me and I care for him. I bought lingerie, the real thing from Victoria's Secret, something that's called Brazilian panties at ten bucks a pop for the littlest scrap of lace you ever saw and some black hipkini panties with *sexy* scrawled right there in front in case he forgets and some eyelet babydoll jammies and—"

"You're right." Bebe kissed Charlotte on the cheek. "There is no analyzing love, or even *like,* for that matter. I'll never understand it—it's not for me—but that doesn't mean no one else doesn't." They pushed through the doors. "So with all this romance in the air, why are we at the courthouse again?"

"To get my birth certificate, since I'm traveling out of the country and don't have a passport and . . . and to maybe look around a little."

"Look around as in . . ."

"I did some checking, and after an adoption, the papers are sealed and so is the original birth certificate. A birth certificate is then issued with the child's new name and parents. I don't know what Jaden's new name is, but I want to look at the birth certificates all the same, to see if I'm missing something, and I need you to pull strings so I can do that. I don't think 'pretty please with sugar on top' is going to get me very far. Cops have great pulling abilities." She nudged Bebe. "And I'll treat you to chili fries."

They located the records office, and Bebe got access to the birth certificates on the computer in the back room, where they could pore over them together. The room, tucked away in the back, was yuck green and smelled musty from lack of use. Not many people in Savannah got off on birth-certificate snooping.

"Well, here we are," Charlotte said, pointing to the monitor as she and Bebe sat on the most uncomfortable chairs in all of Christendom. "Me and Prissy and BrieAnna and no Jaden and no you because yours was an out-of-state adopt—"

Charlotte stopped, mentally calling herself every name for stupid. "I'm sorry I said that. I know how you hate talking about Dara Fitzgerald, spawn of the devil. She should be pickled and fried."

Bebe grinned. Except the grin didn't reach her eyes. It

never did when it came to her adopted family. "Did you know Dara got paid for adopting me?" Bebe blurted, then looked surprised that she said what she did.

"Crap." Bebe stood, sat back down, then rifled through her black pleather Kmart-special purse and pulled out a squashed, bent cigarette with half the tobacco falling out that must have been there for a year. She lit up, the jolt of nicotine calming her, her eyes softening, the smoke circling in the dingy room, breaking more laws than Charlotte wanted to think about. Bebe smoked? Then again, that wasn't the only thing Bebe kept to herself.

"I've thought about this," she said in a low voice. "Why would a woman who despised me so much keep me around when she had six brats of her own? Why adopt me period, and why have the cops drag me home all those times I ran away? Money. Everything's sex or money. I think Dara must have gotten paid as long as I was under her roof."

"But your bio mother and/or father could have shuffled you off to foster care for free or given you up for adoption for free. Why pay someone to care for you?"

"Ah, now that is the question I never intend to get the answer to, because if I found my real parents, I'd have to shoot them." She laughed a not-funny laugh and took another drag on the cigarette. "All I know is that after Dara and her clan, I am finished with family forever, except for the three of you, of course. I'm single and loving it. No one on my turf, no one telling me what to do and when to do it. No entanglements of any kind. She sighed deeply and brightened. "Now let's go get those fries."

They stood, and Charlotte hugged Bebe tight, not worrying whether she'd wrinkle her suit. The ugly things had some advantage. "I'm sorry you went through all that. Sort of like Cinderella does Savannah."

"Except no glass slipper."

"Everybody gets a glass slipper."

Bebe held out her arms, her ugly gray poly-blend suit that could traverse a car wash without wrinkling or wilting hanging loose on her lithe frame. "I know what I want and where I'm going, and I'm up for a big promotion. Hey, life is good . . . now."

"What if Jaden's like you?"

"A cop in a gray suit?"

"What if she had a miserable life like yours and she's pissed at the world that no one helped her? Oh Be, what am I going to do? How can I walk away from this baby without knowing? Maybe she's happy, but maybe she's miserable and alone. The four of us have always had each other. Jaden's had no one. That's so sad."

"Hey, I'm not pissed or sad. I'm so happy I could be twins. Besides, we're out of options. You've asked around, I've asked at the station. No adoption papers, no birth certificate. Zip. Otis may have left her part of the hotel, but unless he said who the heck Jaden is, it's over, honey. The girl is nowhere to be found."

"Or . . . maybe she's just waiting to be found." Charlotte scrunched her eyes closed, trying to think . . . and not about Griff and going to Bermuda! She studied the computer screen again. "The reason I came here is because that woman in the morgue that I saw . . ."

"Your hallucination pals?"

"Okay, maybe she wasn't a ghost and maybe it was my imagination, but the idea came from somewhere, from something I heard or saw along the way. But all the same, she said Jaden's adoption was here in Savannah. What if one of those birth certificates we saw was Jaden's? We know of three adoptions that year. Us. The same age, within the same four months that Jaden would have been adopted." Charlotte took a deep breath, feeling her stomach cramp. "Dear God, Bebe. What if Jaden is . . . BrieAnna."

"Yeah, right."

"If there were other adoptions that year, we would have befriended them, or at least heard about them over the years, since it was always a big deal. We were the band of bastards, the outside orphans. We heard it all. In this town, it's what blood runs in your veins that counts. Look at Harry Jasper."

"Local drunk, doesn't have two dimes to rub together and mooches off everyone. He hit me up for twenty bucks yesterday in front of the Pig."

"And you gave it to him because his great-great-great-granddaddy is Stonewall Jackson. Harry is royalty, gets invited to every Oglethorpe society party, even the Christmas one at the Telfair. Gus Tillman made a killing in the stock market last year, bought the Milliken House, donated a wing at the animal shelter, and still can't get a reservation at the Pink House on Saturday night because he's a come-here from Dallas. We've never heard of any other orphans, have we? We know Jaden isn't you because of the New York adoption and because Otis would have never tolerated the way Dara treated you. My mom was RL's no-good sister. And it can't be Prissy because neither William nor Adie was black."

"Char, honey, what if whoever adopted baby Jaden just moved away when she was a baby?"

"There is that, or there's the fact that BrieAnna's was a rich private adoption and Otis would have placed Jaden, a best friend's daughter, in the best home he could find. He gave up any connection for the baby's safety."

Bebe stared off into space, pulling more drags off the cigarette, turning the trapped air in the little room blue.

"Oh . . . my . . . God."

"I know."

"Oh . . . my . . . God."

"You got to quit saying that. You're freaking me out."

"There's more."

"Girl, I can't do more right now. It's been a pretty packed day already."

"Char, if you can figure out this connection and you can't even find your way out of Target . . . someone else can come up with it, too."

"Is there a compliment in there somewhere?"

"That puts Brie smack in the middle of murder and missing jewels, though we aren't absolutely positive about Brie being Jaden. We could be wrong, you know. Maybe we're wrong. Wrong would be good."

"Griff hired me to find Jaden because he thought if I tracked Brie down, it would be easier than him showing up saying, 'Ta-da! Guess what! You're Jaden, and you and I own a hotel together.' RL knows it's Brie and had a conniption when I took the job because he didn't want Griff going after Brie because he knew of the danger she'd be in."

"How in the world does RL figure into all this?" She faced Charlotte. "Because he's the one Otis hired to take the baby to the grandparents?"

"Yeah. I wondered and wondered who that was, and no one knew. And when the grandparents rejected the baby, RL arranged the adoption. He's one of the few people in Savannah who keeps his mouth shut. Everyone knows that." Charlotte closed her eyes. "We're right about all this, I know it. So many things are adding up."

"How do we find out for sure? If RL's kept it quiet all these years, he's not about to spill it now. He wants things to go on as they are."

"And so does Griff. He's obviously had a change of heart about telling Brie and is more than willing to keep the hotel for himself. Good grief, I've got the hots for a no-good, middle-Georgia-redneck louse."

"Not necessarily."

"No, trust me, it's the hots all right. I know the symptoms. Sweaty palms, blurred vision, mushy insides."

"I mean, maybe he's not such a louse. Things are heating up over this will and Griff's afraid for Brie, too. You had that file stolen right out from under you."

"And I did get pushed into the street."

Bebe's head snapped around, looking her straight in the eyes. "When?"

"Just this morning. Scared me, too. I think it was more of a warning to stay away from this case." Charlotte snatched the cigarette from Bebe and took a drag, choked, then squashed the thing out in the garbage can and fanned away the smoke.

"Here's what we'll do," Bebe said. "I'll get my apartment painted, and that gives me a reason to move in with Brie for a few days, to keep an eye on her. You snoop around RL's stuff and see what you come up with. Do it tonight, before you leave."

"Right after the séance. If we don't go, Prissy will be honked off and we'll hear about it till the middle of next year and beyond."

Bebe raked back her shiny straight blonde hair and let out a long breath. "You're doing Bermuda, Brie's sniffing after a gangster and now we have a séance? When did that happen?"

"Don't you ever check your cell messages? Something to do with a business plan and no one willing to work on the morgue. Prissy's counting on gossip about the séance . . . exorcism . . . voodoo . . . whatever to get around so that everyone will believe all is now well with the morgue and she can get her contractors. It shouldn't take long. Wave a magic wand or spin a dead rat, and ghosts are gone."

"Guess that means bye-bye to your Mutt and Jeff hanging out in the casket room."

"They were more like *Designing Women* meets *Hill*

Street Blues. Why didn't I think to ask them their names? How did our lives ever get so complicated?"

"Because Otis wrote that blasted will and changed everything for a lot of people. He should have left things darn-well alone."

Charlotte clicked off the computer. "Yeah, but he didn't."

Chapter 11

Sam took the front steps of the morgue two at a time, then banged the dull brass knocker that needed work along with every other inch of the place. He gave another whack and the door opened to . . . "Prissy St. James, just the person I'm looking for." He stepped into the main hall. "What the hell do you think you're doing?"

Her big brown eyes rounded as she chewed and held up a plate of something chocolate and gooey. "Scarfing," she mumbled around a mouthful. She swallowed as Vince and Anthony came into the room, and she nodded at Vince. "He bakes. The to-die-for kind, in case you didn't get to sample his fare at the event. This is leftovers, and I don't mean of the meatloaf variety. I think it's a bribe to get me to leave, but it's not happening. Nice suit."

She licked the fork, the sight of her pink tongue on the silver stroking it's way upward and then down made him light-headed and instantly hard. Hell, most of the time he spent around Prissy left him in a perpetual state of hardness. Did she have any idea what she did to him? Obviously not, because he was no match for icing and chocolate.

"Real butter and double-sifted sugar is the key," Vince added, puffing out his purple shirt–clad chest.

"I'm sure it's great," Sam said with perfect honesty and a twinge of regret that he didn't have time for leftovers, too. He faced Prissy, trying not to focus on the little dab of crumb at the corner of her mouth that he wanted to kiss off more than he wanted oxygen. "I should be at work, but then I heard about a séance, here, tonight? Not only is no work getting done at the bank because of all the gossip, but you're turning this place into a sideshow. At this rate, I'll never get the board's approval for your loan."

"Well, I'll be." Prissy looked to the brothers. "See, I told you it would work. Am I a genius, or what? It got all the way to the bank, and not just the bank, but the bank president. I should be in PR."

"What got to the bank? It wasn't your business plan." Sam ran his hand around his neck, willing himself to calm down over a damn cake smear.

"News of the séance via the kudzu vine. The more people hear about it, the more they'll know the ghosts will be gone and my morgue can get funded."

And suddenly Sam didn't care about the vine or the bank or leftovers because he was staring at the most beautiful creature God saw fit to put on earth. His insides stirred, his muscles tensed and he wondered if there was a god of weak erections so he could pray to him.

"This is all because of you." Prissy put down the plate, parked her hands on her hips and leaned toward him, adding some stern to what she intended to say, except her blue blouse gaped in front, offering him a peak at delightful cleavage and delicious skin and filling his head with a scent of something . . . wicked. He tried to refrain from panting. Anthony gave him a subtle man-to-man kind of look.

"I'm working on the business plan," Prissy said. "But I hit a snag. Seems that even though I had the nuns at the morgue on Saturday night in full nun regalia of black and white and thought that would override any and all ghost stories connected with this place, Charlotte's encounter of the ghostly kind outdid me. I think the EMS people blabbed. Can't say as I blame them. Everyone loves a ghost story, and it probably spread like greased lightning. So, until the morgue is declared a ghost-free zone for evermore, we're back to square one, with workers refusing to come. And are you listening to anything I'm saying here?"

Hell no! Or at least, not much, with this lovely scenery. "Of course I'm listening."

"So I started the rumor about the séance to get rid of any lingering spirits. "Great idea, huh?"

Great rack!

"Now I'm off to find a séance person."

"Do you really believe in that stuff? Does anyone?"

"Oh for the love of Mike. It's the Low Country, Sam. Here spirit things aren't tourist shops to buy dolls to stick pins in. Here it's for real. Didn't you read *Midnight in the Garden of Good and Evil*? The good hour; the evil hour? How getting what you want goes beyond handing over your credit card?"

She took a deep breath, making her lovely breasts rise and fall and driving him nuts, though considering this conversation, he'd already arrived. "You're off to find a mambo? You're getting mixed up in something that could be dangerous. Have the nuns say a novena. Much safer."

"Not flamboyant enough. If word gets out—and it always does—that we had a séance and house cleansing and whatever else they do to get the house spirit-free, it should help. And just how did you know a mambo is a voodoo priestess?"

Damn. This is what happened when he was distracted, and no one distracted him like Prissy. "Heard it somewhere. This is a little over the top."

"It's either this or give up on the morgue, and I can't do that."

Vince waved his hands in the air. "We've tried and tried to tell her we can rehab the morgue ourselves."

Prissy said, "There's not three feet square in the whole place that doesn't need work. If you do it yourselves, you'll be having your own funeral here when you're ninety-nine and the place still won't be done. That's bad business. I'm trying for good business, the very reason you went and hired me."

Anthony fidgeted. "Of course we must keep up appearances of a good business. Everyone should know we are working in here and that is all." He looked to Vince. "Perhaps we should do that now, before the place is overrun with more people tonight. There never seems to be any end to them, just more and more." He sighed. "This is not the way it was supposed to be. Not the way we planned."

Vince and Anthony took off, and Sam wrapped Prissy in his arms and kissed her. Chocolate never tasted so good, so sweet, so erotic. How'd erotic get in the mix? Then he considered who he had his arms around, and erotic was just the way he liked it.

"What are you doing?"

He touched the corner of her mouth, the sensitive skin there so delicate, so sensual. "You had a crumb."

"You had a testosterone surge."

"That, too."

Her tongue traced the spot; his dick went painfully hard. Suddenly realizing the effect she had on him, she blushed, her dark skin rosy and fresh and warm. God, he loved her warm, and he wanted her that way, his skin to hers, pressed tight together, all hot and sweaty and—

"Why, when it comes to you and me together, everything circles back to sex? Even ghosts and a séance get us back here."

"Is that such a bad thing?"

Her eyes lit with passion and a good dose of desire. Oh baby.

"Except we're in limbo, Sam," she said in a soft voice. "And the only way out, and to see what we're all about, is if I give you that blasted business plan and get the loan fair and square. Then you won't think I'm using you, and neither will anyone one else in this town. Your reputation as a sensible and uncompromising bank president is intact right now, but if this loan thing doesn't work out, I don't know what we'll do. I don't want to keep sneaking around in hotel rooms and morgue hallways."

"So this job isn't just about repaying the nuns?"

She shook her head, her long loose curls swishing across his arm holding her and dancing in the sunlight streaming into the hall. "Not entirely."

"And all your dreams aren't about kitchen appliances?"

"Not entirely."

"Well, damn."

"Is that a good damn or a bad one? I suggest good. You don't want to get on the wrong side of a gal who's going off to look for a mambo."

"Good, definitely good." And it had nothing to do with believing in voodoo; she had him with her dazzling smile. "But you can't do this looking alone, Prissy. Like you said, there's the good and the evil side. Who knows who you're going to meet up with. Where are the fearsome three-some?"

"Bebe's a cop, Charlotte has a case, Brie has a gala to benefit the literary foundation over at the Hamilton Turner House and is up to her eyeballs in champagne flutes and caviar. Can you come with me?"

"Bank presidents don't do voodoo, and I thought we needed to keep apart."

She unknotted his tie, her fingers at his throat intimate,

the scent of her hair intoxicating. She slid off his coat, then stood back and admired her handiwork. She ruffled his hair and he rolled his eyes up trying to catch the damage.

"Better." Her lips mated with his. "Now you're incognito. Not the stuffy bank president at all." She swiped chocolate from her plate. "I could draw a mustache on you."

Shit! "If the bank's home office in Atlanta hears of this . . ."

"We won't be traveling in economic circles."

"I am on my lunch hour."

She smiled and kissed him, then yelled, "Bye, Anthony. Bye, Vince. I'll be back soon with candles, incense and maybe a full moon, oh my."

She said to Sam as they closed the door behind them, "The brothers are really nice and friendly and hospitable, but I don't think they like me being here. In fact, I don't think they want to rehab the morgue at all. But for some reason, they need me here, too. I don't get it."

Sam opened the door to his car and dropped a kiss into her hair. "Honey, if having a séance in a morgue to get a business plan together can make sense, anything can."

Prissy laughed at the comment, not sure when she'd been so happy, and it wasn't just the job or the prospect of really getting the business plan done but mostly Sam Pate. She liked him, and it wasn't just a passing fancy, but more. They didn't see eye to eye on a lot of things and he was making her jump through all kind of hoops to get the loan, but he wasn't a phony to her or anyone else. He was the sort of guy who always dotted his i's and crossed his t's with everyone. What you saw was what you got. Okay, he was a stuffed-shirt bean counter, but he was also down to earth and she could depend on him. And he was terrific in the sack!

"So," he said as he slid into the Beemer as if he owned it. Heck, he did own it. "Where does one go in Savannah to get a mambo?"

"Head down Drayton back to town. This is some sweet car. Being a bank president has definite perks."

"My dad was in banking, and so was his dad before that. I think my first toy was a calculator."

"Did you ever think about being something else?"

He laughed, the little lines at the corners of his mouth crinkling, his hands sure and strong on the wheel . . . just like they were on her. The man was made for sex. "That's not the way things are done in the Pate clan except for my sister. Two years ago, she ditched the corner office at Wachovia Bank and ran off to New York to be a jazz singer. That just about gave my parents a heart attack." He glanced her way. "So, pretty girl, where do we go from here?"

The question hung in the air between them and it had nothing to do with finding a mambo. He stopped for a light and touched her hair, sending little shock waves through her whole body. "I'm doing everything I can to give us a chance."

He stole a quick kiss. "I know. I want us to have a chance, too, and I don't want anything to happen to you. Be careful."

"That's why you're here with me now?"

"Except I only have an hour for lunch."

"Right. Lunch." The light went to green, and she pulled a notebook from her purse. "I already got a lead. LulaJean is the nurse–slash–jazz singer who helps take care of Charlotte's daddy, who messed up his leg. She takes care of a lot of sick folks and knows what's what. I sing backup for her from time to time down at the Blue Note, so we're friends, and she gave me a name."

"You sing at a jazz club?"

"I do backup at a jazz club. Big difference," she said with a light lilt in her voice, but Sam didn't follow her little joke. In fact, he looked serious.

"Do you do it very often?"

"Couple times a month." She pointed to Julian Street. "Turn right. We're going to the Hampton Lillibridge House. In the sixties, Minerva did an exorcism in this house to get rid of a pesky ghost. He was a worker there when the house was moved and got killed and didn't rightly want to leave. Minerva is the cook there still even when the place gets sold, Minerva goes with the house. Sort of a homeowners' guarantee that the workman won't come back. And she's a great cook."

Sam parked the car in front of the white clapboard that was more New England sea-wharf style than Savannah gray stone. Prissy got out and followed him up the steps. He took the stone walkway edged with coral bells, their spikes of tiny pink flowers dancing in the breeze, around to the back.

"Wait," Prissy said, taking his arm. "How'd you know this was Lillibridge House?"

"I . . . must have seen it in a book or on one of those ghost-tour brochures. They're everywhere."

"How'd you know Minerva would be around back?"

"She's the cook, Priss, and the kitchen is in the back. Not rocket science here." His voice was strong and confident as always, but the look in his eye said something else. Something . . . unsure. "Come on," he said. "I've got to get back to the bank."

Except she felt there was something else going on with him besides an extended lunch hour. Prissy knocked on the screen door, which was painted haint blue, the blue that kept away unwanted spirits. The nuns had the porch in the back of the nunnery painted the same color. Like Sister Armond said, when it comes to the hereafter it's best for everyone if the hereafter stays there.

A gray-haired lady in a white apron came through the back door and onto the porch. She glanced at them through the screen, smiled, her wrinkled face flushed with happiness. She opened the door to them. "Ah, and here be Miss Prissy St. James, after all these years."

"You . . . you know who I am?"

"Well now, I'm supposing I do." And Prissy had the feeling that she knew Minerva, too. Strange. Then again, everything associated with the morgue was that way.

"Can we speak with you for a minute?" Sam said. "I promise we won't keep you from making that apple pie you have started."

"How'd you know that?" Prissy asked Sam, the woman seeming all-too-amused by this.

He stopped dead, his eyes troubled, then he nodded at the apron. "Flour here." He pointed to a small spot nearly the color of her apron that Prissy hadn't picked up on at all. "And . . . and I can smell the apples from here."

Prissy sniffed, and smelled the blooming pink azaleas by the back door. Sam gave Prissy a quick kiss. "Look, I can see you are in capable hands and completely out of harms way, so I'm not worrying about you anymore. And . . . and good-day to you, Ms. Dupree," he said to Minerva. "A pleasure to meet you."

Then as if the devil himself was chasing him, Sam all but ran back down the walk to his car.

"What is his problem?" Prissy said more to herself than Minerva. "How'd he know so much about you?"

"Ah now, honey," Minerva said, pulling Prissy down onto a stone bench surrounded by yellow lilies and the first buds of jasmine. "He be knowing more than you even think he does." She took Prissy's hand, the connection like a zing of electricity, riveting Prissy to the woman, to the spot. "I am profoundly happy to be meeting your acquaintance. Been so many years now."

"Have we ever met before?"

Minerva smiled, her eyes sad and a little glassy. "But yes

we have. When you were but a babe. But that was long ago, and you're here now all grown up, so there is no sadness in the moment." She touched Prissy's cheek, the stroke caring, loving. "I'll be coming to the morgue at eleven. I'll be needing things." She gazed at the sky. "A full moon tonight. 'Tis a good thing for what we're needing to get done. A powerful sign it is."

Prissy couldn't tell where Minerva's hand stopped and hers started, as if they simply flowed together as one in the peaceful garden.

Minerva said, "We'll be in need of a round table now, black candles in groups of three in the center, for love and protection. White candles to circle the room, for the power of good light to circle us. And we'll be needing a bit of incense—"

"Cinnamon, for warmth," Prissy heard herself say, not knowing where it came from. "Frankincense, to expand the consciousness; sandalwood, to stay focused." Prissy dropped the woman's hand and scooted back, falling off the bench. Minerva laughed, a happy sound that drifted out into the garden.

"Holy crap, how did I know that? And I think I killed your . . ."

"'Tis a blue hosta and it'll survive. And how do we be knowing anything?" She took Prissy's hand and brought her back onto the bench. "We listen to our hearts and to the hearts around us. And if we don't, then we have trouble." She cut her gaze to where Sam had been. "There is no finding our way if we be saying no to who we are." Then she kissed Prissy on the cheek, filling her with a sense of peace and love. Not even the sisters tucking her in at night or reading her to sleep gave such a feeling. Peace. Peace. Peace.

"Bathe in milk water, wear beads at your neck, flowers in your hair. You are lovely, in here." Her gnarled finger pointed to Prissy's chest. "And here as well." She held Prissy's chin for a second. She nodded, her eyes shining, then she went back inside, the screen door banging shut. Prissy felt as if she'd been to some foreign place. Calcutta, maybe. It was the most foreign land she could think of at the moment, except for right here in this lovely spring garden in Savannah, where she'd lived all her life.

Charlotte folded her arms and eyed Prissy across the round table sporting the twelve black candles and sticks of incense stuck in a piece of the chocolate cake she'd had earlier. If ghosts didn't come out for this cake, they were hopeless. "Okay," Charlotte said. "I get the rest of this layout—except for the cake, but I'm not one to argue about chocolate—but what's with the flowers in your hair?"

Prissy touched the pansies and tulips she'd wound around a metal coat hanger and shaped into a ring. A pink tulip petal dropped onto her nose. "Minerva said I should wear flowers tonight and take a milk bath. What if I start to sour?"

"What if cats start following you around? So where is Brie with those white candles? It's almost eleven."

"I'm here, I'm here," Brie panted, rushing in, arms filled with bags. "I got glass globes to put the candles in. They'll look so much nicer that way."

Charlotte helped Brie set them around the room. "I'm sure the ghosts will appreciate it."

"Good taste is always a matter of importance, in this life and in any other," Brie countered as Bebe came into the room.

"Why are you bringing a basket of vegetables?" Charlotte asked her.

"Minerva left me a message to bring it, so I did. Said to be sure to bring eggplant. Ghosts like eggplant. And whatever Minerva wants, I do. Though I seriously considered bringing marinara sauce for the eggplant. Did I ever tell you about the time she helped me find that missing kid? I passed her on the street and she looked me dead in the eyes and said, 'Look in the old warehouse.' Amazing."

Brie arranged the black candles on the table. "I think tonight we should refrain from any and all references to death, and that is not to avoid morgue humor so much as to be politically correct. No need to offend anyone . . . or anything, considering the circumstances."

Anthony and Vince brought in the last of the chairs and set them around the table as Sam walked into the room. "You came?" Prissy asked. "I didn't think—"

"I wanted to make sure you all were safe. There's something about this that concerns me."

"Then be it a good thing you are here, man," Minerva said from the other side of the room, none of them having heard her come in. Chills snaked up Prissy's spine, and she suspected she wasn't alone in that. Minerva's long blue caftan swished as she walked to the table and gazed out the big windows. "Open them to let out the spirits."

Sam, Anthony and Vince did as she asked. Minerva flipped off the wall switch, casting the room into darkness except for the moonlight streaming in and falling across the table and the candles. A breeze stirred the air, an owl hooting in a nearby tree. "It is the hour before midnight," Minerva announced in a strong voice that belied her age. "It is the hour for doing good, and that is why we are here. Everyone sit."

They did as asked, leaving Minerva the only one standing. She lit a small bunch of . . . weeds? "Sweetgrass and lavender," Minerva announced. When the flame caught, she blew it out, the sweet smell filling the room as Minerva walked around waving the bundle in the air.

Now wash this room, be making it clean,
Making it fit for spirits dream.

She threw the bundle out the window, and Prissy said a quick prayer that it wouldn't land on a dry bush or ghosts would be the least of their troubles. Minerva sat, took a pink candle from a gray cloth bag, lit it, then lit the twelve black candles on the table.

Spirits, spirits, be hearing us now,
Come to this, our table round.
Let us feel your presence flow,
It's the time for you to go.
We bring you food to take along,
Leave us now, you should be gone!

She clapped her hands, making everyone at the table jump right out of their skins. Guess that was the levitating part of the ceremony. Minerva handed Vince the pink candle, his eyes huge in the candlelight, hands shaking, the flame doing a little dance, making things eerier . . . if that was possible!

She said, "Man, this is your house. Give light to the circle to protect us."

Vince nodded. "Protect, it is a good thing." Looking a little terrified and a lot nervous, he made the sign of the cross, then lit the white candles. He handed the pink candle back to Minerva, and she lit the incense sticks, waited till each caught, then blew out the flames, leaving the tips glowing in the dark, the slow swirl of smoke curling in the moonlight. A mix of spice and tang wafted through the room as she pulled a blue glass bottle from her purse and took a swallow. She passed it to Prissy.

"Potion?"

"Martini."

Prissy took a swig, deciding she'd never needed a martini more in her life. She passed it to Charlotte. The bottle made the rounds, and Minerva said, "Eye the pink candle, child. Keep your eyes there, eyes wide. Now join hands. We are the inner circle of life." Her lids closed.

Oh, Lordy! Now what? What had she gotten herself into? What had she gotten them all into?

Minerva chanted,

> *You spirits come, you let us see,*
> *Be hearing us now, so let us be.*
> *Spirits here of house possessed,*
> *Leave us now, we do request.*
> *Get you gone and not stay with us,*
> *Get you gone and vanish into dust!*

Prissy held Charlotte's hand tight, focusing on the candle, as Minerva hummed and chanted, her head rocking to and fro, till she suddenly stopped, stared, then stood. If her head started spinning, Prissy was so out of here.

"Cha! Bloodfire!" Minerva said. "It's not going to be working tonight. The spirits are not cooperating." She gazed out the window to clouds passing in front of the moon, cutting the light. "A bad sign it is." She looked back at the group, zeroing in on Charlotte, her old finger pointing. "Ah, but it is you that is the true trouble."

Charlotte's jaw dropped. "Me? I don't even live here. I'm an innocent bystander."

"But the ghosts do plenty live here. For a long time now. And are not about the leaving. They're worried about you, child. And not taking leave of this place till it's settled."

"Till what's settled?" Charlotte asked. "What have I done?"

"A man, a woman, on a little couch."

"Holy crap! See, see?" Charlotte gasped. "I told you all it was for real."

"And what you have done is not for me to know, only you, dear. Only you."

"But I've been good lately . . . sort of, except for sleeping around a little," Charlotte said. "What do they want?"

Minerva flipped on the lights. "It is over for now." She shivered. "But it is only being the start for all of you." She clapped her hands again. "Take care. It is a fearful time."

Prissy stood and waved her hands in the air. "Wait. There's no place for a fearful time right now. You can't just do nothing. You have to get the ghost out of here, or lie and tell everyone you did. How am I going to get workers, make this job happen? How am I going to get a business plan and a Viking stove?"

Minerva snuffed the pink candle with her fingers, then did the same to the black ones. "There is no budging the spirits. They will have their way. They've been holding fast to this place for years. They will go in their good time, but it is not for us to say when that's being."

Prissy pointed to Anthony and Vince. "It's their place. Just look at the real estate tax bill. They should have a say who interlopes." Prissy said,

> Oh spirits or ghosts, we hold you dear,
> But now we want you the hell out of here!

Minerva chuckled, then faced Charlotte. "I'll be on my way now. Luck be to you, child. Luck be to all of you. You'll be needing it plenty." She held out her arms, circling them around Prissy, Bebe, Charlotte and Brie, and said,

> Together old, together new,
> it is this bond that sees you through.

Then she kissed Prissy on the cheek, snatched up her martini bottle and bag, and left.

Prissy faced Sam. "What in the world am I going to do now? How am I going to get the morgue together?"

"You!" Charlotte said. "You're worried about a business plan while I have ghosts on my back. What's that all about? I was sort of hoping the settee duo was a figment of my head-conking, but I guess not."

A sudden knock at the door made them all jump again. Brie put her hand to her heart. "Mercy me. My nerves are done shot for one night."

Anthony opened the front door an inch and Sister Ann pushed inside, nearly knocking him over. "Holy mother," she huffed. "Minerva just called and said you needed me. Actually she said you needed all the sisters, but they're watching *Grey's Anatomy* on TiVo, so I got sent. What's up?"

Prissy massaged her forehead. "How do you feel about being a roofer?"

"About the same as I do about getting a root canal. Why?"

The lights suddenly went out. Prissy stomped her foot and said into the darkness, "Okay, that's enough. I've had my fill of ghosts messing up my life for—"

One of the lit globes flew through the air, crashing against the far wall, splintering into a bazillion pieces. Everyone screamed, and Sam rushed to the spot and stomped out the flames running across the tattered rug. He picked up another globe and held it high, casting the light around. "Prissy, are you okay? Is everyone okay?"

They all looked at each other. "Everyone present and accounted for," Prissy said.

Anthony grabbed another globe and Vince grabbed his brother's arm. "We know the way around the house and will locate the fuse box in the basement. As Prissy said, this is our place. If we are not back in five minutes, call the police . . . or the coroner."

Prissy held her breath, her heart pounding in her ears,

waiting for a thud or scream or something not good from the basement, but instead, the lights popped on. Everyone cheered as Anthony and Vince came back into the room.

"Well done," Sam said.

They sat at the table and Anthony set out glasses, and Vince poured bourbon, then raised his glass, as did the seven others. "*A vita lunga.* To long life."

"Amen," Sister Ann added, and Prissy threw in, "Which has been cut considerably short for all of us tonight by many, many years." She tossed back the shot, choked, eyes watering, and felt better. Or maybe she just didn't care so much.

Charlotte rolled her glass between her palms. "I never knew ghosts could be all this trouble. Those two sweet people in the basement didn't seem like the cut-the-lights-and-fling-candles type. More the next-door-neighbor type of ghosts. And why are they so interested in me?"

"They didn't do it," Sam said in a low, steady voice, staring at his empty glass, then stroking his chin. "Too much is going on here for it to be a ghost. Someone . . . someone alive . . . doesn't want this place to open. They want it to themselves for whatever reason, and they're trying to scare off Prissy and anyone else who gets involved."

He peered at Anthony and Vince. "Whoever this is has scared off owners before, but now you're here and have Prissy on board, and Prissy is like a dog with a bone about getting this job done. They're looking for something."

Prissy gasped. "Like the necklace. With all the talk about Otis's will stirring, someone's going after it."

Sam poured another bourbon. "Looking at the history of this place, I'd say someone's been looking for it a long time and hasn't found it yet and doesn't want anyone to find it before he . . . or she does."

"The killer," Bebe said in her I'm-a-cop voice.

Charlotte added, "Minerva said these were fearsome times. Terrific."

Anthony and Vince exchanged uneasy looks, then Anthony poured another round for everyone. "I must tell you all, the tree that fell was cut, not just blown down by the storm. When the men came to clear it, they showed the saw marks. Not all the way through, but enough to make it go in a breeze or storm. A storm was predicted for the night of the party."

Sam nodded. "The game plan is to make the place look haunted. No work will get done, and Anthony and Vince will have to sell."

Anthony's jaw clenched. "We are not going to sell. We cannot do that. It is out of the question. We will do the work ourselves."

"Or not." Prissy looked at Sister Ann. "The nuns aren't afraid of this talk, so we'll use them as contractors."

Sam shook his head. "Too dangerous after all that's gone on here."

"Nonsense," said Sister Ann. "We sisters do pretty much everything at the nunnery ourselves, are regular viewers of the DIY Network, know the folks at Home Depot right well. We're dependable, hardworking, cheap, and we need the money. Seems there are more runaway teens than ever these days. And with the sisters knowing each other, there's no chance of a stranger sneaking in."

Prissy jumped up, kissed Sister Ann on the cheek, then ran over to Sam. She sat in his lap and threw her arms around him. "Well, there you go. One terrific business plan. So, what do you say, big boy? Are we in?"

"You're sitting on my lap; my decision powers are compromised." Then he grinned and gave Prissy a quick kiss. "The home office is not going to like this. It's the most unorthodox business plan I've—"

"And all for me," Prissy laughed. "My hero. You, Sam Pate, are the best."

He kissed her. "Why do I feel like I'm going to regret this?"

"You're not," Prissy said. "I promise it's gong to be the best decision you ever made."

Chapter 12

Charlotte hurried down the deserted sidewalk toward her car. The full moon dodged in and out of clouds and the evil hour ticked on. Considering how rotten the good hour went, she couldn't imagine where this one was headed. If she turned the corner and ran into anything that looked ghostly, she'd die of fright on the spot and get this whole ordeal over with. Instead she ran into . . . "Griff?"

He enfolded her in his arms as if he hadn't seen her in years instead of hours. "Are you okay? I was entertaining clients in the hotel bar and overheard something about a séance at the morgue complete with Minerva, flying candles and the electricity getting knocked out. What the hell's going on at that place now?"

"Prissy's PR campaign is in the toilet, I'm in serious doo-doo with the resident ghosts and . . . try to envision nuns in hard hats. I am so ready for Bermuda."

"I'm not sure what all that means but I'm on board for the last part." He kissed her right there under the street-light. It felt like something from one of those old musicals that RL watched with that Gene Kelly guy except she and Griff didn't burst into song and dance about. She wrapped her arms around his middle and held fast, grabbing fistfuls of his starched white dress shirt, which accented his early spring tan and his very fine build. She laid her head on his chest, the steady beat of his heart making her feel . . . loved?

Yeah, loved. That was the word all right. She smiled, letting herself enjoy the moment, one she'd waited for a long time and never really thought would happen, especially with Griffin Parish!

"Let me drive you home."

"I have my car and RL is waiting up." And, she added to herself, I have sneaking around to do for info on Brie being Jaden. Maybe there wasn't anything. Maybe her instincts were operating in Target-shoe-department mode, except cop Bebe came to the same conclusion.

"Hey, you with me here, girl? What are you thinking about?"

He kissed the top of her head, then tipped her chin, peering into her eyes. She hoped he didn't peer too hard.

"Something bothering you?"

"Just the séance," she lied. The fact that he knew all along that Brie was Jaden and didn't level with her hurt. They could have worked on this together, figured out how to tell her. Then his eyes took on that smoldering-man look that made women's toes curl. Charlotte shoved the Jaden/Brie argument aside. Griff did what he thought was best for Brie's sake, that was all there was to it . . . she hoped.

He smoothed back her hair, his gentle touch making her whole body feel alive. He kissed her temple. "I want you right now, Charlotte. Here, in the middle of East Gaston, on this beautiful spring night." He kissed her other temple. "Almost as beautiful as you. Let's do it in your car."

"The car?" She laughed. "There are police all over this city. We'll get caught."

"Not if we're quick. I think I could do quick." He took her keys and unlocked her car and nodded inside. "Consider it foreplay for Bermuda."

She held his shoulders. "It's late, Griff. I have to check on RL."

"Right, RL." His hand slid between her waistband and her blouse. "You have great skin, smooth and silky and made just for me."

She stroked his chin and kissed him right below his lips, enjoying his stubble against her lips. "How many times do you shave a day? You're always so neat and together."

"Move in with me and find out."

She stared up at him. "Move in?"

"My apartment's big enough. We can share." He kissed her long and deep, his tongue seducing hers. "Get RL squared away, then come on over. Where did you tell him you were going for the next three days?"

"Bermuda. I just didn't say with whom, and he's assuming Brie or Bebe or Prissy and it's better that way. Your mama and my daddy have one thing in common—not liking us together. I think it's a class thing. Your Camilla doesn't think I'm good enough and RL doesn't want me hurt." She stood on her toes and kissed him on the lips, his mouth opening a fraction, her tongue teasing his this time. "But they're both wrong. You taste of brandy."

"And you of whiskey."

"It was a whiskey kind of night. I bought sexy undies . . . not for tonight, but for Bermuda."

He grinned, the edges of his mouth crinkling, his face soft and happy. She took a step back before she gave in to his sex-in-the-car idea and jumped in headfirst, dragging him with her. She got a little dizzy just thinking of Griff's weight pressing down on her, his everything pressing into her. "I'll see you in an hour," she said, a little breathless and a lot turned on.

"I'll be waiting at the bar. Think horny thoughts." He embraced her, lifting her off the ground and whirling her around, holding her body tight to his, this getting more and more like Gene Kelly all the time. His eyes danced; her heart sang. "This is my girl, my Charlotte. One hour, or I'm coming after you."

He put her back down and ran his hand possessively over her rump, cupping it underneath, giving her a hint of the upcoming nightly attractions. She got in the car and powered the window down. "See you soon, Biscuit."

"Biscuit?"

Her turn to laugh. "Wait till I tell you why. Secrets are so much fun." *Sometimes.* She gave a little finger-wave and drove off, watching him in her rearview mirror, standing on the sidewalk looking more handsome than any man on earth, and she nearly drove into a police car stopped for a traffic light.

Yes, officer, I am intoxicated . . . intoxicated by love. Was that corny, or what? This whole thing with Griff was sort of corny. The secret-love thing, getting whisked off her feet—literally—by a man she'd wanted ever since she knew what wanting a man was all about.

"I did it," she said aloud on a giggle. "Griff Parish and Charlotte are an . . . item." The evil hour wasn't so evil after all. She pulled into her driveway, then strolled up the sidewalk doing a little twirl along the way because she had to do something happy. For an evening that got a little dicey along the way, it sure ended up okay.

Reruns of *M*A*S*H* blared from the TV. RL sat slumped in his La-Z-Boy chair, legs propped up, breathing steady, dead to the world. Time to snoop . . . or not. Should she leave this alone? But could she, considering how dangerous things had gotten? She couldn't run off to Bermuda with Brie in a mess. What kind of a best friend was that?

Taking the rechargeable flashlight from the outlet in the hall, she headed for RL's room. This was not a proud moment in the life of Charlotte deShawn, not that she ever intended to own up to what she was doing. She'd tell RL she found out about Brie being Jaden another way . . . whatever that could be.

Her heart thumped. What if RL caught her? She'd hate that. It would be a broken trust, and she and RL were close, closer than any other father and daughter she knew. Always had been. Maybe because he was a single dad or he was trying to make up for his sister abandoning her. Whatever the reason, RL was the best dad around. Everyone said so.

Skulking back to the door, she took one last peek. RL was still sleeping like a hound in the shade. She hurried back to the closet, took a deep breath and opened it.

Okay, RL needed to update. When she got home from Bermuda, she'd introduce him—wheelchair and all—to new friends, J.Crew and maybe Mr. Gap.

She rummaged through the closet . . . shoe box, shoe box, shoe box, old golf bag, older tennis racket, lime green bowling ball, Abs Buster from the shopping network . . . RL was working out? Who knew? A plastic crate of photos. She grabbed one. Little girl and daddy at Christmas with matching Santa hats and nothing else matching. Like RL said, she took after her biological father, whoever that was. But it was a really great green velvet dress.

Flipping on the flashlight, she aimed it into the back of the closet. Baseball bat, Rollerblades and a pogo stick. Pogo stick? Robert Lee deShawn, the early years. And a metal box, a fireproof one.

She froze, the little hairs on the back of her neck standing straight up. Her heart, beating like a hammer, slammed her ribs. This was important, she knew it. And it was something RL didn't want to share, or even trust to his office safe. A Pandora's box—once opened, the contents out, there was no putting it back. She should have gone to carpet school.

"Walk away," said a little voice. "Grab it," another

whispered. Brie needed to know. Charlotte crawled between the pogo stick and the bat, snagged the box, then scooted back out of the closet, her foot bumping into something unmoving that hadn't been there before. She didn't have to turn around to see what—or who—it was.

Sitting down on the floor cross-legged like when she was little, she sat the box in her lap and turned her eyes to RL. He stared at the box, looking tired, not just the kind of tired that made him want an extra hour of sleep, but the tired-clear-through kind that deepened the lines on his face and made his eyes dull and glassy. A worried tired. The worst kind of tired. She'd never seen him this way before, even when money was tight or he'd messed up his leg.

"What are you doing?" His voice was low, planned, like he'd expected this conversation and dreaded it for a long time. Sort of like the time he told her what sex was all about, except worse.

"I need to find out who Jaden Carswell is, and not just because it's a job, but because now it's personal. I think BrieAnna's Jaden, and I think you know that, too, and that what's in this box proves it."

"Forget the box, Charlotte. Put it back in that closet and pretend you never saw it. No good's going to come from it, I promise you that, girl. Leave it be."

"There's a missing necklace that rightfully belongs to Jaden Carswell. Someone killed to get it once before and he . . . or she . . . is still after it now. Brie needs to know so she can protect herself. I understand why Otis had her adopted in the first place and why you helped. Otis got his friend's baby the best care out there and away from a murderer. But when Otis died and left Jaden half the hotel, it opened everything all up again."

RL rubbed his hand over his face and said more to himself than her, "Why couldn't Otis leave well enough alone? Why this? Why now?"

"He knew it couldn't be a secret forever, especially after he was gone. This was his way of getting the truth out and keeping her safe again. Once everyone knew who BrieAnna was, everyone would be looking out for her—you, Griff, the three of us."

RL took a labored breath. "Charlotte, for once in your adult life just listen to me. BrieAnna is not Jaden Carswell."

"Of course she's Jaden. It all makes sense. She was adopted by a prominent family Otis approved of, the time line is right, you and the Parishes have never gotten along and I think one reason is because Camilla wanted the baby far and way from Savannah and any chance of laying claim to Magnolia House. You and Otis wanted to keep an eye on her. It was the perfect solution."

"Put the box away."

"Don't you see, if I can figure this all out, anyone can, and that puts Brie in the middle of trouble."

"You didn't figure it out, Charlotte." He gripped the armrests of his wheelchair, his face hardening. "I'm telling you, dammit, that BrieAnna is not Jaden Carswell! Trust me, and leave it the hell alone."

Damn? Hell? Charlotte looked from the box to RL. His face looked tortured, and suddenly the earth stopped right in its tracks and nothing in the universe moved. Her heart slowed, her blood went to ice. The photo of her and RL in Santa hats stared up at her from the floor. "I never saw pictures of my mother. Not one."

She nudged the crate at her elbow. "No baby pictures of us together, no pictures of her at all." She swallowed. "If I open this box, what . . . what am I going to find?"

"I love you, Charlotte," his voice cracked. "Always have, always will. You're my daughter, my little girl."

Putting pieces together as she went, Charlotte said, "When Adie's parents said they didn't want Jaden, you brought her home and . . ."

"Then I told everyone you were Barbara's baby," RL said in a slow voice as if each word took something out of him. "My sister had gone off and I hadn't heard from her in years. I figured it was a safe lie. Otis was fine with it. In fact, we cooked up the idea over a brandy while you slept right here in the living room. But Camilla blew a gasket."

RL gave a tired laugh. "You should have seen her. I think smoke came out of her ears. It was the one time Otis put his foot down, and he and I made it happen."

"And you lied to me for thirty years." She was numb. She couldn't feel any of her fingers or toes. "How could you do that?"

"I kept you safe . . . we kept you safe."

"You should have told me. When Otis died, it would have been a really good time, don't you think?"

"And I'd lose you to the Parishes and their fancy hotel and way of life." He waved his hand over the room. "This is no competition for Jags and the country club, girl. I love you. I was . . . afraid. I am more than ever. I don't want to lose you, Charlotte. You're my whole life, have been for thirty years."

"You think I'm that shallow?" She held out her arms, giving him a full view of her blouse and jeans, which were not the kind with "Lucky" stitched on the butt. "This is not country club attire, and that's fine by me."

"You're a young woman. That stuff matters."

"I'm *your* daughter, that's what matters, and I've always trusted you. And now I find I can't trust you at all." She slapped her hand over her mouth to hold back the tears. Pulling herself together she managed, "Griff knows, too, doesn't he?" It wasn't even a question. "He and Camilla are all in a sweat over me inheriting Magnolia House. No wonder she tried to run me over."

"What?"

"I have good reflexes; I jumped." She stood and put the

box on the nightstand, staring at it for a minute, neither of them speaking. "That's why you didn't want me to take the case."

"I knew this would happen. And there's murder and robbery surrounding your life."

"I'll help you get into bed and then I have an errand to run."

"I can get myself into bed. Don't be doing this, baby girl. We can put the box away. It's not too late I swear."

"It's done, Daddy. Over with. Putting that box away won't make the truth go away."

He looked at her with sad eyes. "Don't be too hard on Griff. He did what he thought was best. We all did."

"Yeah, right. Best for who? You wanted to protect me. Griff . . . Griff wants Magnolia House." She stepped around his chair, walked to the front door on legs that felt like jelly and went out into the evil night. Minerva knew . . . and RL and Camilla and Griff. And she didn't. Damn them all for not telling! How could RL do this? How could Griff do this? Easy as pie, that's how.

Heart pounding, she ran through the back alley, past the grimy Dumpster from where she'd seen RL and Griff, past the carriage house where she and Griff kissed for the first time and into the now-deserted gardens with the cobalt-blue umbrellas folded down tight. Pushing open the back door, she entered the Magnolia House hallway, Griff's office on one side, Daemon's on the other, everything perfect . . . till now. Jaden Carswell's resurrection was about to make everything a whole lot less perfect around here.

Running down the hall, she suddenly stopped, then retraced her steps to the photographs on the wall, the one with Otis, William, Adie and Magnolia House behind them. She touched the picture. She didn't have a mother who left her after all, or a father who cut and run. Adie and William loved her. The three of them were a family. Adie and William were a handsome couple. . . . Nice suit on dad. Double-breasted, wide eighties tie with stickpin. She looked closer—a horseshoe stickpin. And Adie had a locket? It was hard to tell in the dim hall light, yet . . . And Adie had curly hair!

Charlotte touched her own curls and her breath lodged in her lungs. The casket room? "Oh . . . my . . . God . . ." she whispered out loud. Or maybe when she saw these pictures she simply transferred the images? Yeah, maybe that was it. After a good crack on the head, who knew what happened that night, except . . . She rested her head against the cold glass, her heart hurting, as if someone squeezed it too tightly. She missed them, dammit. She never knew them, yet she missed them terribly. At least she knew now, something that wouldn't be if left up to RL and Griff. Damn them! This was her life, her mama and daddy. Damn them all.

Making her way to the perfect lobby with the perfect black-and-white marble floor and brass chandelier, crossing the sitting area with the custom-woven navy-and-gold carpet sporting a pineapple, the icon of Southern hospitality, she entered the bar area. Griff sat on one of the lovely mahogany stools with fine leather upholstery.

"You no-count, no-good rat." She was panting so hard the words were a whisper. She didn't want to whisper, she wanted to yell. And throw things. "How could you?"

Smiling, Griff stood. Taking one look at her, he suddenly wasn't smiling at all. "Oh shit."

"All you have to say is *oh shit*? I know what you did, you double-crossing scoundrel."

"Look, Charlotte."

And she did look . . . as he stumbled backwards after she punched his jaw and bruised her hand. *Ouch!* She had no idea how she did it, but she did and she wasn't one little bit sorry. "Why did you do this? Damn you!"

"Fall for you?" He rubbed his chin. Good, she hoped it hurt. He deserved it. They all deserved it.

"This is my fault. How could I believe that after all these years you were whisking me off to Bermuda? What were you going to do there, marry me?"

He just stared at her.

"Lord have mercy, you were! And you knew I'd be fool enough to agree to it. So that's why all the flattery." She said in a singsong voice, " 'Oh, Charlotte, you're so pretty. Oh, Charlotte, my girl, my sweetheart. Oh, Charlotte, you complete stupid ass!' Marrying me was the plan all along. Then you'd get the other half of the hotel. That's it, isn't it. You'd get my half!"

"I wanted to marry you and *give* you half of the hotel outright. When you suggested we call off the search for Jaden because it was too dangerous, I figured everything would quiet down, we'd get married and you'd get your half of the hotel that way. And we'd be together and you'd be safe. That was the most important part of all. I swear to God almighty, it's the absolute truth, Charlotte."

"The truth is, you hired me to find myself because you didn't think I could do it. Then you'd have Jaden declared dead, put the search to rest and the hotel would be yours free and clear. Except I got too close and you needed to get the hotel by marrying me." She picked up a bowl of fancy nuts and flung them across the bar. "You lying whoresome bastard!"

"You're adding it up all wrong."

"I found the evidence in RL's closet. A box, a little metal damning box." She came to him and poked him in the chest. "You played me from the get-go. And now you know what you can do with your precious hotel. You can stick it where the sun doesn't shine. I don't want it. For sure I don't want you. I . . . I don't want anyone."

She started for the door, stopped by the counter and took a handful of mints, since theoretically they were hers. Least, half of them were.

"Wait," Griff said, catching up with her in the foyer. "I wanted to make this will situation right, Charlotte, and keep you safe. Okay, it didn't start off that way, I'll admit that. At first I figured you'd eventually find out who you were . . . which seemed a lot better than me telling you out of the blue. This way, you'd find out bit by bit, then I'd buy out your share of the hotel. Except I fell for you."

"Bull honkey."

"And things got risky. I realized that at the morgue party. I looked at that fallen tree and someone had cut it. Going with the Jaden-dead idea and giving you half the hotel by marriage was a good plan."

He held her shoulders and looked her in the eye. "I swear that's the truth, and so is the fact that I love you."

"I think you were going to marry me all right, and when we got back, I'd find out who I was and you'd have the hotel. If I divorced you, you'd fight me for it and stand a good chance of winning because I could never afford your entourage of lawyers, and you made the hotel what it is, and blah, blah, blah. Or maybe you'd want me to sign a prenup where the hotel belongs to you no matter what, and like a dope I'd do it because I wouldn't know half was mine. No matter what, I was getting the short end of the stick."

She smacked her palm to her forehead. "And I fell for it all. I'm nothing but a little fool." She put her hand to his chest to stop him from getting closer, except the feel of him, reminding her of what she wanted and would never have—Griff—made her sad clear through. Well, fuck! And that was never going to happen again either!

"Don't you dare go and follow me, Griffin Parish. We are done, finished. You slept with me, you made me fall for you, and I did and I hate you for it and I hate myself, too."

"Made you?"

"Well, you sure made it easy. You're too handsome and too good a kisser and too smooth a talker and . . . and just too everything." She slammed her fist against his chest. "I hate you so much I could . . . spit wooden nickels." And don't you dare cry, she ordered herself.

"I fell for you, too, Charlotte, and wanted to give you what you deserve."

"What I deserve is top prize for stupidity for not figuring this out sooner." Pushing past him, she left the hotel through the glass doors with their shiny brass doorknobs and kick plates and stood on the sidewalk . . . alone. In fact, she never felt more alone in her life. She pulled in a deep breath, the betrayal of people she loved and trusted like a rock in her gut. She started for home, then stopped dead. Where was home? Did anyone really love her, not just want her around for their own agenda—having a daughter, getting a piece of real estate?

She gazed up at the beautiful hotel of white cornerstones, arched windows and black wrought-iron railings. This wasn't her home, but neither was the gray clapboard on Habersham. Where did she belong? Who was she? What was she going to do about all this?

A tear trickled down her cheek and she swiped it away, but more tears followed and she couldn't swipe fast enough. Well, she couldn't stand on the street corner in downtown Savannah and blubber like a weak-kneed Yankee. She turned toward Oglethorpe Square, walked past RL Investigations, then trudged down Drayton toward Forsyth Park and the morgue, where this all started. She needed answers, to figure out who she was and what she should do about it all.

*   *   *

Griff raked his hand through his hair, the young night clerk staring at him wide-eyed across the marble counter with the usual bouquet of fresh Savannah flowers. "Never fall in love, Jasmine. It's not worth it."

She gave him a sly smile. "Of course it is, Mr. Parish. No matter what you did, she'll be coming around, you wait and see now. She's just a smidge peeved. Women get that way from time to time. All you men know that."

More like the woman was rip-roaring furious, and not that he blamed her at all. He felt terrible Charlotte found out who she was and not from him. Then again, was there any good way? "Charlotte, you're really Jaden Carswell and someone may be trying to kill you" seemed a bit dramatic. Then again, getting punched in the jaw was, too. He blew it. Nothing worked out the way he wanted it to. And worst of all, he lost the woman he cared about most in the world.

He glanced at the bar, closing for the night, everyone acting busy as can be with shutting down. But he knew that no matter how discreet and loyal his staff was, the fact that Charlotte was indeed Jaden Carswell, the long-lost daughter of William Carswell, cofounder of Magnolia House, went well beyond what could be kept under wraps. Phones were ringing all over Savannah this very minute.

Why in holy hell did Otis open this can of worms?

Griff headed for his office, flipped on the light and locked the door behind him. He sat at his desk and pulled a glass and a bottle of Wild Turkey from the bottom drawer. Pouring a measure, he tossed it down, then did another. Closing his eyes, he let the liquor warm his stomach and numb the pain creeping into his bones and his heart.

He opened his eyes and the lights were out . . . sort of, because Otis sat in his favorite chair, reading lamp on, legs crossed, a swirl of Cuban-cigar smoke curling into the air.

Griff blinked.

"Well, boy, you sure did get your titty in a wringer on this one."

"Otis?"

"Know anyone else who's as good looking as me?" He chuckled, his big-barreled chest shaking under his best brown suit. He pulled another puff off the cigar, the red tip glowing. "I guess you're pretty pissed at me about now and I'm not saying I'm blaming you one bit."

"I think *you* got my tit in that wringer. And yeah, I'm pissed as hell but . . . but I have to say, it's great seeing you. Damn, I've missed you."

"I miss you, too, son." His gaze met Griff's, making Griff feel warmer and more settled than any shot of alcohol ever could.

"I figured I needed to come here and explain myself. My going off and leaving you in such a state wasn't fair. I didn't rightly know how to tell you who Jaden was, and then, before I figured it out, my ticker gave up the ghost." He laughed. "Bad choice of words."

Griff leaned back in his chair. "Hell, I'll manage, and you don't owe me anything. You gave me this hotel—least, half of it." He grinned. "You were always there for me, Otis. Always. You were a great dad." He held up his glass. "You still are. You gave me this city and taught me to love Savannah as much as you did. Every statue, every square, every incredible house some stupid son-of-a-bitch wanted to tear down and turn into a fucking parking garage or dollar store or God knows what else. You got the ball rolling to save this city." He smiled at his dad. "She's a beauty, Otis. There's no other like her anywhere."

"We made a pretty damn good team, boy." Otis held up his cigar in salute, then pulled another drag. He tapped the ash in the waste can by the desk. "Still do. But the thing with Jaden and the hotel gets kind of complicated. You see, I needed to do right by William, with us being partners and all. Except Camilla would have no part of Jaden being around and inheriting Magnolia House, and truth be told, she had a point. Without her money, there'd be no hotel. I had the prestige of being a go-getter, along with a family name that dated back to when Oglethorpe himself landed on this here scrap of land. She had the cash and you, and big plans for both."

He smiled at Griff the way he did so many times in his life. "It was a good marriage for that. Love isn't the only reason for a wedding." He winked at Griff. "But it is the best reason. Like you and Charlotte. You're good together, boy. I think in my heart I always knew you would be. I watched her grow up, I watched you. It's a fit. Hand in glove, just like me and William."

"We *were* a good fit. I screwed it up."

"When it comes to love, things often do get screwed up, so you just have to go about unscrewing them. I never got the privilege of marrying for love of a woman. I did it for love of a hotel, love of a dream. For you it can be different. But the first thing you have to keep in mind right now is protecting Jaden." He shrugged. "Charlotte."

"She hates my guts, Dad. She thinks I'm out to get her half of the hotel, and I have no idea how to get her to believe otherwise."

"And at first she was right."

"Yeah. Fuck."

He chuckled. "All in good time, Griff. But right now, you take care of her. Do whatever it takes, with or without her cooperation. There's still a murderer hanging around, and a missing necklace and—"

There was a hard knock at the door, snapping Griff's eyes there.

"Griffin?" It was Camilla. "I need to talk to you. And let me in right now. I'm not dressed properly." She rattled the locked door.

When Griff looked back to Otis, the lamp was still lit but he was gone. Or did Griff, in his semi-inebriated state and need to talk to someone, just dream Otis being there? Griff would have gone with that, except for the lingering bit of smoke floating in the lamplight and the dot of ash in the waste can. In spite of more door rattling, a slow easy grin lit Griff's face. "Bye, Dad. You take care now, you hear."

He opened the door and Camilla hurried in, huffing. "Look at me." She waved her hand over her front. "What if someone saw me dressed like this?"

"You have on a skirt and blouse, Mother. The fashion police will not be offended."

"Well, I do not go out in public looking like some bag lady on the street corner, but I simply didn't have the time to get into a suit and do my makeup properly." Camilla pursed her lips. "She found out, didn't she? I heard everything. She's going after the hotel."

"I take it you're referring to Charlotte . . . or Jaden, if you prefer. And it is her right."

"Right? What right? You and Otis worked like dogs to make a go of this here place and I used considerable money, and I am not about to stand around while some Johnny-come-lately barges in for a piece of our pie."

"Her parents were killed trying to finance the hotel. I'd say she paid her dues, wouldn't you?"

"Buy her out. Get rid of her. Charlotte deShawn is trouble."

"I think that feeling's reciprocated."

"And I'm not caring one little bit." Camilla tapped her foot. "So, what exactly do you intend to do about all this, Griffin? Things cannot stay as they are."

"That is the one thing we agree on, Mother."

Chapter 13

"Hey, woman, want a ride?"

Normally Charlotte would have ignored a crack shouted out a car window in the middle of the night as she walked. Except tonight was not normal—when was the last time she even used that word?—and the voice was Prissy's and the car was Bebe's old silver PT Cruiser with a million miles on it.

"I'm fine," she called back. "Go home, go to bed, let me be."

The Cruiser pulled to the curb and Bebe, Prissy and Brie spilled out. They linked their arms together and through hers, and the four continued walking as Bebe said, "Sweet thing, this is no place for a midnight stroll."

If she told them she was heading for the morgue, they'd have a stroke and she'd get a lecture, and she was in no mood for either. "I needed to clear my head, and since you all are here, I'm guessing you know the reason why."

Bebe nudged her. "In this part of town, you have a good chance of getting your head bashed in. Let's go home. I have the margarita bucket chilling in my freezer."

She stopped and looked at each one of them. "Okay, you tell me, where is home these days? Magnolia House, RL's? I . . . I want to go to the cemetery."

Brie gasped. "Honey, it ain't all that bad. We'll get you through this."

"Oh for heaven's sake, not that. I just need to start over. Look what happens when you go snooping into your past or it comes along and bites you in the butt. Big trouble. We all need to swear again never to look back. I'm choosing a new name. Rachael. Rachael is good. Always wanted to be called Rachael, after that chick on *Friends,* and maybe be a size four and have a fling with Brad Pitt. Now there's a new life I could get used to."

"You can't just wish your life away," Bebe said. "Trust me, I know. I've tried."

Charlotte gave her a determined look.

"Right, Bonaventure Cemetery it is."

Brie bristled. "Well, I am not cutting my finger. This is a new dress from the Neiman Marcus spring catalog, and if I bleed on it, it'll be ruined."

Charlotte gave her a determined look.

"Oh, all right, I'll cut my finger . . . but just a nick and just for you, and I hope I don't pass out again."

Charlotte looked at Prissy, who held up her hands in immediate surrender. "Hey, I'm not saying a word. You got squashed flat by a tree for me and went to a séance with flying things. I owe you. I'm in."

They piled into Bebe's car, detoured to Bucky's twenty-four-hour drive-through for nourishment and headed for Skidaway Island, which really wasn't an island so much as a break in the land. "This is a lot easier than riding here on our bikes," Prissy mumbled around a mouthful of cherry moon pie.

"We must have been nuts," Bebe added.

"We still are," Brie laughed, and reached for a pie of her own.

They turned off 80, made some more turns, then eased onto Bonaventure Road, a narrow street nestled in a resi-

dential area that didn't look very cemeterylike at all. Bebe
stopped the car at the iron gates, quiet settling in around
them. "Well, they're still locking the place up. I think we
walked along the edge of the river and slid in around the
end post perched over the riverbank."

Brie sighed. "Gee, I'm just getting to like this idea more
and more all the time."

Frogs grunted, crickets chirped and insects rubbed their
legs together or flapped their wings or humped their mates
or did whatever they did to make their insect sounds.

"We have to ditch the car or the cops will come looking." Bebe backed up to a gravel road and parked to the
side, behind a tree. She took a flashlight the size of a small
kid from under her seat and slid out of the car. They
headed for the river.

"Last time, we sat around Johnny Mercer's grave," Brie
said. "I'm getting sand in my new shoes. Can we just do
any grave this time? I mean, after all, dead is dead."

Prissy stumbled and Charlotte grabbed her. "I wouldn't
say that too loud around here."

Stepping over weeds and around mole holes that were
probably snake holes, which Charlotte refused to think
about, they followed the wrought-iron fence to the river.
The moon laid out a shimmering ribbon of white across
the water, a gargantuan freighter motoring silently to the
ports beyond. One by one Prissy, Brie, Charlotte and Bebe
slid around the last post.

"This was easier last time," Prissy said, holding on to
the pillar for dear life so as not to fall in the drink.

"There," Brie said, pointing to an obelisk. "Graves by
the river. Let's do it. They're close, with a view. Prime dead
real estate."

They swiped sand from a slab of granite, and sat.
Charlotte cracked open a beer and chugged half the bottle.
Her head started to spin, just the feeling she wanted. She

pointed the longneck at the obelisk, aiming straight up. "Reminds me of Griff, except not so pointy. The man is hung."

They all choked and laughed, then Brie sobered. "Well, at least you have a good memory. Mine, not so much. In fact, it's pitiful. I got together with Beau. Fixed him dinner at my place—chocolate strawberries, steamed asparagus, filet mignon—"

"We don't care what he ate, honey, unless it was you," Prissy said.

"Not exactly." Brie held her index finger straight up, then curled it down."

"No! He's still not . . . performing?" Prissy gasped, hand to heart. "The man has a reputation . . . and a legendary do-da, or so I hear."

"Only if he do-das himself, because I sure don't have the power. He wouldn't even take off his clothes. He stood there in my candlelit living room fully dressed while I undid my blouse—you know, that one-button-at-a-time way. Then I flipped my hair—the hair flipping always works, which I thought it was by the telltale bulge in his pants. But then he blushed, the bulge deflated and he give me a sloppy kiss on the cheek and ran off. Ran!"

"Next time try oysters," Prissy said, then Brie continued, "The trouble is, in spite of all that, I like him. He's cute and . . . shy."

"Beau Cleveland? Shy? He's a ladies' man from kindergarten days." Bebe shook her head. "Bulgeless, huh. How sad is that?" She shook her head. "This has been the night of extreme revelations."

"And he's considerate, and he brought me daisies he picked in some field and got poison ivy, and what am I going to do?" Brie wailed.

"You need a plan," hiccuped Charlotte. "A win-him-over plan. A seduction plan. Sexnapping."

Brie sighed. "What is that?"

"Have no idea, but it sounds fun." She gulped the rest of her beer, feeling a little sick, but that was better than feeling betrayed and angry. "And I need a plan to get on with my life that does not include parents in any form or seduction of any kind. I'm done with seduction." She eyed the monument. "And that is most unfortunate indeed."

She put down the beer. "It's time." She rifled through her purse. "Anyone have a knife?"

"I think I have a pin." Brie dug into her purse and held up the safety kind. She gritted her teeth, closed her eyes, jabbed and yelped, then stuck her finger in her mouth and mumbled, "We so need a new ritual."

Prissy gulped her beer and pricked, handed it to Charlotte, who passed it off to Bebe. Charlotte held up her thumb, the red dot on the end. "To us. To never looking back at those who abandoned us. On to the future, whatever the heck it may be."

"Wait!" Bebe shook her head. "You can't do this, Charlotte. Not this time. You can't turn your back on who you are and where you came from once you know. You're Adie and William Carswell's daughter and there's no denying that. They gave their lives for Magnolia House, and Otis confirmed that when he left it to you. You can't just walk away from it all because it screwed up your life, and a bloody thumb doesn't change anything."

"Watch me."

"And then there's RL," Brie added. "I know you're pissing-mad at him now, honey, but he needs boatloads of therapy, and with the money you'll have at your disposal, you can afford the best for him, not scrounge around for bargain-basement treatments. A real rehab center. Least, sell Magnolia House to Griff; don't just hand it over free and clear. Plus, that will totally frost Camilla's cookies to no end. That alone is reason enough," Brie added with a chuckle.

"I'm bleeding here," Prissy said. "Are we going to do this blood-swear thing or not?"

"We can't," Bebe said in a soft voice. "It's over. Least, for you all. I know I'm truly done with the past, but that's me. I've worked like mad to get on with my life and I'm making it just fine."

Brie added, "And I have a wonderful mama and daddy, and I'm not about to upset things in my life. I am who I am and I'm right happy with that. I'm leaving the past alone, too. But Char, you're different."

All eyes turned to Prissy. "Now you make this big decision after I'm leaking red fluid here."

"Oh for heaven's sake." Brie pulled a tissue from her purse, tore it into fourths and passed them out. "Can we go now? I'm getting eaten alive by mosquitoes. And if I take one more bite of pie, I'll get a zit for sure."

Prissy set the six-pack and moon pies in the middle of the gravestone. "It's been a night of good, evil and everything in between. These things aren't exactly wings of bats and eyes of gnats or whatever, but beer and moon pies have got to carry some weight with the spirits, at least in Savannah, to make things right." She took Brie's hand, and Brie took Charlotte's, who took Prissy's. Brie said, "To friendship forever."

"Amen," Prissy added and made the sign of the cross.

"Why did we ever do this blood pact in a graveyard anyway?" Bebe asked.

Charlotte stood and shook the sand from her pants. "Because our pasts were dead and buried, and we swore to keep them that way." She gazed at the other three. "But that's not the way it is anymore."

"You're going to be okay," Bebe said and hugged her. "You're going to be just fine."

"Don't know if I'd jump straight to fine, but I'll darn well be something."

On the way home, Charlotte did some fancy talking and convinced them she wanted to spend the night with RL. After dropping her off at the gray clapboard, she watched the Cruiser fade down the street.

No dancing this time as she made her way up the walk. How could things change so quickly—in the blink of an eye? Unlocking the door, she peeked in at RL asleep in the La-Z-Boy, an infomercial droning on about something called the Bullet. The only bullet she was interested in was one right between Griff's eyes, for what he did to her. Except she couldn't stop thinking about what he did to her in another way, a really great way. A sexy way.

Blast the man for being so fine in the sack! And for being so fine in other ways, too, like when he came looking for her at the morgue, watched over her when she had a concussion and paid her hospital bill.

The huge live oak hung low, draping the front yard in deep shadows. She turned for the office; she'd spend the night there. A car motored, a twig snapped. Probably a Palmetto bug tromping around. Each year they got bigger, for sure uglier, a glorified roach.

She picked up the pace and turned down State Street. She should have gone down Broughton—better light, bigger street, not so many bugs in the shadows. The sidewalk narrowed, an overhead porch cut the light from the streetlamp, which wasn't all that bright to begin with. Great for ambience; sucked for safety.

Okay, this was crazy, no doubt fallout from spending time in a graveyard. She'd walked these streets all her life, knew every cobblestone and crack in the sidewalk and . . . and she was yanked into a doorway and flattened against the wall and . . . Oh shit, where was her pepper spray when she needed it?

"Mind your own business," a man growled in a foul beer-smelling voice.

"What business?"

He pushed her down, knocking her head on a protruding mailbox, and ran off. She staggered to her feet, tried to focus and spotted another person in the doorway, another guy, bigger this time. That was it! No more shoving, flattening, threatening. If Hillary Clinton could run for president, Charlotte deShawn aka Jaden Carswell could defend herself against some thug. Though what one had to do with the other she wasn't sure, but at the moment it sounded good. Taking a breath, she charged.

Griff stood in the doorway as Charlotte growled, "I've had enough!" And just as he was about to ask her enough of what, she dove at him, knocking him against the parking meter, beating him with her fists, biting his shoulder, kicking his knee . . . least it was just his knee.

"Stop! Stop! My god, woman, you're going to kill me before the night's over."

"Griff?" She froze. "What are you doing here?"

"Getting the shit beat out of me." He rubbed his knee. "I think I need crutches."

"I didn't know it was you."

"You were just practicing in case it was, is that it?" A police car pulled up, lights flashing, cop climbing out. "What's gong on?"

"I fell," Charlotte said. "Griff was helping me up."

"Some reason you're walking around at this hour?"

"My office is at the next corner. I'm putting in an early day or late night, depending on how you want to look at it." She gave him a wide-eyed innocent look. How'd women do that? Be guilty as hell and look as if they were all sugar and cream, pure as the driven snow.

The cop shined his flashlight in Griff's face, making him scrunch his eyes half-closed, then blink. "Mr. Parish?" The cop cut the light and stuck out his hand. "Danny Richmond. I was your night doorman through four years of college."

"Right. Doorman. You drove that sixty-four Mustang convertible and dated the cute redhead who was always hanging around and flirting. Marry her?"

"Dumped me."

"Lots more where she came from." He shook Danny's hand.

"You take care now, you hear, Mr. Parish." He tipped his hat and took off."

Charlotte rubbed her head. "Do you know everyone in this city?"

He gave her a sideways glance. "Some better than others." He dragged her into the light. "You have another bump on your head. That gives you a matched set. What the hell happened in that doorway? I was two blocks away and saw someone go after you."

"I got shoved. Probably a purse-snatcher."

"And you didn't tell Danny because . . ."

She propped her hand on her hip and pushed back her hair. "Are you following me?"

"I left you a million messages. You weren't picking up. I didn't have a choice."

"What part of 'I don't want to talk to you, I don't want anything to do with you' don't you get?" She started off and he fell in step.

"I finally got Bebe, and after promising to donate three cases of wine to the next police auction, she said she'd dropped you off at your house. You weren't there, so I headed for your office."

"You bribed Bebe? I can never bribe Bebe. I've tried on many a speeding-ticket occasion."

"She's worried about you. And what the hell were the four of you doing out at this hour anyway?"

"Eating. So you tracked me down. So what now? What do you want?"

Searching for the right words, he ran his hand over his chin. "I wanted . . . needed . . . to talk to you again, try and straighten things out between us."

"Like in, you want to sweet-talk me out of my half of the hotel? Well, I do have news on that score. I'm not giving it to you, but you can buy it from me and it's going to cost you a whole lot of money."

"You still have your purse. It wasn't a purse-snatcher, was it?"

She took out her key for the building. "Go home, Griff. Leave me alone."

"To spend the night by yourself, with whoever's after you? And obviously someone is." He took her arm. "You're coming home with me."

"Fuck you."

He couldn't keep the grin off his face. "That can be arranged."

"Oh, for crying in a bucket, Griff. I've had enough of you and your macho crap for one day, probably even for a year, maybe a lifetime. I'm going up to my office and going to sleep, and you're going back to your fancy hotel and—"

"*Our* fancy hotel."

"Go home and start selling stocks and bonds or stuff on eBay or whatever it takes to get me my money. And leave me be."

Chapter 14

"No way." Griff stepped inside.

"Why are you doing this?" Charlotte said as she flipped on the inside hall light and climbed the stairs, their footfalls echoing. He paused and looked at her. She didn't get how much danger she was in. "Because the real you is out there for everyone to see. Jaden Carswell's back, alive and kicking, and there's a murderer who's managed to elude the police for thirty years. He doesn't want you going after him or the necklace, and he's not about to hang tight and twiddle his thumbs waiting for you to cross his path."

"He's safe. I wouldn't begin to know where his path is. Right now I don't know where my path is."

"And that's the rub. You're blundering around here—"

"I am not a blunderer."

"You're like a pinball, bouncing here and there, and sooner or later you'll hit the thousand-point spot and really be in hot water."

She slipped her key into the door, except it swung open on its own, the interior dark, a little red dot glowing from the floor. "Like now," Griff said, shoving her behind him.

She stepped in front of Griff and flipped on the light. "Holy shebang, the place was hit by a tornado."

She took a step, and he grabbed her arm, staring into

her green eyes, which didn't trust him as far as she could throw him. "What exactly did your purse-snatcher say?"

"Since you're not going to shut up till I tell you, he said something about—"

"Mind your own business and get out of town?"

"Well, the first part, but . . ." Her eyes narrowed. "How'd you know?"

He turned her around to face the far wall, where those words were scribbled in red marker. "Guess he wanted to make sure you got the point."

"He misspelled *business*. One s. Not only is he rude, he's stupid, and if I would have been five minutes sooner, I would have caught him."

Griff's heart heaved. "Or he would have caught you. Your situation is not improving, Charlotte."

"I know, you're still here pestering me."

"Why not take a vacation for a few months?"

"Why not take a long walk off a short pier?"

He picked up the desk chair, she grabbed the lamp. "I think he killed my coffee pot." She set it back on the shelf.

"Are you afraid yet?"

"I jumped over afraid and landed on pissed. Whoever this person is, he has managed to screw up my life for years now, and I think I'm getting tired of it." She gave Griff an even look. "Unless . . . unless whoever did this isn't the killer and wants me out of the way for other reasons, like trying to frighten me away from my new life so he can sell the hotel dirt-cheap and run. Sound like anyone you know? Anyone who would stoop low enough to lie and connive? You were in the area; you could have hired that thug. It fits except for the spelling part, especially a word like *business*."

"You think I'd resort to this?"

She gave him a sassy look. "You resorted to marrying me in Bermuda, sweet cakes."

"I wanted to marry you, dammit. Still do. Be a hell of a story to tell our grandkids."

"Grandkids? With you?" She made a strangling sound, then pointed a stiff finger at the door. "Out."

He sat on the couch, propped up his feet and leaned back on the armrest. "I'm staying, sweet cakes."

"I'm calling the cops."

"I know the cops."

She stood over him trying to look determined and strong and in charge. Mostly she looked tired and lost. "Do you have any idea how messed up my life is right now? In fact, I don't have a life, or I have one too many lives. Charlotte deShawn, Jaden Carswell, and a whole bunch of people aren't thrilled with me being either one. Your mom, you, my grandparents, the killer and/or robber, and that could be a whole new list. Any of them, or you, could have done this. Now go away and let me figure this out on my own."

"I hurt you and I'm sorry about that, but this is not my doing and we both know it." He sat up, snagged the waistband of her jeans and pulled her off balance. She yelped, grabbed the air, grabbed him instead, then landed flat on top of him as they flopped back on the couch . . . eyes to eyes, body parts to body parts, lips to lips. The lips part was too much temptation, so he kissed her. The sexy body parts were a lot of temptation, too, but they were covered. Damn covered. Little sounds of protest gurgled in her throat, but she kissed him back, making him smile. After a night like this, a smile was much appreciated.

She rested her forehead against his. "I should slap you silly."

"We're both too tired for much physical exertion, silly or otherwise." He wrapped his arms around her. "Someone's following you and you should be afraid because I'm damn-well afraid for you."

"I can't even think about that right now. I don't have

enough free brain cells to take it on. I need to find out who I am, how I got here, then maybe it will make sense. But Otis is dead, my parents are dead and RL sees me as his little girl. No one knows squat."

"Well, then that brings us to breakfast with your grandparents. They're staying at the hotel in room . . ." He suddenly realized she was asleep, her forehead balanced on his, her breathing slow and easy. He kissed her again, his lips skimming hers this time, her body sinking into his just the way he liked it. "Good night, pretty girl."

"G'night," she whispered back, not really awake. He scooched against the back of the couch, then curled her in against him. The lights were still on, the place still a disaster, but he and Charlotte were together, and that mattered more than anything. He kissed her hair, promising he'd do whatever it took to keep her safe. He loved her, and somehow he had to make her realize it, and that was his last thought till a shaft of morning light pierced through the window straight into his eyes and his skull.

His gaze met Charlotte's, but she wasn't cuddled close to him. She was sitting in a chair, her eyes wide and worried and watching him.

"Good God, now what?" He struggled to a sitting position. "If this day is going to be anything like yesterday, I'm wearing a suit of armor."

"I called them. I'm having breakfast with my grandparents in fifteen minutes. I know I should have grabbed a shower and changed, but if I did, I'd chicken out. Want to come along? It is your hotel. There could be bloodshed."

"Our hotel, and you can shed anything you want. Thought you hated my guts."

"Oh, I do. Just not as much as theirs. Want to come anyway? You can freeze ice on the Rayburn's collective asses, save electricity for the hotel. How could I have grandparents like that? What happened to gushing over how big I've gotten?" She frowned. "Never mind. Don't want to hear that one either. But I have to go. They're the only living links I have to Adie and William, and trying to piece together who my parents were and who I am and what happened."

He stood. "Here's the deal. I'll come if you agree to move into the hotel."

"I'm in the middle of a personal crisis here and you're bribing me to get what you want? You're getting pretty good at it."

"I'm doing it for your own good. If it was for my own good, there'd be cohabitation involved. And just for the record, this is more like coercion. Look at this place, Charlotte. You can't stay here. You don't even have coffee."

"I can move back home or in with Brie or—"

"In case you missed something, you're a dangerous commodity to have around, sweetheart. Wherever you go, trouble follows, and it's no accident. Someone's after you in a big way. You don't want to bring RL or the girls into a dangerous situation. That means you're stuck with me. The hotel isn't all that big and I have staff to keep an eye on things if someone lurks."

"No." She held up her hand, shaking her head. "Absolutely not." She stood. "How do I know you won't be crawling into my bed every night? Didn't you just say something about cohabitation?"

"How do I know you won't be crawling into my bed?"

She made an X over her heart. "Cross my heart and hope to die a quick and sudden death because that's never going to happen, not in this lifetime, not in any. But somehow I don't think it's about bedhopping so much as setting me up to toss my sorry self over the balcony and inherit Magnolia House outright. How can I trust you after what you did?"

"I'm no lawyer, but I think next of kin inherits, meaning your half of Magnolia House goes to RL. And I never lied to you so much as not leveling with you."

"I'd rather sleep in the park."

He gave her a get-real look.

"Okay, you got me. There are bugs and I'd freak out. But right now we're going to be late; we have to go."

Tucking in his shirt, which looked more dishraggy than starched, he hurried to catch up as Charlotte rushed down the hall. "I don't even have my suit coat."

They clambered down the stairs. "We'll tell Grammy and Grampy you're Griff's messy twin."

"Nervous?"

"Petrified." They rounded the corner onto Broughton. "What will your staff do with me moving in?"

"Duck. They remember the flying nuts."

"You know that carriage house around back? Can you turn it into a honeymoon suite, with trellis, private garden and veranda with lots of Southern charm? I could probably draw you up some plans, increase the value of the hotel, make you pay me more for it."

He pulled her up short just inside the lobby. "That's a really good idea." He smiled down at her. "The girl can't find her way out of Target, but give her a hammer and nails and she's there."

"Builder genes from William. Guess I know more who I am than I think I do." She waved her hand around the hotel. "Construction, it's in the blood."

"Maybe we should make a martini bar. Specialty martinis are the rage. Chocolate martinis, dirty martinis, apple-tinis."

Daemon put his hand on Griff's shoulder and said, "Well, as I live and breathe, the two most talked-about people in all Savannah."

"It's about to get worse. The Rayburns are expecting us for breakfast."

Daemon frowned. "Edwina is in a blue suit looking like General Patton, Shipley is in a tan sport coat. The staff already shoveled the snow away from their table. You'll have to try mighty hard not to get frostbite. Have a good time now, you hear."

Daemon left, and Charlotte grabbed Griff's arm. He wished she held on to him for some other reason than nervousness over meeting long-lost grandparents. But that wasn't going to happen. He was damn lucky to get her in the hotel. "Ed and Ship can't be that bad."

"They sent an orphaned baby away from their doorstep, and that baby was me. In my opinion, they passed *bad* a long time ago."

"You could just turn around and forget meeting them, but you'd walk out on your best source of finding out about yourself."

"That's not the only reason I want to meet them." She took a deep breath. "What if they had something to do with the murder?"

"They're Patton and the tan sport coat, not killers."

"They were here to stop Adie from selling the necklace. They could have hired someone to get it and things didn't go as planned."

"That was their daughter."

"I'm their granddaughter and look what they did with me. These are not stellar parents here."

"You're going to accuse your grandparents of murder?"

"Oh, of course not, I wouldn't do that. I'm just going to hint at it a little."

"Oh boy." Griff followed Charlotte out into the garden. She smiled sweetly, way too sweetly, as she approached the table. "Oh Grammy, oh Grampy, yoo-hoo," she said in a little-girl voice. "It's me, little Jaden, all grown up." She waved. "Long time no see."

The couple stared bug-eyed. Guess this wasn't the way Bostonians greeted each other for breakfast. "J-Jaden? Is that really you?"

"Jaden Carswell." Charlotte yanked out a chair and sat

down. Griff pulled his chair and parked. "Now I want to hear all about why you disowned my mother and William and me."

The bug-eyed look was back. Actually it never left. "Aren't you going to introduce us to your—"

"No."

One of the waiters approached, but Griff waved him away. This was too good to interrupt.

Grammy stammered, "Well, Addison, your mother, simply married someone we didn't approve of, so we severed ties."

"Simply?"

"She knew how we felt, Jaden," Grampy added. "Then she inherited the necklace and—"

"The Kent Shelton necklace of thirteen white diamonds and thirteen yellow," Grammy said with a huff. "That is not *just* a necklace. Her grandmother gave it to her when it should have gone to me. She bought it with family money from a friend who got it from who-knows-where. When Addison said she was going to sell it, well, we simply couldn't let that happen and we came here to stop her. But someone stole it, and Addison and William and you paid a high price for trying to save this hotel and that's all there is to it."

"All?" Charlotte ground out.

Grampy folded his hands on the table. "I know this sounds a bit harsh, but Addison went against our wishes knowing full well what the outcome would be. She didn't care about us or our feelings. She chose William. It was her preference, with all the consequences it entailed."

"And," said Grammy, "that necklace would have been a family heirloom, something passed down from generation to generation, ensuring the success and place in the world of the Rayburn Family. When you have something that fine, that cherished, you don't sell it off. You protect it at all costs, for yourself and your family. But Addison didn't get that. She only had eyes for William."

Grammy smiled sweetly. "And now that you're all grown up, as you say, I think we can be friends, don't you? You are our granddaughter."

"Actually," Charlotte said as she stood, her knuckles blanched white as she made a fist, "I'm Charlotte deShawn, because that's all I know how to be, and I'm an investigator and I wouldn't be leaving town for a bit if I were you. There's a murder to be solved and I intend to do it."

"And there's a necklace to be found," Grammy added. "My necklace."

"Or mine," Charlotte said, raising her left brow a fraction so Grammy knew she meant it. "As we agree, I am all grown up now. I'm no lawyer, but I think an inheritance goes to the next of kin. I'm the kin; I'm the child. You have a nice breakfast now, you hear."

Griff followed Charlotte out into the hallway, then detoured her into his office. "Holy shit, girl, you were doing okay till you laid claim to the necklace. What the hell are you thinking? If they did go after your parents for that damn thing, they'll come after you."

She kissed his cheek. "I know."

"You know? Charlotte, honey, you have some guy pulling you into doorways, and now the grandparents from the Black Lagoon are after you. You might as well have a bull's-eye painted on your back."

"Not a bull's-eye. Anything but that. But what if what happened in the doorway and Ship and Ed are all the same package?"

"And maybe they're not."

"If the police can't figure it out after all this time, I have to do something to kick it up a notch. I'm the only one who can. I owe it to Adie and William and myself to figure out what happened."

He pulled her into his arms and kissed her. "You should have told me."

"I was sort of winging it as I went."

"Good thing you're staying in the hotel, because I'm staying in your room. I have the keys. We hit a little snag, but you'll trust me again, Charlotte. We're going to fall in love like we've always meant to be."

He slid up her blouse and ran his hands across her delicious back as he kissed her like a man who knew what he wanted, because he did. "I want you, Charlotte. Now more than ever." He kneaded the soft round of flesh.

"Or . . . do you want my hotel?" Her gaze met his. "Like Grammy said, when you have something so valuable, you do anything to protect it, keep it, make it yours forever."

He stepped away from her. "You're the valuable treasure here, Charlotte. I swear it. I want to make things right and pick up where we were before you decked me." He touched her cheek. "I want to get back where we were, in bed, making plans, making love. And right now, you seem pretty damn receptive."

"Maybe I've got the hots for you because you have the hotel, *my* hotel."

This time it was his brows doing the arching. "You're kissing me because of Magnolia House? Because you want it?"

"Where do we end and the hotel begins, Griff? It's all running together. It's such a big part of your life and now mine, and you've never shared it with anyone but Otis. Suddenly I'm in the picture and you can't like that."

"I'm intentionally working you for the hotel?"

"I don't know whether it's intentional or not, but it's there in both of us. Heck, we're standing smack in the middle of the place. You, me, Magnolia House and a custody battle—that's what it boils down to."

"I don't want a battle, I want you."

"And I want you. At one time it was a simple attraction, but now everything is different. The question is, why?"

"Shit!"

Chapter 15

Panting, Sam flopped over on his back, a spring breeze drifting over his naked body, covered with a fine sheen of sexually induced sweat . . . the best kind of sweat. "Prissy St. James," he finally managed. "Sex with you is better than maple syrup on a stack of blueberry pancakes with a side order of grits."

Staring up at the ceiling in sublime exhaustion, she laughed. "You're comparing me to food."

"The best food, sugar. The kind my grandma used to make, God rest her soul." He cut his eyes to Prissy. "I think I'm getting hungry all over again."

"Room service?" She walked her fingers across his rib cage.

"Or Sam service."

"Definitely Sam service." She giggled as he rolled out of bed and disposed of the condom in the bathroom.

"I'm going to grab a quick shower." A cold quick shower, he added to himself. "I've got to get to work." He flipped on the water. He never did things like this, pleasure before work, but now . . . Now he had Prissy in his life and nothing was the same. When he came back into the bedroom, Prissy was lying across the bed like some centerfold, front side down, her hair tumbled around. "You've got the best derriere in all of Georgia."

"What took you so long, big boy?" She crooked her finger at him. "I'm lonely in this big old bed all by myself."

"Oh, girl." His insides stirred. "I don't have time for this."

"Just for a minute. One teeny-weeny minute."

"Liar." But he lay down and she rolled onto her side, letting his eyes feast on her. How could he say no to this? "I'm going to be so late."

"And the sisters will have to start working on the roof without me." She ran her finger over his mouth. "But everyone will survive without us." She winked. "Wanna play?"

"We played all night. I'm all played out. Don't even have an opening kick left in me."

"Then I'll play, just a little, and see if you want to join in. Give you something to remember me by all day while you're at that big, impressive bank of yours." She slowly dragged her finger down his handsome face. "You have such fine lips. Did I ever tell you that?"

"About twenty minutes ago."

"Deserves repeating." She kissed his top lip, then the bottom, sucking it into her mouth, letting him savor the way she tasted, the way her lips mated with his, as if they were meant to be that way since the dawn of time.

"And your chin." She kissed him there. "I love your morning beard."

"I just shaved."

"I'm fantasizing. And your chest. I love that morning and night and every time in between." She twirled her finger in the tight curls of hair there, teasing and tickling. "Oh my stars, you do have a nice broad chest, Sam Pate." She kissed one nipple, then the other.

"Are you enjoying yourself?"

"Immensely."

He sighed, "Me, too, baby, me, too."

"And abs," she cooed. "You have delicious abs." She

licked the indent of his navel, then licked lower, his solar plexus quivering. "Every time I'm with you, I want to eat you up." Her finger stopped at his dick. "You are one mighty fine specimen of the male species."

"I can't believe what you do to me, Prissy."

"Sugar, I can't believe what *you* do to me," she said in a slow Southern drawl. She grazed her palm over his expanding erection. "I love watching you get hard, knowing it's just for me."

"I can't keep up with you."

She wrapped her fingers around his shaft and he sucked in a quick breath. "You just went and lied to me, Sam Pate. You're keeping up mighty fine indeed." She kissed the tip. "You make me all warm and wet inside just when I feared I might not have any warm and wet left in me."

"Prissy, what are you doing?

"Breakfast." She rolled over onto him and took his erection deep in her mouth.

The earth wobbled, and every breath of air rushed out of his lungs in one swoop.

"I've never done this before," she said as she kissed one side of his erection, then the other. "Never appealed to me till now." She grinned. "Till you. I want to be intimate with you in every way possible. I want you to take me every way you can think of. You're so hot, so hard." She straddled his legs, her damp sex resting on his thighs.

"Dear God, Priss," he hissed as her mouth and tongue stroked his dick, her long chestnut-brown hair cascading down around her face like some glorious waterfall.

"I want to appreciate every inch of you." She winked at him. "And there's a lot of inches here to appreciate."

"Flatterer."

She added another lingering kiss. "Maybe a little, but not much. It's all you."

He took her by the shoulders and pulled her up, her face

to his now, her eyes bright and happy, hair tousled, evidence of their fooling around. "Enough."

"There's never enough between us. I think there is, then this craving for you that's deep inside me starts up and I want you over again."

"I'm a craving?"

"An addiction."

He turned over, him on top now, straddling her hips.

"Something's come between us and it's grand and glorious. "I'm getting desperate here."

He folded his arms. "You're desperate? Look at me."

"Oh, I am. Do I get what I see?"

"All in good time." He took her wrists and together brought them over her head, taking in her flat stomach, nicely slim hips and the inviting pink tips of her breasts. "Oh, honey, you are one fine lady."

She shook her head. "I can't hold on much longer, Sam. I'm in the mood now."

"Just a bit longer, honey." And he bent his head and sucked her left nipple deep, his mouth opening wide, his tongue lathering her sensitive skin over and over and over, her sweet moans filling the room, making him all the harder.

"Sam," she panted, her hips arching in invitation. "Now, blast you."

"Remember the craving. The more you want it, the better it is, and I intend for it to be very, very good for you." He suckled the other breast, his tongue lapping her nipple into a hard bead. He nipped the tip, and another moan escaped her parted lips, making desire shoot through him. He kissed her. "Did you like that?"

"Wonderful. Peachy. Incredible. Now I want your dick!"

"Such talk." He smiled, adding a bit of the devil. "But I want more kisses." He brought her arms down to her sides, scooted back and kissed the dark patch of curls at the apex of her legs.

"Okay, I'm kissed. Now do it," she said in an exhale of pent-up air. "I'm about to explode." He nestled himself between her legs. "I'm so ready for you, Sam. I want you so much."

He stroked the inside of her thighs, making her legs relax, the scent of sex drenching the air. "So soft, so smooth."

"So wordy. You'd think you were in politics."

His pushed her legs apart. "That's it, open for me, honey. Let me have you." He bent her legs and pushed back on her knees, opening her wider still. He massaged the inside of her thighs, placing firm palms against there. Then he bent his head and kissed her hot, swollen sex.

"Sam? Oh God, Sam!" Her hips lurched off the bed. He suckled her clit, her body thrashing and arching toward him again for more. Then he plunged his tongue into her hot, wet passage. "Sam, I can't . . . hold . . . on."

"Let it happen, baby." His tongue took her again. "Let me make love to you. Let me pleasure you."

Her body tensed as an orgasm ripped through her, shaking her to her very core. Nothing could be better than making love to Prissy, and then he filled her with himself, sliding deep as he cupped her bottom, lifting her. She grabbed the rungs of the brass bed, her hips thrusting to meet his as he pumped into her again, till she found her release for the second time and he imploded in spirals of raw passion more intense than anything in his life.

Euphoric. No other word came close to loving Prissy. Loving? Did he? Breathing hard, he rolled over, taking her with him. "Look what you started."

"Look what you finished." She started to giggle and he joined her.

"Now I really do have to get to work, and with this grin

on my face, it's not going to take a genius to figure out why I'm late."

She set her chin on his, their mouths nearly touching. "I'm singing tonight at the Blue Note. Come?"

He closed his eyes and she asked, "Is something wrong? If you like jazz, this is the place. It's just a hole in the wall down on Bay, but you'll love Jimmy, and I'll introduce you to LulaJean and—"

"And bank presidents, especially young ones on the way up the corporate ladder, go to the country club or the black-and-white cotillion or the Pink House for dinner or—"

"Meaning I'm not good enough for you?" The tone of her voice ripped at his heart.

He opened his eyes. "My family is one of those that scratched and clawed their way off the tenant farm. My daddy went to night school, my mama taught piano. Daddy made something of himself and expects me to do the same. I realize that what I do after I walk out of that bank at five o'clock is my business . . . but it's really not. I have to play the game, Prissy. Be the image."

"You have to be the snob."

"Snobs have the money. Someone in an Old Navy T-shirt swilling beer at the local watering hole is not what wins over investors and depositors."

Her eyes lost some of the fire from before. "What about me?"

His stomach rolled. Yeah, what about Prissy? She was not the mate of choice, that was for sure. "You're perfect," he lied. "You were raised by nuns." He grinned.

"And I'm an orphan with no connections and for sure no money. That's why your helping me with the business plan means so much. It's my ticket to decorating and rehabbing big houses. I can make decent money for a change and help the sisters help other kids. I owe them so much."

"Except your great business plan isn't working. After the séance, the word's out and no one will work on the morgue, and I know you have the good sisters helping but that's a temporary fix. They're not established contractors."

"Can't you just loan us a little money? After all, the morgue is worth something as collateral."

"It's more of a white elephant." Her face filled with disappointment and he felt like shit. "Let me see what I can do."

"Really?" she squealed, the happy look back.

"It won't be much, but it'll be something, I promise," he said, thinking about what underperforming stocks he could liquidate for her. She wouldn't have to know it was a personal loan. Then she'd feel obligated. He knew all about how that crippled the soul, and the last thing he wanted was that for Prissy.

She kissed him. "It'll be fine, whatever it is. We'll make it work. We'll pay it all back." And he felt in his gut she would. Prissy was like that, a survivor and a fine woman, taking care of herself and others. That was admirable. Unfortunately banks didn't give diddly-squat about admirable.

"What are you thinking about, Sam Pate?"

"You know, my grandmother was a lot like you."

"I miss family, more than I thought. Oh, the sisters are my family for sure, but Charlotte finding out who she is has got me wondering."

"Thought you four swore you all didn't care."

"Who am I really?" Prissy sat up. "I'm thinking about going to see Minerva. She seemed to know about me, and about you, too, before you hightailed it out of there like your hair was on fire."

"She's a little scary, honey."

"That woman is whole lot scary. Heck, she talks with

ghosts and whatever else is out there. But she knows me, I can tell. And not just the Prissy St. James of today, but another one. One I don't even know."

"Be damn careful what you wish for, girl." He had no idea where that came from, and Prissy gave him a questioning look. "Meaning?"

"I'm not sure."

Prissy sat on the edge of the bed. "I want to know about me, like why I have instincts about things. Why I know if a person is good or rotten to the core, or if Sister June left her sewing basket in the living room or in her bedroom, or when Bebe's insurance is due and she forgot to pay the bill. I just know." She took his face in her soft, sweet hands and gazed into his eyes. "I know just like you know."

"Me?"

"Your voice sounds surprised, but your eyes don't show it. There's more to Sam Pate than youngest bank president around. There's another side. I can feel it."

Her eyes closed, and a tremor ran through him. He could sense her energy, her goodness, her love for him, flowing into him. But he didn't want these feelings. He wanted his job. And if it ever got out that . . . He took Prissy's hands in his. "Maybe you're coming down with a cold and that's what you feel."

"There's something about us beyond what's normal. It's the reason we were instantly attracted, why we jumped each other's bones in the elevator without even knowing names. We connect, Sam. I tried to ignore who I am, what I am, for a long time, but it won't go away, and I'm betting it's not leaving you alone either."

He stood, shaking off the moment. "Nope, you're wrong about that one, Priss, least on my side. There's only one side to Sam Pate—the logical, accounting side. The bank side."

"You knew where Charlotte was when that tree came down. You knew she was safe."

"I wanted to console you, honey. I took a guess." He headed for the closet, where his white button-down shirts hung in a nice straight row. This was his life, what he'd worked for, what was expected of him. He couldn't afford a reputation as a wacko . . . about him or those he spent time with. Why couldn't Prissy be just a normal woman? Except then she wouldn't have the fire, the excitement, that made her Prissy. Still . . . "I can't hear you sing tonight, Priss. I just remembered I have to work and it can't be put off. I'll call you around midnight, if that's okay."

"You can't come? You're not listening to me." She sounded frustrated. He felt like a jackass.

"Tomorrow night we can have a romantic dinner up here, what do you say?"

"I say, you're just like Robert Larson, my high school boyfriend. He also thought I was weird, and wanted me just for sex."

Oh shit! "That's crazy talk, Prissy." Sam tossed down his shirt and took her in his arms, loving that she was here with him. "I want to be alone with you. The two of us together."

Maybe, Prissy thought to herself. Then the *maybe* felt more like a *maybe not*. There it was again, that feeling, the intuition, the gut reaction to what was really going on. Sometimes it was a good thing, and sometimes—like now—it was not so much. Sometimes she didn't want to know everything. At the moment, dumb and happy beat the heck out of knowing and miserable.

The rat bastard was lying. She wasn't good enough for him, not good mate material.

He kissed her on the forehead. "I've got to skedaddle. Are we okay?"

"I'll talk to you after my set at the Blue Note."

He kissed her again, and she headed for the shower. When she came out, Sam was gone, and in more ways than one. She kicked her shoe, missed and stubbed her toe on the dresser. Hopping around on one foot, she decided nothing was going right today, and if anyone knew such things, she did . . . and so did Minerva.

It was time Prissy St. James found out why she was the way she was, and it went way beyond the spirituality of being raised in a nunnery. She dressed and headed down Broughton, the rush-hour traffic giving way to mid-morning Slowvannah meandering. She turned onto St. Julian and stood out front of Hampton Lillibridge House, with dormers and slant roof. No wonder it was haunted. A Yankee built the damn place.

She stared at the path that led around to the back . . . to Minerva. Prissy felt like those Hansel and Gretel kids from the fairy tales Sister June used to read to her. They went into the woods and left bread crumbs to find their way out. Except the birds ate the bread and the kids were totally screwed. If she followed the path, would she be screwed, too? Lost and not be able to get back?

"Are you wanting to talk to me, child?" Minerva asked as Prissy came around the house and down the path. Her hair looked as if lightning had struck, her blue apron spotted with flour, but her eyes . . . those gray know-it-all eyes . . . were sharp as ever.

"I'm not sure."

She laughed. "An honest answer, now."

"A coward's answer." Prissy pulled in a deep breath. "Do you know who left me on the nunnery steps?" she blurted out. *Please say no. Please say no.*

"Ah, that I do," Minerva said as she sat down on the third step, looking at Prissy eyes to eyes. "Now the question being, do *you* want to know?"

"Can you give me a clue? Like, is it a good thing I should know or a bad thing I don't want to know? What if I ask you questions and you tell me whether I'm hot or cold. Like a game." She felt good about that. "Yes, a game."

"Ah, a game, you're saying? But that be not one of a guessing kind, more one of knowing. A game you can count on."

"Numbers. Cards!" Prissy gasped, nodding like one of those stupid bobble-head dolls. "Cards. That's it. I was won in a card game. Poker."

Minerva laughed. "Best give it another try."

Minerva put out her wrinkled old hand and Prissy took it, feeling some of those bread crumbs fading away and a sense of walking deeper into the forest growing stronger. "Picture cards with numbers." Her gaze fused with Minerva's, and Prissy's hair actually tingled as she whispered, "Tarot."

"Ah, but now we are getting somewhere, no?"

"I've never done Tarot."

"But alas, someone has. That someone being close to you."

"You?" Prissy said, squeezing Minerva's hand tightly. "And my mother. Ohmygod, you're my mother!"

"Grandmother, child. Your mother is—"

"Dead . . ." Prissy gasped, feeling a terrible sense of loss that pained her clear through. "At the morgue. It all fits together, doesn't it?" It wasn't even a question; Prissy knew it to be true.

"Your mama's been dead some twenty-five years now, girl, but she went to the morgue when she was alive, not when she died."

"Why would she leave me on the steps of a nunnery? Why not let you raise me?" Prissy closed her eyes, then snapped them open, a shiver running down her spine. "Murder . . . and a necklace and my mother. It's all connected somehow. But how? Why?"

"That necklace . . . Well, no one found it. Then they come looking for your mama, knowing what a fine woman of the spirits she be. She said she could find their necklace. But she couldn't. All she saw was sunlight. So much sunlight. The police went digging up the courtyard and all the grounds at the morgue and finding nothing. Your mama was shamed, everyone here thinking she a fraud, a fake. They laughed and made the jokes. Not wanting that for her baby child, she left you on the sister's steps, to break the curse for good, and made me swear on your life I wouldn't come looking. Then she left here and never came back. All these years I've been keeping watch. 'Course the truth being that you getting raised by the good sisters didn't break any powers. You have them, child, just like your mama, just like me. You know, could tell every time I be looking at you all these years."

Prissy couldn't breathe. She couldn't have moved if someone yelled, "Your clothes are on fire!" Minerva patted her hand. "Then you came looking for me, to be doing that séance. I knew you had the feelings. We were of the same blood." Minerva stood and hugged her tightly. "A pretty child you are, too. Like you mama all over again."

"The sisters didn't know?"

"I give my promise to your mama and I not be going back on that."

"What do I do now?"

"That be for you to figure out, but have it for the good, not the evil, child. Can be for either, you know."

She took Minerva's hands, feeling giddy with happiness. "I have a grandma."

"And I having a fine granddaughter now."

"Can I tell the sisters? And Charlotte and Bebe and BrieAnna?"

"I be proud if you did. Are you afraid of what people say?"

Prissy's heart sang. "All my life I didn't know who I was or why I felt the way I did. Now I do, and I have you, too. A bonus."

A tear trickled down Minerva's cheek and she laughed. "Never thought I'd be sitting here today talking to you."

"But we are. Isn't this incredible? Do you like peach ice cream?"

"Being my favorite."

This time Prissy laughed. "I'll meet you down at River Street Sweets tomorrow at noon. My treat." She stood. "Now I'm going to tell the sisters I have a grandma and they have a new member of the family. You're going to love the sisters. Wait till you taste Thanksgiving dinner!"

LulaJean belted out "Take Me I'm Yours" as Bebe, Charlotte and BrieAnna stared at Prissy across the little round table with a candle dripping wax in the middle. Brie finally managed, "You're who? You're what?"

"It's the truth. Minerva's my grandmother."

"All these years, so close to you. I get why she didn't own up but—"

"But then you went to her." Charlotte grabbed Prissy's hand. "I'm so happy for you. Minerva is such a step up from Ship and Ed." Her eyes brightened. "You know what we should do now? The lottery . . . what numbers do we pick? And maybe we should go to Las Vegas. We have Prissy the all-knowing with us. We can't miss."

Prissy rolled her eyes. "Oh good grief. If it worked like that, I'd have gotten all A's in school and cleaned up on the stock market. All I can do is sense things, like I've always been doing."

Charlotte arched her eyebrow. "Truth be told, you don't exactly know what you can do, do you? Remind me to keep on your good side."

Bebe folded her hands on the table. "Are you all starting to see a pattern here?"

Charlotte looked from one to the other. "Priss is the resident soothsayer, I can't find my way out of a one-way street, Brie's got the hots for a bad boy and you have a horrid wardrobe."

Bebe said, "Not that. The murder? The missing necklace? It's the common factor. Look, Charlotte's parents lost the necklace, Prissy's mom tried to find it. That's two for two in the *Who Am I?* book of four orphans. That leaves me and Brie." The candle flickered, drawing their eyes to it.

Prissy shivered, and Charlotte said, "I usually don't believe in coincidences, but in this case I do. It's just the circumstances. Period."

Prissy looked from Char to Bebe to Brie. "Not period and the list is growing. We were all adopted at the same time, we're the same age, none of us knew diddly about where we came from and now . . . Now there's more to link us."

"Link who?" Sam said as he planted a kiss on Prissy's cheek.

She turned and squealed, "You came!"

"How could I not? My favorite girl is singing my favorite music. And the girl's looking particularly hot in that pink dress."

"I thought you had to work?"

His eyes danced. "I'll finish up tomorrow morning." He nodded to the stage. "Someone up there is waving at you, sugar. I think it's showtime." He kissed her cheek. "You sing pretty now, you hear."

"I'll sing for you." Prissy jumped up and threw her arms around him. "You came, you really did. It means so much to me. I love you, Sam Pate."

"God, Prissy, I love you, too," he whispered in her ear. "With all my heart."

How could a day get any better than this? Prissy wondered. She spent it with her new grandma and her incredible boyfriend, who would soon be more than just a friend. She was sure of it—until the candle on the table flickered. A breeze, she told herself. That's all. Nothing could ruin tonight.

Sam whistled "Angel Eyes," the song Prissy sang just for him tonight, least that's the way it felt even though the Blue Note was packed. He was falling in love, or closer to the truth, he already fell. He could make this work, his business side and his Prissy side. The trick was to keep them apart, and in a small city like Savannah, that would be hard. Still, he could do it . . . somehow he'd manage. He entered his apartment, turned on the light and came face to face with . . . "Dad? What are you doing here?"

"Waiting for you." He stood. Every pleat, every crease perfect as always. "What the hell do you think you're doing, Sam?"

"What are you talking about?"

His eyes flashed. "Visiting psychics, going to séances, dating some undesirable woman who's penniless and raised by nuns, and then tonight, going to some dive to hear her sing? Have you lost your fucking mind?"

"You're spying on me?"

"I'm keeping track so you don't screw up, and thank God I am. You've lost all sense of priority. You're not a banker; you're a damn joke." He crossed the room and turned. "You're committing business suicide. But that's not going to happen. Your mama and I made sacrifices to get you where you are, and you are not throwing yourself away like your sister did. You are not associating with this little nothing woman I've heard about when you're capable of so much more."

"Prissy is a fine woman, Dad. She reminds me of Grandmother."

"For Chrissake, Isabella was a nut-job, and Prissy is a detriment to your position and your station in the community. Tomorrow night is the Sawyers' Spring Garden Party, and you are attending with their daughter as your date and you are going to be Mister Charming and you're telling this Prissy person you will not be seeing her again, end of story." His dad's eyes narrowed. "And above all, you will not ever mention your little problem to anyone. Or have you already done that?"

"No, I've kept it to myself."

"Well, thank God for that much. My flight back to Atlanta leaves in an hour and I have to get to the airport. You do what I tell you now, you hear. Your mama and I didn't pay all those hefty tuition bills to Vanderbilt for nothing. We raised you to be someone important."

The door closed behind his father, and Sam sank into an overstuffed chair. "Shit."

Chapter 16

Charlotte held the bag of chips in her teeth and the other food bag in her left hand while she pulled open the screen door, pushed in the front door and slid inside, a move perfected by living her whole life in the gray clapboard. No TV blaring, blinds drawn, uneaten fried fish on the coffee table. "RL?"

Nothing.

"Daddy?" Panic stabbed her in the gut. Where was he? What happened? Was he in a depressed stupor in his room? "Dad? RL, where are you? Answer me right now, you hear me."

"For crying in a bucket, can't a man take a leak around here without all hell breaking loose?" RL pushed his wheelchair around the hall corner. His eyes widened. "Charlotte?"

Her heart slammed her chest. "Who the hell else calls you Daddy? You scared the liver out of me."

His eyes teared and he swallowed hard. "No one else calls me Daddy. Only heard the RL part around the john flushing and washing my hands."

He stared at her and she stared back.

"I'm sorry," they both blurted at the same time.

"Me, too," they blurted again. Then Charlotte bit her bottom lip, "I really am sorry. I shouldn't have walked

out. Nothing ever gets settled by walking out. You taught
me that. You taught me everything."

"You had a right to leave. I shouldn't have kept you in
the dark for so long." She kissed him on the head and put the
bags on the end table. "Come to feed your old man?"

"What old man? Don't see any around here."

He laughed and it sounded wonderful, curing some
dark place in her heart that she feared wouldn't go away.
Then she realized she was the one who had to make it do
that.

"Going to give me a heart attack with that stuff, you
know that, don't you?" He rolled up to the table and
peeked inside the bags. "Lordy, that smells good."

"This is a bribe, Dad. Seems to be a lot of it going around.
But I need to talk to you. And I want you to do me a favor
and listen to me and please do what I ask. Do it for me."

"There's a whole passel of *for me*'s in there, little girl.
Oh my, is this fried okra? You know how I love fried
okra."

"From Magnolia House. The chef made it up special for
you this morning along with fried oysters and a gumbo
that's to die for and lemonade—the real deal, not some
frozen concentrated goop." She sat on the sofa and took
RL's hand, looking into his blue eyes, the ones she trusted
all her life, and now she so wanted him to trust her.
"You're my dad. In fact, I just told that very thing to the
Rayburns, who are pond scum, though you already knew
that, and I'll thank you till my dying day for not leaving
me with the wicked witch of Boston and her sidekick."

RL nodded, snagging a piece of okra. "Pretty much my
take on the situation, too, and you're welcome. And I already knew you told them to pound salt and you're a
deShawn. I do have my sources." He winked. "Good girl.
Now what's the rest of this here bribe for?" He chomped a

fried oyster and arched a brow in approval. "Bet it's a doozie."

"I made arrangements for you to go to the Abbot Physical Rehabilitation Center in Atlanta." She held up her hand so he wouldn't start griping. "Big Al's on his way here to get you, and he'll visit and I'll visit and you'll be up and walking in no time. It's the best, Dad. You need the best."

He put down his fried oyster. Not a good sign. "Not going to happen, little girl. I'm not taking your money from Magnolia House. It's your inheritance."

Well damn. Now what? Plan B, except she didn't have a plan B, since plan A looked like a shoo-in. "I . . . I found the necklace."

He brought the fried oyster to a halt halfway to his mouth, meaning he didn't put it down, meaning she was onto something. "And that's not an inheritance. That's blood money." Least that part was true enough. "Money Adie and William died for. Money I want no part of. I'm selling the necklace and using the money for you, and what's left I'm giving to charity."

"You really found the necklace?"

She crossed her fingers behind her back. "Scout's honor."

RL stroked his chin. "First I've heard of it."

"Keeping it quiet. It's safer for me that way. Sent it to New York for appraisal and to find a buyer. Let something good come from all of this, something positive for Adie and William and me." She rolled her shoulders. " 'Course I could just turn it over to the Rayburns."

"Like hell. Your mama and daddy . . . your other daddy"—RL grinned—"would flip in their graves. Where'd you find the necklace? Everyone looked high and low for that thing for years."

Oh gads. "The old settee. I saw it the night of the storm when I stumbled into the casket room. There it was, tacked back under a fold of old upholstery. Thirteen white diamonds, thirteen yellow, set in platinum. I went back for it the next day."

"And you didn't tell me?"

"I wanted to surprise you when I got the appraisal back." She smiled. "See, it's all taken care of." She kissed his cheek and hurried into his bedroom, pulling suitcases from the closet and making a racket before he asked any more questions she had no idea how to answer. She yelled, "I'll get you packed and ready to go. Eat up now, you hear. Big Al will be pulling into the drive any minute now."

"You told him what?" Griff stared at Charlotte across her room at Magnolia House as she hung clothes in the closet. Damn he loved having her here. It wasn't moving in together but close to it, and he'd put her in a room far away from Skip and Ed so they wouldn't bother her, and that was really a nice pink blouse she just put away. And was that a yellow halter top? He had a thing for women in halter tops. Well, just one woman . . . Charlotte.

"What else could I do? RL wouldn't go to the therapy center unless I promised the money didn't come from selling you my share of Magnolia House. The money had to come from somewhere. Your bank account may support that kind of lie, but mine sure doesn't."

"So you invented the necklace story."

"He bought it, that's what's important."

She opened a drawer and dumped in panties of every color imaginable, and he imagined Charlotte in every single one of them . . . then out of them. He swallowed. She dropped in bras, and he had the same thought and swallowed again.

"Except now there's a little pressure to find the damn thing."

"Find what damn thing?"

"The necklace? Are you okay?" She folded a black slip, then a cream one with lace.

He lost okay when he saw that pink blouse. "Is it hot in here?" He loosened his tie.

"Feels fine to me." She ran her hand over the cherry mantel adorning the little fireplace in her room. "Magnolia House is beautiful. I've never been in one of its rooms before . . . except yours, of course." She laughed. "Couldn't afford it."

She dropped shoes in the closet. Good. Nothing sexy about gym shoes. He said, "For Otis and me, it's a dream come true."

"Dreaming is good, and that's what I must have been doing when I bought these things." She pulled a pair of black stilettos from her luggage and held them up. "I don't know why I bought heels this high. Brie wants to borrow them for the Sawyer's garden party tonight and—"

He tackled her, sending them both across the bed. "No."

"No? Tossing a woman onto a bed usually means yes, yes, yes!"

"The shoes are yours. Actually I think they're for me. You in them are for me. Damn, woman."

She let out a deep breath. "What are we doing, Griff? On again, off again."

"And right now I'm on, and liking it a whole lot." He smoothed back her hair. "What do you want to be doing, Charlotte?"

"I'm still mad at you. I don't know if I'll ever get over it. And can I really trust you? That's the big question, isn't it. Trust."

"Before the will got in the way, we were doing pretty good. In fact, given a little time, I think we would have wound up right here where we are now. Can't we just go back to that?" He kissed her, his lips on hers like coming home. "Oh sweetheart, this is nice."

"I know." Her lips softened, her face lost the edge of worry that had been there since she flung the nuts. Her body relaxed under his, and he kissed her again.

"We're actually in a bed for a change."

"Is that a proposition?"

"I'm crazy about you, Charlotte. Always have been."

"The question is, are you crazy about me just to get the hotel?"

"We're going to have to work on that suspicious streak. The only thing I want to take advantage of is your lovely body, right here and now. You're gorgeous, Charlotte, and you're fun and exciting . . . sometimes too exciting . . . and I want you in my life. I don't want anything to get in the way of that. And I don't want anything to get in the way of you in my bed."

"Our bed."

He smiled. "I like the sound of that." And he slid her white sweater over her head. "And I like the looks of this, of you, a lot." He kissed her left breast just above the bra line.

"Shouldn't you be working?"

"I am. We'll see where it leads."

She closed her eyes. "I'm so confused. Us together, us not together. Us wanting to be together no matter what."

"Let's just go with what we have right now and forget the hotel." He kissed her left shoulder and slid down the strap, his lips following.

"You're going to wrinkle your suit."

"God, I hope so." He slid down the other bra strap till she grabbed the knot of his tie, pulling his face to hers. "If you're playing me, Griff Parish, I swear . . ."

"And I swear this is a time-out. A break. No worries." He kissed her on the lips. This was it, she was it, the woman he was supposed to share his life with, just like Otis said.

He slid his hands under her and unsnapped her bra. "This, or not? It's your call. Walk away, or not?"

Her gaze met his. "No promises, no bribes, no mind games?"

"Just us."

She scooted from under him and out of the bed and stood, the bra falling off. "Well, there you are. Nothing can be done now. Once a guy sees your boobs, you have to screw him, everybody knows that."

He felt his smile clear through to his heart. "Then it's a done deal." He laughed. "Care to show me what else goes with this deal?"

She looked shy, then playful, and the playful won out. "I suppose I can do that." She kicked off her left sandal, which landed on the bed, the right one falling on his chest. Slowly she unzipped her jeans and peeled them down, then she stepped into the stilettos. "Is that deal enough for you?"

"Pink panties and black stilettos, my favorite outfit. How did you know?"

"It's every guy's favorite outfit. Google 'dressing for guys' and this is what pops up." She cocked her left hip, assuming a provocative pose, and ran her fingers through her hair, letting the auburn curls spill down.

"Where'd you learn how to do this?"

"Instinct." She put her finger in her mouth, sucking the tip, making him as hard as the post at the end of the bed. Her gaze zeroed in on the bulge in his pants. "I think I want to switch things around."

"Honey, there are shoes and undies. Nothing's left to switch."

"Wanna bet?" Before he knew what she meant, she straddled him, her voluptuous breasts firm and creamy right in front of him, ready for him. Her panty-clad hot sex over his dick. He reached for her, but she ground her heat against his arousal and he nearly went blind. "Whatcha got there for me, big boy?"

"Something that's not going to wait."

She unbuckled und unbuttoned his pants.

"This isn't helping."

"Depends on your point of view." She pulled up his dress shirt and kissed his left nipple, her breasts skimming his chest.

"I want to do that."

"You can't kiss your own nipple." She nipped the tip, and bolts of lust shot straight through him from head to toe. "That's what you have me for."

"Do I have you, Charlotte? Dear God, I hope so." He stroked the sides of her breasts, her eyes now dark jade.

"Yes," she said in a breathy low voice that constricted his chest into a tight knot of wanting. "Absolutely, least for right now." Then she slid up his front, dragging her nipples over his chest, and kissed him. His heart soared, his body in fever pitch, his dick on red alert. He rolled her over, him on top now.

"I wasn't finished."

"We have a lifetime to let you finish." He kissed her. "And it's going to be great. Right now I want to make love to you. Incredible love. Love you'll remember all day and into the night, until I take you again, right here in this bed."

"Again," she breathed on a whisper. He stripped off his coat, then his tie and shirt. She sat up and slid off his belt, dropping it onto the floor. Her hungry gaze met his, her hands lingering, pressing against his pulsing dick as she drew down the zipper. The sound filled the room, the promise of what was to come turning his blood to white-hot fire.

"I want you, Griff."

He kicked off his shoes and yanked off his pants all at once. She leaned back, dangling a stiletto off her left foot. "Care to take off my panties? Or shall I?" She laughed. "That's a line I never used before. I don't think I've used many lines at all." She nibbled her bottom lip. "But leave the shoes."

She eyed his erection. "And if I keep saying things like *that,* I don't know what in the world I'll do with all of . . . *that!*"

"It's going to be a hell of a good time finding out." He sat next to her, the golden afternoon sun slanting in through the blinds across Charlotte's lush body. He cupped her left breast on the side, the nipple pinking with excitement. "You are so lovely."

He licked her right nipple, then sucked it into his mouth, the sweet nub against his tongue incredible, her gasp of pleasure pure heaven.

"Griff . . . the undies?"

He smiled down at her. "Patience."

She eyed his strained state. "I don't think either of us has much left."

He eased down the lacy slip of material to the mysterious, secretive, enticing tangle of hair. He planted a soft kiss there, making her gasp again . . . or was it a sigh? "Don't ever shave it."

"It's summer and bathing suits and—"

"Leave some for me." He kissed the sweet bit again and traced the outline with his forefinger as he watched her eyes darken to black. He slid inside. She closed her eyes, her hips arching to take more. "I want you," she moaned. "Oh, Griff. Now."

He pushed deeper, adding another finger, her delicious juices drenching his fingers, her passage giving way to his possession. "Let me have you, baby. Let me please you."

Her hips pressed against his palm, his thumb to her clit.

Her eyes opened, not focusing, wild with desire. "I want to come with you full inside me."

"You will, I promise." Then he pushed deeper, his thumb stroking and massaging more, adding pressure. Her body tensed, her eyes wide. "Let go, Charlotte. Let me love you."

"But . . ." Her body quivered, then tensed again, in glorious orgasm. "You're so beautiful, Charlotte." And that he could bring her to this state made him want her all the more.

"Now?" She whispered. "Again . . . and again . . . with you."

He kissed her. "With me, only with me." He slid her panties off and took a condom from his wallet.

"Let me," she said, rolling to her side. "Except I want to feel you naked first."

"But—"

She ignored him and cradled his erection in her palm as she looked into his eyes. "Holy shit!"

He laughed.

"What the heck am I supposed to do with—"

"Oh, honey, let me show you." And her lovely mouth took his dick deeper than he thought possible. He wanted to say his control was almost gone, his wanting her overflowing and the mix at a critical state. Except no words would come.

His brain melted, his body throbbed and she took him again, then once more. He grabbed fistfuls of sheet, his teeth clenched. "Char," he finally managed, holding on by a thread. "Now. Right now, honey."

She slid on the condom and this time he took her, her legs over his shoulders, her sweet pussy wide and wanting and wet. His body ignited with love—yes, it was love, all-powerful, all-consuming—for Charlotte deShawn. His . . . she was all his. And he was hers.

He held her tight, not wanting to lose the moment. He'd

HOT AND BOTHERED 233

remember it till he died. This woman, this time. "There's no one like you, Charlotte. I love you. I do. Completely. Nothing can change that."

He gazed down at her, saw tears forming in the corners of her eyes. "I love you, too, Griff," she said in a hushed voice that melted his heart. "I do. I don't ever want to lose you. I couldn't bear it."

He kissed her. "You won't have to, I swear it. We've been through a lot and we're going to work things out. We deserve to be in love. We deserve each other." He rolled over, taking her with him. "Marry me."

Her eyes sparkled, her smile brighter than the sunlight. She nodded as if the words wouldn't come out. "Yes!" she finally managed. "I'll marry you, Griffin Parish."

"We'll elope. You name the day." She laughed with happiness, then rested her head on his chest. "You thrill me, you know that. You always have. Whenever I saw you, whenever I was someplace and you came into the room, or I came into a room where you were . . . you thrilled me. And now I know it will happen for the rest of my life."

She planted a kiss on his chest. "You're wonderful."

He held her tight, tired to the core. The kind of fatigue from a long search that ends when you finally find what you were after. He felt her body relax against his, her breathing slow, and he let himself sink into sleep, the sleep of contentment from knowing that when he awoke, Charlotte would still be there.

Charlotte grabbed the phone, cursing whoever was on the other end for interrupting her sleep. Make that interrupting their sleep. Their, as in she and Griff together. Holy cow! "Prissy? What's the matter?" Charlotte was instantly awake. "You sound terrible. I'll be right down."

"What?" Griff said when she hung up and rolled off of him. She'd so much rather be rolling on.

"I don't know." Charlotte pulled on her panties. "Prissy said my name in that tone like the world just came to an end." Charlotte pulled on her slacks. "I've got to go on a diet. Do you know how hard it is to live in Savannah and not plump out?" She glanced at Griff. "No, I suppose you don't."

"You need to climb back into bed so I can take those slacks off and we can do what we just did all over again."

She put on her sandals while giving him a kiss. "Tonight. I promise. And we're going to be together a lot from now on."

He gave her a devilish grin. "I know."

"Not just in bed, sexy man, but for the hotel, too." She slid on the other sandal. "I don't have to sell my share to afford RL's therapy. Actually selling's not the answer at all, because I can't use the money for that. I promised." She kissed Griff full on the lips. "So I guess it's 'Howdy, partner,' from here on out. But like you said, we'll make this work."

She grabbed her purse from the nightstand and ran out the door and down the staircase past the picture of Robert E. Lee on his horse Traveller. In the lobby, Charlotte looked for Prissy till Jasmine nodded toward the bar. Charlotte mouthed a thank you and headed in that direction.

The bar was sparsely occupied, the after-work crowd not in yet, the tourists still out doing the city. Charlotte slid up onto one of the mahogany stools next to Prissy, who was gulping something tall and lethal-looking. "What happened?"

Prissy held up her finger in a wait-till-I-kill-this-off gesture. "Ah," she finally managed, followed by a burp. "That was darn tasty." She swiped her hand over her mouth. "What happened is, Sam, that no-good Yankee pig-stealer, broke up with me"—she checked her watch—"two hours and fifteen minutes ago."

"But . . . but I was with you last night. He came, he gushed, he clapped, he said he loved you. I heard it. I'm a witness. A guy doesn't do that and then tell you to take a hike."

"Wanna bet?" Prissy motioned for the bartender to give her another.

"What did he say?"

"'Prissy, my love, we're not a good fit.' Then I found out he had no problems finding a replacement fit right quick. The Sawyers' party is tonight and Sam is Amanda Sawyer's date. How do you like them apples?"

"Oh, honey, after five minutes of the laugh that strips skin off lizards, he'll come crawling back to you, begging forgiveness. Men get scared when they find *the one*. He has cold feet, is all."

"Sam's cold feet are from my lack of a nice fat bank account or stock portfolio to warm them up. Jasmine overheard our breakup at lunch in the courtyard. Men always break up in public places so you don't cause a scene and you don't shoot their sorry butts. Anyway, she told me Sam's daddy flew in last night, stayed till Sam came home, then left ten minutes later. She thought maybe that had something to do with him calling it quits, and I'm sure she's right. Sam's daddy is all about doing well, making money and being important."

Prissy held up her fresh tall drink. "And an orphan raised by nuns is none of those things. I think Daddy gave Sonny a facts-of-life talk."

"You're not an orphan. You have the sisters, the three of us and now Minerva."

"The local mambo. This is not the proper image for a bank president and for sure no competition to Amanda and her mommy and daddy's millions, or is that billions?"

"We just can't sit here and take this. I say we get Minerva

to whip up some revenge. Roses are red, violets are yellow, may Sam's dick turn into Jell-O."

Prissy moaned, and plopped her head on the bar. "That was just plain wrong."

"Hey, I'm not the one with the gift around here. That's you and Minerva. Bet you could come up with something powerful if you set your mind to it."

Prissy straightened up, supporting her head in her hand. "You've been reading way too much Harry Potter."

"This is the Low Country, and you know as well as I do, a lot of strange stuff happens in these parts. Mr. Wallace lost all his money after he divorced Deloris for that cupcake from Beaufort. You think Deloris didn't have a little something to do with that?"

"Yeah, she had Billy the-ball-buster Branson for an attorney."

"Sam's got it coming, Pris."

"I love him."

"Tough love, baby, tough love. He has really great hair and I bet he really likes his hair."

"You want me to mess with his hair?"

"A little retribution is good for the soul."

"How do you know I can do this?"

"How do you know you can't?"

Priss pulled a picture from her purse and whined, "Me and Sam over at City Market. One of the street vendors took our picture." She sniffed.

Charlotte took the picture, tore it in half and put Sam's pond-sucking half on the bar. She placed Prissy's palm over the picture. "Okay, say something."

"I think you've lost your pea-picking mind."

"Say something else. Something . . . hairy." Charlotte plucked a sable-brown strand from Prissy's collar. "Sam's?"

"He kissed me goodbye."

"Aha! It's a sign." Charlotte picked up Prissy's hand and laid the hair across the photo. She got one of the lit candles in a blue globe from a table and brought it over to the bar. "Okay, we're all set. Close your eyes, concentrate."

"I can't think of anything. My brain is pickled."

"Good grief, Harry never had this trouble. How about . . . You've been so mean, I was your girl . . ."

"So unto you this curse I hurl."

"That's it, that's it. Keep going."

"Your hair so grand, it all will fall, that's what you get for being an asshole. Amen. I fudged the end."

"You're just starting. That was great."

The bartender stared, his eyes covering half his face. He held up his hands as if warding off . . . something. "No charge for the drinks." He grabbed the bill, tore it in pieces, threw it in the air, then hurried off.

Prissy said, "I wonder if it will work. I feel kind of bad."

"Hey, you got free drinks. It's already worked pretty well."

A man hurried up to Charlotte. "Ms, Charlotte deShawn? I'm the Parishes' attorney, James Hall of Hall, Mackie and Hall. I need you to sign these papers right quick, since you are now half-owner of Magnolia House."

Charlotte grinned. "Doesn't that sound superb? Half-owner. Little old me." She batted her eyes, feeling giddy. "You really want me to do this here at the bar? Don't we go to your office or something?"

A reassuring smile spread across Hall's round face. "A lot of business has taken place at this here bar, and it's important to get your name on the banking statements, the checking accounts and the like so the hotel can continue to function." He put the papers on the bar and handed her a pen. "Simple stuff, very straightforward."

She read, "Griffin Parish or Charlotte deShawn. That

sounds terrific, doesn't it?" She picked up the pen, and Prissy grabbed it away and threw it across the room. "What are you doing?"

"This is not okay." Prissy hiccupped. "That *or* part means Griff can conduct business without you knowing squat. It should be *and*."

The attorney's smile broadened. "Complete nonsense, this is—"

"A ploy to get Charlotte to sign over god-knows-what." Prissy said to Charlotte, "If it read *and*, then Griff would have to get your blessing for everything, like transfer of money, hotel holdings. You'd also have to sign, not just him. When I had to get that freaking business-proposal stuff together for Sam the low-rent, no-count needle-dick—actually, that part's not true, but I'm pissed—for rehabbing the morgue, I read so much legal mumbo jumbo, my eyes crossed. This *or/and* thing is a biggie. Rates right up there with that plus or minus sign on pregnancy tests. One little line makes a heck of a difference."

A few customers from the crowd at the bar nodded in agreement, and Charlotte felt as if she'd been hit by a truck. For a second she couldn't speak. "Griff's trying to get me to sign off on the hotel?"

"The operation of it."

"But we just . . . He just . . ."

The attorney shook his head. "You're making too much of this. Both your names are on the deed and on all bank papers."

"But only one name is required to do business," Prissy ground out, eyes bloodshot but determined and staring at Hall. "Charlotte has no idea at the moment what the business is all about, and by the time she gets up to speed, she could be cut out entirely."

Hall tried a patronizing smile this time. "You're just a wee bit tipsy now, sugar."

"Don't you sugar me, you . . . you overpaid, unethical swindler." The crowd applauded, but Hall pushed on with, "You have no idea what you're talking about." Except his eyes held that oh-shit look.

Charlotte crumpled the papers on the bar into a ball and placed the crinkled mess into Hall's hand. "Give that to Griff." She took Prissy's drink and dumped it on Hall's head. "You can give him that, too."

"How dare you," Hall sputtered.

Charlotte handed him a napkin. "No charge. It's already paid for. And the last time I saw the lily-livered jackass Griffin Parish, who's trying to cheat me out of my hotel and make me a laughingstock, he was as naked as a jaybird in my bed. Damn."

They watched Hall head for the door as Griff came in from the foyer. He sat beside Charlotte. "Was that Hall? Is it raining? He looked drenched." He stole a quick kiss. "So, sweetheart, did you sign the papers?"

Chapter 17

"Sweetheart?" Charlotte said to a perfectly pressed Griffin Parish who had obviously changed. Something else was about to change around here, and by God, this time for good. "How could you? And that's the second time . . . as in two . . . that I've said that."

"What happened?"

Charlotte slid from the stool. "You'd think I'd learn. But noooo, I keep falling into the same stupid trap involving your desk or my bed or something to do with great sex that completely warps my brain and kicks any good sense I have straight to the curb."

"Charlotte, the papers are legal documents to get your name on the accounts. It's not a trap. It's the truth."

"It's like . . . like Sears and Roebuck. Two names, but who does anyone hear about? Sears. Whatever happened to Roebuck, huh? I'll tell you what happened. The poor schmuck probably signed legal papers with *or* instead of *and,* then it was bye-bye Roebuck. You, Griffin Parish, think I'm Roebuck."

"I think you're drunk."

Prissy burped, then raised her hand. "Honey, that would be me."

Griff spread his hands to Charlotte. "What the hell's this all about?"

The bartender leaned over the bar to Griff, pointing to Charlotte and then Prissy. "Don't give them any grief, boss, unless you fancy a toupee."

He stood. "Charlotte, you have to be a little more specific because I don't have a clue what's going on here, so I can't fix it."

"Like you didn't know Hall had those papers reading Griffin Parish *or* Charlotte deShawn instead of *and* Charlotte deShawn, giving you free reign over the hotel without me?"

"It was *and*. I looked them over."

"Not to worry. I'm getting an attorney. Billy Branson comes to mind." Charlotte grabbed Prissy's arm and hauled her out of the bar, into the lobby and out the main door, the warm spring sun chasing away the chill of being double-crossed again. Well, sort of.

Prissy held her head. "If I ever drink again, shoot me."

"If I ever look at Griff again, return the favor. How can I keep making bad decisions when it comes to him?"

"Because you're in love, and that's the worse betrayal of all."

"I thought he cared, Priss. I did. In my heart I could feel it, the two of us together, and all the time he was scheming one way or another to get the hotel. Maybe not out-and-out ownership this time, but control. How could I be so wrong? I think we should rename the place Charlotte's Folly."

"Or the Kiss My Ass." She shook her head. "Where'd that come from? I'm a terrible drunk."

"And I'm a terrible judge of character."

"You caught the affliction from me. I hope Brie's doing better with Beau."

"Miss Charlotte," Daemon called as he followed her

through the glass doors out to the now-crowded sidewalk. Here's a letter for you. Someone must have left it on the counter. I was busy with guests, so I have no idea who put it there."

Which was a nice polite way of saying everyone in the hotel was glued to the Griff and Charlotte Show. Daemon handed over the envelope, her name printed on the front. "I know it's none of my business, but I'm mighty sorry you and Griff seem to be having difficulties. You two make a handsome couple in every way. You get along right well except when it comes to the hotel business. Then things go straight to pot."

Daemon headed down Broughton, and Charlotte tore open the letter. "It's from Anthony and Vince. They found something in that casket room about the necklace." Charlotte put her hand to her chest, her heart racing. "Do you think they found it, Priss?"

"Lordy, I hope so, or you'll be so deep in credit-card debt from RL's therapy, you'll never see the light of day. Why didn't Vince and Anthony just call you?"

"I never gave them my cell number and RL's not home. And everyone in the whole blessed city knows I moved into the hotel today and now they know Griff and I just had another blowup. Come with me to the morgue. My car's in the alley, and it'll get your mind off you-know-who."

"The sisters have been working there all day, and I never made it back after the drama in the garden. I should go check it out, see what I can do to help. Maybe the sisters are the ones who unearthed the necklace."

They headed for her Chevy, and Prissy asked, "So are you going to stay in the hotel or move out? If you move, you look like a weak-kneed brat who didn't get her way. But if you stay, you'll have to look at Griff, and the jump-his-bones factor comes into play."

Charlotte fired the engine. "No jumping, no playing, no

Griff and no bones . . . especially the one between his legs. I am done with that man and all his attributes no matter how much I'll miss them." And I will so miss them, she added to herself with a frustrated whine.

They headed up Drayton, and Prissy curled into the seat. "Well, here we are again. Manless. It's not that I have to have a man in my life, I just happened to like the one that was there except . . ."

"Except he's going to be as bald as the underbelly of a bullfrog and just as ugly?"

"Nope, with or without hair, Sam will still be handsome. But if that man is so shallow that he chooses money over me, and if he is such a chicken-shit to not stand up to his dad for the woman he loves . . ." She tossed her hair and tipped her chin. "Then I am much too good for the likes of Mr. Sam Pate, and he can eat dirt and die."

"Amen!" they shouted together as Charlotte turned into the driveway.

"Wow," Charlotte said, gazing around. "The place looks so much better with all the overgrown trees and shrubs cut down. You can actually see how beautiful it is, or will be."

"The sisters are getting some of the teens staying with them to help. A group project." They took the front steps and rapped the knocker. When no one answered, they headed around back to the entrance there. The late-afternoon sun dappled through the trees, the lush tropical feel of Savannah settling in for the summer.

"This door's open," Prissy said, going in. "Yoo-hoo, Anthony? Vince?" She tried the light switch.

Charlotte stood in the doorway. "I think this is the door I went into on the night of the storm. I wonder where Vince and Anthony are." She was suddenly shoved inside, landing on all fours with the door slammed behind her. Prissy said, "Why'd you close the door? Now we can't see a thing."

"I didn't close it. Someone made that choice for us."

"No," Prissy whimpered. "This is not happening. I've already had a bad day. I don't need more of a bad day. Where are you, Char? It's as dark as a tomb in here, and that is not morgue humor, it's fact. The door's locked. I can't budge it. Why would someone want us in here? Anthony? Vince? What's happening?"

Charlotte scrounged around in her purse, pulled out a penlight and flashed it around. "Maybe Anthony and Vince want to scare us so we don't come back and they can have the morgue to themselves. Maybe they're looking for the necklace."

"I thought of that, too. They're so . . . secretive. Or this could be Camilla's work, to get you out of the running for the hotel and her son. Or the Rayburns'. Get rid of you, they get the necklace. Do you realize how many people want you . . . gone? You're racking up quite a list there, Char."

Charlotte pushed on the outside door again, then banged and yelled, mostly because she had to do something. "I've got a plan."

"Thank God. I was freaking out."

"If you can make Sam's hair fall out, you can chant a door open."

"Good grief, here we go again. Look, I don't know if the hair thing will work. In fact, I doubt seriously that it will. I'm more of a sense-things-are-going-wrong kind of gal. That chant at the bar was lame. I rhymed *fall* with *asshole*."

"Chant, dammit. We have to get out of here. Whoever locked us in will be back!"

"Crap."

"That's not a chant."

"Spirits here, you have great might, so help us now to see the light."

"Okay, that was the most pitiful chant ever. It didn't say anything."

"Hey, it rhymed. I was going for the rhyme, since I messed up the last one. Do you smell something?"

"Smoke?"

"Fire! Oh shit, fire! In the corner."

"Where'd that come from?"

"*See the light.* Guess chants have to be more specific. We're seeing light all right, and we're trapped in a casket room with no way out. Chant something else, quick!"

"There was a girl from Nantucket—"

"What are you doing? That's a limerick."

"It's all I can think of! I'm scared. What should we do?"

"Blow!"

Griff took a gulp of beer as a guy claimed the bar stool beside him and ordered bourbon neat. "Sam Pate, right? You're with Prissy St. James."

Sam downed the drink in one gulp and motioned for another. "Was with Prissy."

Griff nodded. "Seems to be the day for that, and it explains why Prissy was three sheets to the wind."

"Prissy was drunk?"

"Just about where you'll be if you keep throwing those things back."

Sam studied the third bourbon in front of him. "Damn."

Griff took another swig of his beer. "She left about twenty minutes ago. Are you looking for her?"

"Not exactly. I'm getting myself fortified for a night with Amanda Sawyer."

"Sweet Jesus," Griff said with a chuckle. "Drinks are on me. I know it's none of my business, but Amanda over Prissy? I'm not following."

Sam shivered, and sipped his drink. "It's the Savannah Low Country Sawyers."

"Yeah, there are more reasons than love to have a wedding. A very wise man told me that." He patted Sam on the back. "Sorry, I really am. You ditch the woman you love for money, I can't get the woman I love because of money. I say we're both royally fucked."

Sam shivered again.

"You're not looking too good here, man. Want me to get you my doctor? He makes calls here to the hotel."

"I got a bad feeling, and it won't go away no matter how many of these things I have." He held up the tumbler and downed the contents.

"Doc will fix you right up. Good guy."

"You saw Prissy about a half-hour ago?"

"Give or take. Something wrong with Priss? Hell, I think something's wrong with you. Great tux, but I got to tell you, you're looking like shit."

"They're in trouble, Charlotte and Prissy." Sam squinted his eyes closed. "Gray building, white fountain, the park, dead people . . . where the hell are they?"

"That's the morgue."

Sam stood. "Yeah, the morgue. We have to go. Right now. Something about a light that got all screwed up."

"How do you know?"

"I just do. I have a . . . thing. I see stuff. For better or worse, and it's part of me no matter what, unless maybe I have a lobotomy, and the way my luck's going, that probably wouldn't help either. Let's get out of here. My car's in front."

"You for real?"

"You think I'd make this crap up?"

"You got a point there."

"You're going to miss your party." Griff nodded at two hairs on the bar. "And you got to quit stressing out. You're going to be bald before your time."

"Been losing hair all day. Like I'm shedding." They hustled out of the bar, into the Jag and Sam hit the gas, his car squealing off down Broughton. "You better slow down. The cops will get us for sure."

"Call 911 in case they miss us."

"Freaking hell. You sure about all this?"

"Yeah. Wish I wasn't. Wish I was at that stupid-ass party having the time of my fucking life."

"No wishing in the world's going to make that happen, my friend. Amanda's laugh is legendary, her mother's worse. Migraine-quality." Griff made the 911 call. "What the hell do I say?"

"A fire at the morgue and two women trapped inside."

"Trapped? Fuck!"

"Around back and . . . and they're blowing on the flames to put them out?" He gave Griff a sideways glance, and shrugged. "It's what I'm getting."

"Spidey senses tingling?"

"Sort of, except no red suit and I can't crawl up buildings."

"Bummer. You are some kind of guy and what the hell have two of the four gotten themselves into? I sure hope you're just drunk and dreaming all this up, and we can turn around and go back to the hotel."

"The girls are in a shit-pot full of trouble that's not their fault. And have you ever known anyone to be this drunk?"

He ran the red light, and Griff's stomach tightened into a hard knot, his heart in his throat, and not because of the driving. If this mess with *and/or* hadn't come up, he might be with Charlotte right now and could help.

He made the call, and Sam slammed to a stop in front of the morgue. "There," he said, pointing to a thin ribbon of smoke curling into the air.

"Sweet Jesus, you're right," Griff said, running from the car, Sam beside him. "Charlotte!" he yelled coming around the back of the building. "Charlotte? Where the hell—"

"The door," Sam said. He kicked a post wedging it shut, smoke leaking at the edges. Sam pulled at the handle until something smashed against it, making him jump back. A settee flew out into the courtyard, Prissy and Charlotte gagging and stumbling right behind it along with billowing smoke.

Bent over, Prissy held on to Sam while gasping for air. "What took you so long?" She glanced up wheezing. "You need to pay attention to that niggling feeling in your gut. It's not acid reflux, bubba."

Sirens sounded a few blocks away, and Griff steadied Charlotte, covered in ash, reeking of smoke and coughing her head off. "I thought we were goners," Charlotte said. She took in another lungful of clean air.

Griff's heart was still racing. "Using the settee as a battering ram was a great idea. How'd the fire start?"

The heavy rumble of fire trucks stopped in the street, sirens screeching at ear-piercing levels. Charlotte exchanged looks with Prissy and yelled over the racket, "A little misunderstanding, is all."

Charlotte opened the door of RL's house, paid the pizza delivery guy and paraded two large everythings to the dinette table in the kitchen. "Soup's on. Come and get it."

Prissy handed paper plates to Bebe and Brie, and they all dug in, enjoying a fresh hot pizza moment. "Is there anything better?" Bebe mumbled around a mouthful, catching a string of mozzarella on her tongue.

"All I can taste is smoke," Prissy said. "My hair still reeks of it, even after five washings. Any more and I'll be Ms. Savannah Straw Hair."

Charlotte tapped the towel turban on her head. "I'm trying the mayonnaise approach. It's supposed to soak up the odor. Bet I gain five pounds from fat osmosis."

Prissy slurped a mushroom. "The good news is, the fire didn't do structural damage to the morgue, just burned stuff in the corner and threw ashes everywhere."

Charlotte gurgled out more box wine into each of the

glasses. "You guys don't really have to stay with me tonight. I'm fine. I can take care of myself."

Bebe snatched a piece of fallen pepperoni from the box. "No way, and since you left the protective yet slightly underhanded arms of Mr. Parish, we're here with you till they find whoever locked you and Prissy in the morgue."

Prissy said, "When we were leaving the morgue, I saw Ray Cleveland on the sidewalk just watching the firefighters and all the hubbub. What was he doing in this part of town? The Forsyth Park area is not his usual haunt."

Brie said, "That necklace was supposed to be his. When it went missing, his trophy wife left him and took their daughter. Beau said she ran off with some land baron from Columbia. The morgue has bad memories for that guy."

Bebe added, "And that goes double if he's the murderer. Could be he tried to get the necklace for nothing and things went wrong. Ray Cleveland's no saint in anyone's book, and maybe he's afraid the firefighters will come across something they shouldn't."

She tried for another pepperoni, but Charlotte got it first. She said to Brie, "How does Beau fit into that picture? And how does he fit into your picture, hmm? Care to share?"

"Well, if you must know, I have plans for Beau, but I'm not going to tell you just yet. There are a few things I have to work out, like how to drive a boat." She refilled her glass. "But as for Beau and Ray," she rushed on before anyone could make a crack about her driving the boat, "Beau was a rebound-relationship baby, and Ray went for full custody. Ray's a lot of things, some shady, some not, all making for great gossip, but I truly don't see him as a murderer. Mercy, he's a nice man. According to Beau, he's a great dad. I like him."

"Honey," Bebe said, "a murderer is just someone, any

someone, who gets pissed off and has a weapon. Trust me on this one. I've seen it all."

Prissy stood, and held out her hands. "Okay, that's it. I've had enough heavy talk for one day. This is getting too much like *The Sopranos*." She shuddered. "We need to watch something fun. We need a little levity. I'll run over to the nunnery and get—"

"What, *Lassie*? *Leave It to Beaver*?" Charlotte offered with a sassy smile.

"I was thinking more of my *Sex and the City* series. I bought it for the sisters. A few episodes of that, and the sisters are thrilled to their toes they're celibate."

Charlotte picked up the pizza boxes for the trash. "I'll walk you out. I want to get rid of these. And Bebe's right— we should hang together for a while."

Charlotte watched Prissy drive off, turned back to the house and ran straight into a solid hunk of man. "Griff. Dear God in heaven, you scared me half to death."

"What's with the hair? Going into fortune-telling?"

"What do you want?"

"I wanted to make sure you were okay."

She held out her arms, the big sleeves of her terry robe drooping down. "See? Okay. Next time call."

He slid his hands into his jeans pockets, his dark hair catching the streetlight, making him more handsome than ever. "And you would have picked up?"

"No." She pulled in a deep breath, hoping to get some anti-Griff strength. "I'm going inside."

"Wait." He grabbed her arm, turning her back, his touch reminding her of what they almost had . . . each other. "Camilla is the one who had the papers drawn up. I knew nothing about it, and I fired Hall and his cronies."

"Couldn't fire Camilla?"

"Moms are stubborn that way. She did it for me, Charlotte. Just like RL kept you in the dark all these years to keep you safe. We don't like what parents do a lot of times, but I think it's one of those things where you have to be a parent to understand. Parents will do anything for their kids . . . least, the good parents will. It's not an excuse; it's an explanation."

He ran his hand through his hair, looking beat. "I should have suspected she'd try something." He let out a deep breath and touched her cheek, melting her insides into sloppy goop. "I don't want us to be over, Charlotte. I wanted a beginning for us."

She kissed him because she had to, just once more. "As long as we have Magnolia House, there is no us, Griff. Something will get in the way. There's always going to be a Camilla problem coming between us, or you'll want a martini bar and I'll want a honeymoon suite or I'll want to paint the foyer puce when you want chartreuse or whatever. It's your hotel. You and Otis saved it and made it what it is, every brick, every step, every piece of flooring. That's the way you'll always see the place. I see Magnolia House as the only part of my parents I have left, and I want a say in how it's run. We can do business, we can do love, but we can't do both. I think we both know that now."

This time he kissed her, his lips lingering, as if he also knew this was the end. "I don't know what to do, Charlotte. I don't know what to say."

"Goodbye, Griff." She turned, and walked back into the gray house on Habersham, feeling more lonely than she ever thought possible.

Prissy took the back stone steps of the nunnery, lit by the single overhead leaded glass light. She pushed the door . . . the one open 24/7 in case someone needed help. How many runaways did the sisters have now? Ten? Twelve? She said a little prayer that the morgue job would work out in spite of all the problems. There were a lot of mouths to feed.

She hurried down the hall, the polished oak floor gleaming as always. Opening the door to her room, she switched on the light, yelped and jumped two feet straight into the air, she was sure of it.

"Sam!" She leaned against her dresser, her heart racing. "Why are you here? You can't just sneak into a nunnery. And what in the world happened to your hair? You're bald as—Oh . . . dear . . . lord!"

"That was my reaction, too, but I'm starting to like it. I'll save a fortune on shampoo and haircuts. I had two gals whistle at me on the way over here. I know bald is in, but it's a mystery how it happened to me." He rubbed his hand over his head. "And as for sneaking, the back door's always open. Everyone knows that. It's not very safe.

"But necessary. God's work, God's house. Where do people go who have no place to go?" She pushed the guilt over his no-hair state away, remembering how the louse broke up with her over a shrimp cocktail and a spring roll. "So why are you here? You're not exactly a runaway."

He sat on her bed, resting his forearms on his thighs, looking . . . relaxed. What was with this? Sam never looked relaxed. Even when they made love, he was energetic.

"Actually, I guess I am a runaway."

"Sam, you're a bank president. They don't run away. Go count some money. That'll make you happy." She pulled clothes from her closet to take to Charlotte's and threw them on the bed. "Better yet, why don't you go and count some of Amanda Sawyer's money." Grinding her teeth, she threw more clothes on the bed. "That'll really make you happy, and will for sure make your daddy happy and probably your mama and aunts and uncles and cousins and—"

He pulled her into his arms, cutting off her tirade. "You, Prissy St. James, make me happy."

"Tough toots, big boy. I'm not playing the other-woman game, I can promise you that. I want you out of my life because I've decided I am way too good for the likes of Sam Pate." She took a step back, straightened her spine and pointed to the door. "Hit the road. Don't let the door hit you in the ass. That means, leave fast."

"I am leaving. I'm leaving the bank, but I am not leaving you. I know I hurt you and I'm sorry, and I intend to win you back no matter how long it takes. Months, years, decades. You're not getting rid of me."

Prissy wagged her finger at him. "You're suffering from rescuers' syndrome, the mistaken assumption that because you saved me, you want me or own me or I can't make it without you or something like that. Choose one of the above. But the deal is, first of all, you didn't save me—a settee did—and second of all . . . Well, I can't think of a second of all. Just get out anyway."

"You don't truly mean that." He smiled at her. "I know."

"Of course I do. Look at me." She growled. "See, that's me angry. Go away."

"I want you forever and you want me too, and the reason I know is the same way I knew where you were today and the same way I knew Charlotte was okay that night of the storm. I just know. All my life I tried to ignore these feelings, tried to pretend they didn't exist because they don't belong in a banker's world. They make people uneasy, and the last thing bankers want is uneasy. They thrive on stability, what they can see, the tangible. Then you walked into my life and there was no more denying anything. We connected. One man, one woman, made for each other. And there we were, face to face, and we both knew this was it. I'm not denying who I am or what I am any longer. And you know I mean what I'm saying."

"What are you going to do, sell pencils on the street corner? You're a banker, for crying out loud."

"I'm going into the investment business. There's an upside to being intuitive. I can't say stock XYZ is going up thirty points tomorrow, but I have great gut instincts. I've done it for myself for years. Now I'll do it for others. It's a good mix. I won't starve, Priss."

"Your father's going to have a stroke. Look how he reacted when your sister took off to do her thing. You sure you can live with that? Your family and what they think is really important, Sam."

"And I'm part of that family. My father and my mother will have to deal. They had the chance to live their lives, and now I'm living mine and I want you in it. I love you, Prissy St. James, now and forever, and you love me, too. I want to marry you and when I come back from Atlanta, I'm bringing a ring. I'm leaving tonight to tell my parents, but I'll be back tomorrow. You can give me your answer then."

She stared at him wide-eyed, her heart beating wildly, her head spinning. "Yes."

"Yes?"

"Oh my goodness! Yes, I'll marry you, Sam Pate." She threw her arms around him, laughing and crying a little, too. "I cannot imagine life without you." She looked him in the eyes. "I love you with all my heart, and we'll have a great life together, I know it. The sisters are going to be so excited, and Minerva, too. And I'm really, really sorry about your hair."

"Why are you sorry?"

"I'll tell you after you bring that ring back from Atlanta."

Chapter 18

Charlotte sat at her office desk, chin in palm, gazing out the window, watching a bird build a nest in the live oak in Oglethorpe Square as Prissy strolled in. "Still no work?"

Charlotte nodded at the overflowing in-box. "Seems that being able to find yourself is a big deal around here. Now everyone wants me to find someone. Do you know how many missing people there are in Savannah? It's a blooming miracle there's anyone left to populate the city."

"Well, honey, you wanted business."

"Truth be told, I'm no better at being a PI now than I ever was. That's RL's turf."

"And now you have Magnolia House."

She grinned, and arched her eyebrows. "I know. And the thing about it is, I love to build, fix up, paint and redo. Wait till you see the plans I drew up for the carriage house and . . . Holy Toledo, is that a rock on your left hand!"

Charlotte jumped up, ran around the desk and grabbed Prissy's fingers. "An emerald, no less. Oh, it's beautiful." She hugged Prissy. "This is so exciting. I take it you and Sam patched things up?"

"We did and I'm so happy, Char. I think I'm delirious, and I want you this happy, too, and Brie and Bebe."

"Do they know?"

"Bebe's on a case. Some big shot in Atlanta wants Ray Cleveland investigated and Bebe's got the case. They sent in some Yankee detective. Sweet mother, will they never just go back North and stay there? Brie's taking boat-driving lessons, and don't be asking because she's not telling. I tried. We're all meeting up tonight for dinner at the Pink House to celebrate. The sisters are coming, and so is Minerva. The Savannah spirits should darn well be leaving us alone with that kind of representation, don't you think?"

"I do."

"Oh, honey, I think that's my line." Prissy giggled and blushed, and never looked happier in her life. "How are you and Griff? Any breakthrough?"

"We have a hotel, we don't have a relationship, and that's the way it is and that's okay. I love Magnolia House and so does he, and every time we get close in the relationship part, something happens with the hotel part and we end up doing battle royale. Sometimes I wish I could go back to two weeks ago, when none of this had happened yet and we were still doing the flirting thing. It was innocent, uncomplicated. We could smile at each other and it felt good. Now I just feel . . . sad."

Prissy sat on the edge of the desk, her beautiful ring sparkling in the sunlight, just like the rest of her. "You can make this right."

"There is no time machine, Priss."

"Make one. Find a way to go back. Sam did for me. It's like the first time we met at the bar and did the horizontal hula . . . actually it was the vertical hula . . . in the elevator, and it was just the two of us and nothing else mattered. He's given up his job for me, and this weekend I'm driving to Atlanta—Sam doesn't know—to talk to his devil parents to try and make things right with them. I even bought a white button-down blouse, tan skirt and pumps."

"Wow, you must love him."

"I'm willing to do what it takes to make us work and so is Sam." Prissy bent over the desk and kissed Charlotte on the cheek. "Sad is not good. It robs your heart and your soul. Find a way for you and Griff. It's worth it if you love him. Guess the question is, do you?" She checked her watch. "Yikes, I have to go. We're plastering the front hall and two viewing rooms this week. They're airing out the casket room to get rid of that smoke smell. It's all shaping up right nicely, Char. It's going to be great, and so are you. See you at seven."

Charlotte tapped her pen on the desk, listening to Prissy's retreating footsteps. "There is no way to make this work," she said to her empty office. Pulling out the plans she drew up for the carriage house, she smiled. Two honeymoon suites with big windows overlooking a garden, private verandas draped in wisteria, king-size beds, hot tubs. She couldn't wait to show it to Griff. That's why she was smiling. She'd get to see him again. They could talk over the plans.

And then he'd show her the plans for his martini bar and they'd be at it all over again. Well, that was just too darn bad. She pulled in a deep breath and closed her eyes. She was going to get what she wanted no matter what it took, no matter what the price. She was going to get this settled today, once and for all. It was time.

Griff gazed at his employees, gathered in the bar. It didn't open till four, so that gave him a half hour to get this business taken care of. As he watched everyone take a seat, he ran his hand over the polished mahogany, remembering when the bar was installed and how proud he and Otis were.

"Okay, everyone," he started. "This is going to be quick, as you all have work to do. I'm leaving as head of

Magnolia House. As you all know, Charlotte deShawn is the other owner of the hotel, and in all fairness, I believe it's her turn to have a shot at the place. So," he rushed on before anyone could ask him a million questions he didn't have answers to, "I'm handing over the deed to Ms. deShawn this afternoon. I expect you to give her the support you've always given me. Without you all, the impeccable staff of Magnolia House, there would be no Magnolia House. Actually, I suppose I never considered you all staff, but more family. And . . . and I'll miss you."

He smiled and nodded at his dazed staff, then headed back to his office. It was done, finished. He opened his office door to Otis.

"Well, boy," Otis said as Griff shut the door. "You went and did it. Think Charlotte will let my chair stay here, so I can keep an eye on things?"

"I'll talk to her about it." Griff sat on the edge of the desk that originally was Otis's. "I'm going to miss this place, Dad. I remember when you bought that chair, at an estate auction out at Shallow Brook Plantation."

"And the desk was from when they redid that there library at the Telfair Museum. You're doing the right thing, boy. Charlotte's a fine woman, a lot like her daddy. She'll give Magnolia House her all. She'll love her like we have."

"And I'll love Charlotte."

Otis took a drag from his cigar then grinned. "And there's the most important thing of all. You be happy, Griff. That's what counts."

A knock sounded at the door and Daemon entered without waiting to be asked. "Mercy me, boy. Since when are you smoking cigars?"

Griff looked back to the maroon leather chair, only a thin line of smoke hovering. "What's going on, Griff? Your daddy must be flipping in his grave that you're giving away Magnolia House."

"I think this is what Otis wanted all along. He left half to Charlotte because he intended for her to have the hotel."

"Well, then, your mama must be flipping, and this will probably put her in the grave."

"Camilla's had her way for thirty years. For sure there'll be considerable ranting and raving and the need for a few bottles of scotch along the way, but she will survive. And Charlotte will be good at running the hotel."

"She has no experience, Griff, not one speck."

"Neither did I nor Otis nor William, and we made it. You were the only one who knew what to do, and now Charlotte has Daemon Rutledge to help her along the way." Griff hugged his manager. "It's going to be okay, Daemon. Change is good. Now you better get out there and answer all those questions from the staff that I didn't answer."

Daemon shook his head. "To have such a fine gift. All this handed to you, then be giving it away."

"Don't know whether it was exactly handed to me. I remember working my ass off. But it's time to move on."

"You're making a big mistake. Think about what you're doing, Griff. No woman is worth Magnolia House."

Griff smiled. "Except Charlotte."

The door banged open and Charlotte stood in the doorway. "What are you doing?"

Griff nodded to Daemon. "Thank you, my friend."

Daemon looked from Griff to Charlotte, shook his head again and left. Griff folded his arms. "Hi."

"Have you lost your mind? The phone lines, cell and land, are so congested, no calls are going though. Your mother tracked me down at the Pig between produce and the bakery. She threw tomatoes and doughnuts at me and called me an interloper. Not quite sure what that is, but it doesn't sound good. You can't give me Magnolia House."

"I want to be with you. I want to give us a chance. Like

you said, we can't have it both ways . . . us and the hotel. Now there's just us."

"No, there's not."

He went to his desk, opened a folder and pulled out the deed. "Here, read. No *ands*, no *ors*, just Charlotte deShawn. One name. It's your turn to run the hotel and it's our turn to fall in love." He scooped her into his arms. "I love you. God, I love you. You have to believe me now. I want us to be together forever. I want to make you happy. Marry me now. No strings, no motives, no agendas. Just us."

She stepped back. "What the hell are you going to do now? Work at Holiday Inn down on Bay Street? They'd probably hire you; you have good references."

He ran his hand through his hair. "I thought this would make you happy. You'd have the hotel, you could run it any way you wanted. Camilla's out of the picture, me out of the picture, no martini bar to piss you off. I thought you loved me."

"Of course I love you."

He grinned. "Okay, I can live with that. But why are you so upset? I don't get it."

She opened her purse, unfolded a paper and tossed another deed on the desk next to his. "Your name only."

"You gave me Magnolia House?"

"It's yours. You made it what it is. Every brick, every board, every employee is yours. Magnolia House is your heart and soul. If I loved you, which I completely and totally do, how could I take that away from you?"

She picked up her deed and tore it up. Then she took his and put it in his inside pocket. She kissed him. "Close to your heart, where it belongs."

He sat in Otis's chair. He couldn't speak till she curled up in his lap. "I can't take this away from you. You're supposed to have it. I want you to have it."

"I'm giving it all to you. There's a catch. When you read

the fine print, you'll see that I kept the carriage house separate. It's in both our names."

"For your honeymoon suites? So you can build them the way you want?"

She kissed him. "Sort of. I'm going to turn it into our house, as in yours and mine. Close to the hotel, yet not the hotel. What do you think?"

"I . . . you. Good God! You're incredible. Just when I think I know every part of you, Charlotte deShawn, you surprise me again. I love you. I didn't know I had this much love in me. We're going to get married, Charlotte. We're going to be happy forever, I swear it."

"And what a great forever it's going to be, Griff."

"Yeah, forever. Finally, at last. They made it happen Char. Otis and William and now you and me."

Epilogue

They were like swarming bees. Every foot of the morgue had someone working on it. Damn them. Why couldn't they leave the place alone? The necklace was still missing even after searching all these years. Giving up now was out of the question. It was there . . . somewhere. So much money. Money to make dreams come true. There was still a way to find it, there had to be. Too much time, too much effort invested to give up now. There had to be a way, a plan that would work no matter who got in the way. And no one better get in the way this time.

Be sure to catch Shelly Laurenston's
THE BEAST IN HIM,
out this month from Brava . . .

Sherman cleared his throat. "I'll speak with you another time, Jessica." She heard his footsteps heading back to the coffeehouse.

When Sherman opened the door, Smitty tossed out, "Just don't call her when we're having sex—which will be constantly!"

Jess waited long enough for Sherman to get inside before she yanked away from Smitty and followed up with a solid fist to his chest. The pain that radiated up her arm afterward, she ignored.

"*What is wrong with you?*"

"Nothin'," he said, looking confused. "Why?"

Smitty wasn't sure what he enjoyed more. Torturing that scrawny dog—and he had tortured him. The poor guy didn't know whether to be horrified or jealous of Smitty and Jessie going at it. Or had his pleasure come from torturing Jessie Ann? All that was fun, but what he enjoyed the most was having Jessie Ann plastered up against him. She nuzzled real nice, even when she didn't mean to.

At the moment, however, she looked real cranky.

"I was helping like you asked."

"You were being a dick," she said while looking down

at the giant watch on her wrist. "And you were enjoying every damn second of being a—oh, my God! I've gotta go."

She ran to the corner and hailed a cab, but before she stepped inside, she ran back over to him.

"One other thing."

"Yeah?"

She slid her hand under his jacket and twisted his nipple until his eyes watered.

"Touch my tits again without permission and I'll rip this off." She glanced at her watch again. "Ach! Now I really do have to go."

Jessie turned and ran back toward the waiting cab. Sure, Smitty could have let her go, but to be honest, he'd never been so damn entertained by a woman before. "So how do I get permission?"

She spun around, jumping back when she realized he stood right behind her. "Stop sneaking up on me! And you don't get permission."

"Why not? You said I was pretty."

"Look, Smitty, while I appreciate your doglike persistence, you need to know that nothing you do or say will change my mind about this. You're part of my past, and these days I'm all about my future. I don't have time or room in my life for you and your casual chats. Understand?"

"Sure."

"Good."

" 'Cause I always love a challenge."

He'd caught her with that when she was halfway in the cab. With one foot in and the other still braced against the curb, she stared at him. "What challenge?"

"You're challenging me to get you back into my life."

"No, I'm not."

"Your exact words were 'I challenge you, Bobby Ray Smith, to get me back into your life.' "

"I never said that."

"That's what I heard." The beauty of wolf hearing. You heard only what you wanted to, made up what was never said but should have been, and the rest meant little or nothing.

"Is there something wrong with you? Mentally?"

"Darlin', you met my family. You've gotta be more specific than that."

"That's it. I'm leaving. I can't have this conversation with you. I can't—"

He saw it immediately. The way her entire body tensed, her eyes focusing across the busy city street, locking on something in the distance. She went from exasperated to on point in less than five seconds.

"What's wrong, Jessie?" He followed her line of sight but didn't see anything that stuck out to him.

"Nothing," she said, her eyes still staring across the street. "I need to go." She went up on her toes and absently kissed him on his cheek. He'd bet cash she wouldn't even remember she did it.

She stepped into her cab and closed the door. She didn't look back at him, didn't acknowledge him in any way. That wasn't like her. Even if it was to give him the finger, she'd do or say something before driving off.

Smitty turned and stared at the spot Jessie'd been staring at. But he still saw nothing that made him feel tense or worried.

So what the hell had worried his little Jessie Ann?

Tensions mount in
DON'T TEMPT ME,
the latest from Sylvia Day,
available now from Brava . . .

"What game are you playing?" he asked gruffly.

"I was staring," she admitted, turning to face him. She appreciated having the light behind her, which shielded her features in shadow while revealing the whole of his. "But then, every woman here was doing the same."

"But you are not just any woman, are you?" he growled, coming toward her.

So . . . he knew who she was. That surprised her. Her mother had insisted they hide their identities. They stayed with a friend instead of at their own property and were using an assumed surname. Her mother said it would prevent her father from becoming angry with them for deviating from their stated destination—Spain. She would have agreed to anything in order to come to Paris. In all of her life, her family had never visited here.

But then . . . If Quinn knew her true identity, why would he pull her away from the festivities in such a public manner?

"*You* approached *me*," she pointed out. "You could have kept your distance."

"I am here because of you." He caught her elbows and jerked her roughly into him. "If you had stayed out of mis-

chief for a few days longer, I would have been far from
France now."

She frowned. What was he talking about? She would
have asked if he had not placed his hands on her. No man
had ever been so bold as to accost the daughter of the
Vicomte de Grenier. She could hardly believe Quinn had
done it, but she could not jerk away because the sensations
elicited by his proximity stunned her. He was so hard, like
stone. She could not have expected that.

As her breathing quickened, she felt herself sway into
him, her chest pressing into his. It was madness. He was a
stranger and he seemed to be angry.

But she felt safe with him, regardless.

For a long taut moment Quinn did not move. Then he
yanked her toward the window, impatiently pushing the
sheer curtain aside so the moonlight touched her face. With
a tug of his fingers, he untied the ribbons of her mask and
it fell away, leaving her exposed. She suddenly felt naked,
but not nearly naked enough. She felt a reckless, goading
need to strip off every article of clothing while he watched.
It was heady to be the focus of such heated, avid interest
from so handsome a man.

He loomed over her, scowling, his mouth set in a grim
line. "Why are you looking at me like that?" he snapped.

She swallowed hard. "Like what?"

Quinn made an aggravated noise, dropped the curtain,
and caught her about the waist. "As if you want me in
your bed."

Mon Dieu, what did one say to that?

"You are . . . very attractive, Mr. Quinn."

" 'Mr. Quinn,' is it?" he purred, his large hands cupping
her spine, making her feel tiny and delicate. Conquered. "I
always knew you were mad."

Her tongue darted out to wet her dry lips and he froze,
his gaze burning.

"What game are you playing?" he asked again. This time, she heard something else in his tone. Something darker. Undeniably arousing.

"I-I think we are both c-confused," she said.

He moved, cupping the back of her neck and the side of her hip, mantling her body with his. "I'm bloody well confused, curse you." He tugged, forcing her spine to arch, leaning over her so that she had no leverage to move.

Every inhale was his exhale. Every movement was an enticement, their bodies sliding against each other in a wanton dance. She felt a fever in her blood, a conflagration that had started with that first smoldering glance in the ballroom.

"Do you want to be fucked?" he purred, his head lowering so that his lips touched her jaw. The caress was divine and wicked at once, making her shiver with delighted apprehension. "Because you are begging for it, witch, and I am insane enough in this moment to indulge you."

"I-I . . ."

Quinn turned his head and kissed her, hard, his lips mashing against hers. There was no finesse, no tenderness. Her mouth was bruised by his volatility and ardor. She should have been frightened. He seemed barely leashed, his emotions swaying from irritation to consuming desire.

She whimpered, her hands fisting in his jacket to keep him close. Enamored with the taste of him, she licked his lips and he groaned, his hips grinding restlessly into her. She surrendered weakly and he gentled his approach, seemingly soothed by her capitulation.

"Tell me what you are involved in," he murmured, his teeth nipping at her swollen lower lip.

"You," she breathed, tilting her head to deepen the contact.

Meet more sexy shifters in Cynthia Eden's
HOTTER AFTER MIDNIGHT,
coming next month from Brava . . .

"I'm an empath, Colin. My gift is that I sense things. I sense the *Other*. I can sense their feelings, their thoughts."

Oh, yeah, he'd definitely tensed up on her. "You're telling me that you can read my thoughts?"

The temperature seemed to drop about ten degrees. "I'm telling you that *sometimes* I can tell the thoughts of supernaturals." She'd known he wouldn't be thrilled by this news, that was why she hadn't told him the full truth the other night. But now that they were working together, now that her talent was coming in to play, well, she figured he had the right to know.

Colin grabbed her arms, jerked her forward against his chest. "So this whole time, you've been playing with me."

The sharp edge of his canines gleamed behind his lips. "No, Colin, it's not like that—"

"You've been looking into my head and seeing how much I want you?"

"Colin, no, I—" *Seeing how much I want you.* Had he really just said that?

His cheeks flushed. "While I tried to play the dumbass gentleman."

Since when?

"Well, screw that." His lips were right over hers, his fingers tight on her arms.

"If you've been in my head, then you know what I want to do to you."

Uh, no she didn't. Her shields had been firmly in place with him all day. Her heart was pounding so fast now, the dull drumming filled her ears. She licked her lips, tried once more to tell him the truth, "It's not like that—"

Too late. His mouth claimed hers, swallowing her words and igniting the hungry desire she'd been trying so hard to fight.